BEYOND
THE PALE

Saladin Ahmed
Peter S. Beagle
Heather Brewer
Jim Butcher
Kami Garcia
Nancy & Belle Holder
Gillian Philip
Jane Yolen

Edited by Henry Herz

Birch Tree Publishing
3830 Valley Centre Dr., Suite 705-432
San Diego, CA 92130
www.birchtreepub.com

With gratitude to my parents and the Author of all things

Praise for Beyond the Pale

"*Beyond the Pale* features a stellar, diverse line-up, brimming with talent and imagination."
 - New York Times bestseller Jason Hough, author of *The Darwin Elevator*

"Beyond the edge of fear and dread, shadows tell each other beautiful and frightening stories. Crack open this book and listen to the voices."
 - New York Times bestseller Richard Kadrey, author of *Sandman Slim*

"*Beyond the Pale* is the kind of thing to keep loaded on your reader in case you need a quick fix of fine fantasy by one of the field's finest fantasy writers."
 - Nebula Award-nominated Greg van Eekhout, author of *California Bones*

"Light a black candle and crack open this collection of short stories from writers who are more than mere wordsmiths. A thrill runs up my spine as I wonder, could these scribes be messengers from in-between worlds sent here to prepare us for our own crossings? The veil thins and the candle flickers. Fiction? I'm not so sure."
 - New York Times bestseller Frank Beddor, author of *The Looking Glass Wars*

CONTENTS

INTRODUCTION

~

by Henry Herz

This is an anthology of fantasy, urban fantasy and paranormal stories that skirt the border between our world and others. Was that my imagination, or did I hear something under my bed? What was that blurred movement in my darkened closet? There is but a thin Veil separating the real and the fantastic, and therein dwell the inhabitants of these stories.

The noun "pale" refers to a stake (as in impaling vampires) or pointed piece of wood (as in a paling fence). "Pale" came to refer to an area enclosed by a paling fence. Later, it acquired the figurative meaning of an enclosed and therefore safe domain. Conversely, "beyond the pale" means foreign, strange, or threatening. You are about to go Beyond the Pale.

It was an honor and delight to work with such gifted authors. I hope you enjoy reading their work as much as I did.

HOOVES AND THE
HOVEL OF ABDEL JAMEELA

~

by Saladin Ahmed

As soon as I arrive in the village of Beit Zujaaj, I begin to hear the mutters about Abdel Jameela, a strange old man supposedly unconnected to any of the local families. Two days into my stay, the villagers fall over one another to share with me the rumors that Abdel Jameela is in fact distantly related to the esteemed Assad clan. By my third day in Beit Zujaaj, several of the Assads, omniscient as "important" families always are in these piles of cottages, have accosted me to deny the malicious whispers. No doubt they are worried about the bad impression such an association might make on me, favorite physicker of the Caliph's own son.

The latest denial comes from Hajjar al-Assad himself, the middle-aged head of the clan and the sort of half-literate lout that passes for a shaykh in these parts. Desperate for the approval of the young courtier whom he no doubt privately condemns as an over-schooled sodomite, bristle-bearded Shaykh Hajjar has cornered me in the village's only café—if the sitting room of a qat-chewing old woman can be called a café by anyone other than bumpkins.

I should not be so hard on Beit Zujaaj and its bumpkins. But when I look at the gray rock-heap houses, the withered gray vegetable-yards, and the stuporous gray lives that fill this village, I want to weep for the lost color of Baghdad.

Instead I sit and listen to the shaykh.

2

"Abdel Jameela is not of Assad blood, O learned Professor. My grandfather took mercy, as God tells us we must, on the old man's mother. Seventy-and-some years ago she showed up in Beit Zujaaj, half-dead from traveling and big with child, telling tales—God alone knows if they were true—of her Assad-clan husband, supposedly slain by highwaymen. Abdel Jameela was birthed and raised here, but he has never been of this village." Shaykh Hajjar scowls. "For decades now—since I was a boy—he has lived up on the hilltop rather than among us. More of a hermit than a villager. And not of Assad blood," he says again.

I stand up. I can take no more of the man's unctuous voice and, praise God, I don't have to.

"Of course, O Shaykh, of course. I understand. Now, if you will excuse me?"

Shaykh Hajjar blinks. He wishes to say more but doesn't dare. For I have come from the Caliph's court.

"Yes, Professor. Peace be upon you." His voice is like a snuffed candle.

"And upon you, peace." I head for the door as I speak.

The villagers would be less deferential if they knew of my current position at court—or rather, lack of one. The Caliph has sent me to Beit Zujaaj as an insult. I am here as a reminder that the well-read young physicker with the clever wit and impressive skill, whose company the Commander of the Faithful's own bookish son enjoys, is worth less than the droppings of the Caliph's favorite falcon. At least when gold and a Persian noble's beautiful daughter are involved.

For God's viceroy the Caliph has seen fit to promise my Shireen to another, despite her love for me. Her husband-to-be is older than her father—too ill, the last I heard, to even sign the marriage contract. But as soon as his palsied, liver-spotted hand is hale enough to raise a pen… Things would have gone differently were I a wealthy man. Shireen's father would have heard my proposal happily enough if I'd been able to provide the grand dowry he sought. The Caliph's son, fond of his brilliant physicker, even asked that Shireen be wedded to me. But the boy's fondness could only get me so far. The Commander of the Faithful saw no reason to impose a raggedy scholar of a son-in-law on the Persian when a rich old vulture would please the man more. I am, in the Caliph's eyes, an amusing companion to his son, but one whom the boy will lose like a doll once he grows to love killing and gold-getting more than learning. Certainly I am nothing worth upsetting Shireen's coin-crazed courtier father over.

3

For a man is not merely who he is, but what he has. Had I land or caravans I would be a different man—the sort who could compete for Shireen's hand. But I have only books and instruments and a tiny inheritance, and thus that is all that I am. A man made of books and pittances would be a fool to protest when the Commander of the Faithful told him that his love would soon wed another.

I am a fool.

My outburst in court did not quite cost me my head, but I was sent to Beit Zujaaj "for a time, only, to minister to the villagers as a representative of Our beneficent concern for Our subjects." And my fiery, tree-climbing Shireen was locked away to await her half-dead suitor's recovery.

"O Professor! Looks like you might get a chance to see Abdel Jameela for yourself!" Just outside the café, the gravelly voice of Umm Hikma the café-keeper pierces the cool morning air and pulls me out of my reverie. I like old Umm Hikma, with her qat-chewer's irascibility and her blacksmithish arms. Beside her is a broad-shouldered man I don't know. He scuffs the dusty ground with his sandal and speaks to me in a worried stutter.

"P-peace be upon you, O learned Professor. We haven't yet met. I'm Yousef, the porter."

"And upon you, peace, O Yousef. A pleasure to meet you."

"The pleasure's mine, O Professor. But I am here on behalf of another. To bring you a message. From Abdel Jameela."

For the first time since arriving in Beit Zujaaj, I am surprised. "A message? For me?"

"Yes, Professor. I am just returned from the old hermit's hovel, a half-day's walk from here, on the hilltop. Five, six times a year I bring things to Abdel Jameela, you see. In exchange he gives a few coins, praise God."

"And where does he get these coins, up there on the hill?" Shaykh Hajjar's voice spits out the words from the café doorway behind me. I glare and he falls silent.

I turn back to the porter. "What message do you bear, O Yousef? And how does this graybeard know of me?"

Broad-shouldered Yousef looks terrified. The power of the court. "Forgive me, O learned Professor! Abdel Jameela asked what news from the village and I... I told him that a court physicker was in Beit Zujaaj. He grew excited and told me to beg upon his behalf for your aid. He said his wife was horribly ill. He fears she will lose her legs, and perhaps her life."

4

"His wife?" I've never heard of a married hermit.

Umm Hikma raises her charcoaled eyebrows, chews her qat, and says nothing.

Shaykh Hajjar is more vocal. "No one save God knows where she came from, or how many years she's been up there. The people have had glimpses only. She doesn't wear the head scarf that our women wear. She is wrapped all in black cloth from head to toe and mesh-masked like a foreigner. She has spoken to no one. Do you know, O Professor, what the old rascal said to me years ago when I asked why his wife never comes down to the village? He said, 'She is very religious'! The old dog! Where is it written that a woman can't speak to other women? Other women who are good Muslims? The old son of a whore! What should his wife fear here? The truth of the matter is—"

"The truth, O Shaykh, is that in this village only *your* poor wife need live in fear!" Umm Hikma lets out a rockslide chuckle and gives me a conspiratorial wink. Before the shaykh can sputter out his offended reply, I turn to Yousef again.

"On this visit, did you see Abdel Jameela's wife?" If he can describe the sick woman, I may be able to make some guesses about her condition. But the porter frowns.

"He does not ask me into his home, O Professor. No one has been asked into his home for thirty years."

Except for the gifted young physicker from the Caliph's court. Well, it may prove more interesting than what I've seen of Beit Zujaaj thus far. I do have a fondness for hermits. Or, rather, for the *idea* of hermits. I can't say that I have ever met one. But as a student, I always fantasized that I would one day *be* a hermit, alone with God and my many books in the barren hills.

That was before I met Shireen.

"There is one thing more," Yousef says, his broad face looking even more nervous. "He asked that you come alone."

My heartbeat quickens, though there is no good reason for fear. Surely this is just an old hater-of-men's surly whim. A physicker deals with such temperamental oddities as often as maladies of the liver or lungs. Still... "Why does he ask this?"

"He says that his wife is very modest and that in her state the frightening presence of men might worsen her illness."

Shaykh Hajjar erupts at this. "Bah! Illness! More likely they've done something shameful they don't want the village to know of. Almighty God forbid, maybe they—"

Whatever malicious thing the shaykh is going to say, I silence it with another glare borrowed from the Commander of the Faithful. "If the woman is ill, it is my duty as a Muslim and a physicker to help her, whatever her husband's oddities."

Shaykh Hajjar's scowl is soul-deep. "Forgive me, O Professor, but this is not a matter of oddities. You could be in danger. We know why Abdel Jameela's wife hides away, though some here fear to speak of such things."

Umm Hikma spits her qat into the road, folds her powerful arms and frowns. "In the name of God! Don't you believe, Professor, that Abdel Jameela, who couldn't kill an ant, means you any harm." She jerks her chin at Shaykh Hajjar. "And you, O Shaykh, by God, please don't start telling your old lady stories again!"

The shaykh wags a finger at her. "Yes, I *will* tell him, woman! And may Almighty God forgive you for mocking your shaykh!" Shaykh Hajjar turns to me with a grim look. "O learned Professor, I will say it plainly: Abdel Jameela's wife is a witch."

"A witch?" The last drops of my patience with Beit Zujaaj have dripped through the water clock. It is time to be away from these people. "Why would you say such a thing, O Shaykh?"

The shaykh shrugs. "Only God knows for certain," he says. His tone belies his words.

"May God protect us all from slanderous ill-wishers," I say.

He scowls. But I have come from the Caliph's court, so his tone is venomously polite. "It is no slander, O Professor. Abdel Jameela's wife consorts with ghouls. Travelers have heard strange noises coming from the hilltop. And hoofprints have been seen on the hill-path. Cloven hoofprints, O Professor, where there are neither sheep nor goats."

"No! Not cloven hoofprints!" I say.

But the shaykh pretends not to notice my sarcasm. He just nods. "There is no strength and no safety but with God."

"God is great," I say in vague, obligatory acknowledgment. I have heard enough rumor and nonsense. And a sick woman needs my help. "I will leave as soon as I gather my things. This Abdel Jameela lives up the road, yes? On a hill? If I walk, how long will it take me?"

"If you do not stop to rest, you will see the hill in the distance by noontime prayer," says Umm Hikma, who has a new bit of qat going in her cheek.

"I will bring you some food for your trip, Professor, and the stream runs alongside the road much of the way, so you'll have no need of water." Yousef seems relieved that I'm not angry with him, though I don't quite know why I would be. I thank him then speak to the group.

"Peace be upon you all."

"And upon you, peace," they say in near-unison.

In my room, I gather scalpel, saw, and drugs into my pack—the kid-leather pack that my beloved gifted to me. I say more farewells to the villagers, firmly discourage their company, and set off alone on the road. As I walk rumors of witches and wife-beaters are crowded out of my thoughts by the sweet remembered sweat-and-ambergris scent of my Shireen.

After an hour on the rock-strewn road, the late-morning air warms. The sound of the stream beside the road almost calms me.

Time passes and the sun climbs high in the sky. I take off my turban and caftan, make ablution by the stream and say my noon prayers. Not long after I begin walking again, I can make out what must be Beit Zujaaj hill off in the distance. In another hour or so I am at its foot.

It is not much of a hill, actually. There are buildings in Baghdad that are taller. A relief, as I am not much of a hill-climber. The rocky path is not too steep, and green sprays of grass and thyme dot it—a pleasant enough walk, really. The sun sinks a bit in the sky and I break halfway up the hill for afternoon prayers and a bit of bread and green apple. I try to keep my soul from sinking as I recall Shireen, her skirts tied up scandalously, knocking apples down to me from the high branches of the Caliph's orchard-trees.

The rest of the path proves steeper and I am sweating through my galabeya when I finally reach the hilltop. As I stand there huffing and puffing, my eyes land on a small structure thirty yards away.

If Beit Zujaaj hill is not much of a hill, at least the hermit's hovel can be called nothing but a hovel. Stones piled on stones until they have taken the vague shape of a dwelling. Two sickly chickens scratching in the dirt. As soon as I have caught my breath, a man comes walking out to meet me. Abdel Jameela.

He is shriveled with a long gray beard and a ragged kaffiyeh, and I can tell he will smell unpleasant even before he reaches me. How does he

7

already know I'm here? I don't have much time to wonder, as the old man moves quickly despite clearly gouty legs.

"You are the physicker, yes? From the Caliph's court?"

No 'peace be upon you,' no 'how is your health,' no 'pleased to meet you.' Life on a hilltop apparently wears away one's manners. As if reading my thoughts, the old man bows his head in supplication.

"Ah. Forgive my abruptness, O learned Professor. I am Abdel Jameela. Thank you. Thank you a thousand times for coming." I am right about his stink, and I thank God he does not try to embrace me. With no further ceremony, I am led into the hovel.

There are a few stained and tattered carpets layered on the packed-dirt floor. A straw mat, an old cushion and a battered tea tray are the only furnishings. Except for the screen. Directly opposite the door is a tall, incongruously fine cedar-and-pearl latticed folding screen, behind which I can make out only a vague shape. It is a more expensive piece of furniture than any of the villagers could afford, I'm sure. And behind it, no doubt, sits Abdel Jameela's wife.

The old man makes tea hurriedly, clattering the cups but saying nothing the whole while. The scent of the seeping mint leaves drifts up, covering his sour smell. Abdel Jameela sets my tea before me, places a cup beside the screen, and sits down. A hand reaches out from behind the screen to take the tea. It is brown and graceful. *Beautiful*, if I am to speak truly. I realize I am staring and tear my gaze away.

The old man doesn't seem to notice. "I don't spend my time among men, Professor. I can't talk like a courtier. All I can say is that we need your help."

"Yousef the porter has told me that your wife is ill, O Uncle. Something to do with her legs, yes? I will do whatever I can to cure her, Almighty God willing."

For some reason, Abdel Jameela grimaces at this. Then he rubs his hands together and gives me an even more pained expression. "O Professor, I must show you a sight that will shock you. My wife... Well, words are not the way."

With a grunt the old man stands and walks halfway behind the screen. He gestures for me to follow then bids me stop a few feet away. I hear rustling behind the screen, and I can see a woman's form moving, but still Abdel Jameela's wife is silent.

"Prepare yourself, Professor. Please show him, O beautiful wife of mine." The shape behind the screen shifts. There is a scraping noise. And a woman's leg ending in a cloven hoof stretches out from behind the screen.

I take a deep breath. "God is Great," I say aloud. This, then, is the source of Shaykh Hajjar's fanciful grumbling. But such grotesqueries are not unheard of to an educated man. Only last year another physicker at court showed me a child—born to a healthy, pious man and his modest wife—all covered in fur. This same physicker told me of another child he'd seen born with scaly skin. I take another deep breath. If a hoofed woman can be born and live, is it so strange that she might find a mad old man to care for her?

"O my sweetheart!" Abdel Jameela's whisper is indecent as he holds his wife's hoof.

And for a moment I see what mad Abdel Jameela sees. The hoof's glossy black beauty, as smoldering as a woman's eye. It is entrancing...

"O, my wife," the old man goes on, and runs his crooked old finger over the hoof-cleft slowly and lovingly. "O, my beautiful wife..." The leg flexes, but still no sound comes from behind the screen.

This is wrong. I take a step back from the screen without meaning to. "In the name of God! Have you no shame, old man?"

Abdel Jameela turns from the screen and faces me with an apologetic smile. "I am sorry to say that I have little shame left," he says.

I've never heard words spoken with such weariness. I remind myself that charity and mercy are our duty to God, and I soften my tone. "Is this why you sent for me, Uncle? What would you have me do? Give her feet she was not born with? My heart bleeds for you, truly. But such a thing only God can do."

Another wrinkled grimace. "O Professor, I am afraid that I must beg your forgiveness. For I have lied to you. And for that I am sorry. For it is not my wife that needs your help, but I."

"But her—pardon me, Uncle—her hoof."

"Yes! Its curve! Like a jet-black half-moon!" The old hermit's voice quivers and he struggles to keep his gaze on me. Away from his wife's hoof. "Her hoof is breathtaking, Professor. No, it is I that need your help, for I am not the creature I need to be."

"I don't understand, Uncle." Exasperation burns away my sympathy. I've walked for hours and climbed a hill, small though it was. I am in no mood for a hermit's games. Abdel Jameela winces at the anger in my eyes and says, "My... my wife will explain."

I will try, my husband.

The voice is like song, and there is the strong scent of sweet flowers. Then she steps from behind the screen and I lose all my words. I scream. I call on God, and I scream.

Abdel Jameela's wife is no creature of God. Her head is a goat's and her mouth a wolf's muzzle. Fish-scales and jackal-hair cover her. A scorpion's tail curls behind her. I look into a woman's eyes set in a demon's face and I stagger backward, calling on God and my dead mother.

Please, learned one, be calm.

"What... what..." I can't form the words. I look to the floor. I try to bury my sight in the dirty carpets and hard-packed earth. Her voice is more beautiful than any woman's. And there is the powerful smell of jasmine and clove. A nightingale sings perfumed words at me while my mind's eye burns with horrors that would make the Almighty turn away.

If fear did not hold your tongue, you would ask what I am. Men have called my people by many names—ghoul, demon. Does a word matter so very much? What I am, learned one, is Abdel Jameela's wife.

For long moments I don't speak. If I don't speak, this nightmare will end. I will wake in Baghdad, or Beit Zujaaj. But I don't wake.

She speaks again, and I cover my ears, though the sound is beauty itself.

The words you hear come not from my mouth, and you do not hear them with your ears. I ask you to listen with your mind and your heart. We will die, my husband and I, if you will not lend us your skill. Have you, learned one, never needed to be something other that what you are?

Cinnamon scent and the sound of an oasis wind come to me. I cannot speak to this demon. My heart will stop if I do, I am certain. I want to run, but fear has fixed my feet. I turn to Abdel Jameela, who stands there wringing his hands.

"Why am I here, Uncle? God damn you, why did you call me here? There is no sick woman here! God protect me, I know nothing of... of ghouls, or—" A horrible thought comes to me. "You... you are not hoping to make her into a woman? Only God can..."

The old hermit casts his eyes downward. "Please... you must listen to my wife. I beg you." He falls silent and his wife, behind the screen again, goes on.

My husband and I have been on this hilltop too long, learned one. My body cannot stand so much time away from my people. I smell yellow roses and hear bumblebees droning beneath her voice. *If we stay in this place one more season, I will die.*

And without me to care for him and keep age's scourge from him, my sweet Abdel Jameela will die too. But across the desert there is a life for us. My father was a prince among our people. Long ago I left. For many reasons. But I never forsook my birthright. My father is dying now, I have word. He has left no sons and so his lands are mine. Mine, and my handsome husband's.

In her voice is a chorus of wind-chimes. Despite myself, I lift my eyes. She steps from behind the screen, clad now in a black abaya and a mask. Behind the mask's mesh is the glint of wolf-teeth. I look again to the floor, focusing on a faded blue spiral in the carpet and the kindness in that voice.

But my people do not love men. I cannot claim my lands unless things change. Unless my husband shows my people that he can change.

Somehow I force myself to speak. "What... what do you mean, change?"

There is a cymbal-shimmer in her voice and sandalwood incense fills my nostrils. *O learned one, you will help me to make these my Abdel Jameela's.*

She extends her slender brown hands, ablaze with henna. In each she holds a length of golden sculpture—goat-like legs ending in shining, cloven hooves. A thick braid of gold thread dances at the end of each statue-leg, alive.

Madness, and I must say so though this creature may kill me for it. "I have not the skill to do this! No man alive does!"

You will not do this through your skill alone. Just as I cannot do it through my sorcery alone. My art will guide yours as your hands work. She takes a step toward me and my shoulders clench at the sound of her hooves hitting the earth.

"No! No... I cannot do this thing."

"Please!" I jump at Abdel Jameela's voice, nearly having forgotten him. There are tears in the old man's eyes as he pulls at my galabeya, and his stink gets in my nostrils. "Please listen! We need your help. And we know what has brought you to Beit Zujaaj." The old man falls to his knees before me. "Please! Would not your Shireen aid us?"

With those words he knocks the wind from my lungs. How can he know that name? The shaykh hadn't lied—there *is* witchcraft at work here, and I should run from it.

But, Almighty God help me, Abdel Jameela is right. Fierce as she is, Shireen still has her dreamy Persian notions — that love is more important than money or duty or religion. If I turn this old man away…

My throat is dry and cracked. "How do you know of Shireen?" Each word burns.

His eyes dart away. "She has… ways, my wife."

"All protection comes from God." I feel foul even as I steel myself with the old words. Is this forbidden? Am I walking the path of those who displease the Almighty? God forgive me, it is hard to know or to care when my beloved is gone. "If I were a good Muslim, I would run down to the village now and… and…"

And what, learned one? Spread word of what you have seen? Bring men with spears and arrows? Why would you do this? Vanilla beans and the sound of rain give way to something else. Clanging steel and clean-burning fire. *I will not let you harm my husband. What we ask is not disallowed to you. Can you tell me, learned one, that it is in your book of what is blessed and what is forbidden not to give a man golden legs?*

It is not. Not in so many words. But this thing can't be acceptable in God's eyes. Can it? "Has this ever been done before?"

There are old stories. But it has been centuries. Each of her words spreads perfume and music and she asks, *Please, learned one, will you help us?* And then one scent rises above the others.

Almighty God protect me, it is the sweat-and-ambergris smell of my beloved. Shireen of the ribbing remark, who in quiet moments confessed her love of my learning. She *would* help them.

Have I any choice after that? This, then, the fruit of my study. And this, my reward for wishing to be more than what I am. A twisted, unnatural path.

"Very well." I reach for my small saw and try not to hear Abdel Jameela's weird whimpers as I sharpen it.

I give him poppy and hemlock, but as I work Abdel Jameela still screams, nearly loud enough to make my heart cease beating. His old body is going through things it should not be surviving. And I am the one putting him through these things, with knives and fire and bone-breaking clamps. I wad cotton and stuff it in my ears to block out the hermit's screams.

But I feel half-asleep as I do so, hardly aware of my own hands. Somehow the demon's magic is keeping Abdel Jameela alive and guiding me through this grisly task. It is painful, like having two minds crammed inside my skull and shadow-puppet poles lashed to my arms. I am burning up, and I can barely trace my thoughts. Slowly I become aware of the she-ghoul's voice in my head and the scent of apricots.

Cut there. Now the mercury powder. The cautering iron is hot. Put a rag in his mouth so he does not bite his tongue. I flay and cauterize and lose track of time. A fever cooks my mind away. I work through the evening prayer, then the night prayer. I feel withered inside.

In each step, Abdel Jameela's wife guides me. With her magic she rifles my mind for the knowledge she needs and steers my skilled fingers. For a long while there is only her voice in my head and the feeling of bloody instruments in my hands, which move with a life of their own.

Then I am holding a man's loose tendons in my right hand and thick golden threads in my left. There are shameful smells in the air and Abdel Jameela shouts and begs me to stop even though he is half-asleep with the great pot of drugs I have forced down his throat.

Something is wrong! The she-ghoul screams in my skull and Abdel Jameela passes out. My hands no longer dance magically. The shining threads shrivel in my fist. We have failed, though I know not exactly how.

No! No! Our skill! Our sorcery! But his body refuses! There are funeral wails in the air and the smell of houses burning. *My husband! Do something, physicker!*

The golden legs turn to dust in my hands. With my ears I hear Abdel Jameela's wife growl a wordless death-threat.

I deserve death! Almighty God, what have I done? An old man lies dying on my blanket. I have sawed off his legs at a she-ghoul's bidding. There is no strength save in God! I bow my head.

Then I see them. Just above where I've amputated Abdel Jameela's legs are the swollen bulges that I'd thought came from gout. But it is not gout that has made these. There is something buried beneath the skin of each leg. I take hold of my scalpel and flay each thin thigh. The old man moans with what little life he has left.

What are you doing? Abdel Jameela's wife asks the walls of my skull. I ignore her, pulling at a flap of the old man's thigh-flesh, revealing a corrupted sort of miracle.

Beneath Abdel Jameela's skin, tucked between muscles, are tiny legs. Thin as spindles and hairless. Each folded little leg ends in a minuscule hoof.

Unbidden, a memory comes to me—Shireen and I in the Caliph's orchards. A baby bird had fallen from its nest. I'd sighed and bit my lip and

13

my Shireen—a dreamer, but not a soft one—had laughed and clapped at my tender-heartedness.

I slide each wet gray leg out from under the flayed skin and gently unbend them. As I flex the little joints, the she-ghoul's voice returns.

What... what is this, learned one? Tell me!

For a long moment I am mute. Then I force words out, my throat still cracked. "I... I do not know. They are—they look like—the legs of a kid or a ewe still in the womb."

It is as if she nods inside my mind. *Or the legs of one of my people. I have long wondered how a mere man could captivate me so.*

"All knowledge and understanding lies with God," I say. "Perhaps your husband always had these within him. The villagers say he is of uncertain parentage. Or perhaps... Perhaps his love for you... The crippled beggars of Cairo are the most grotesque—and the best—in the world. It is said that they wish so fiercely to make money begging that their souls reshape their bodies from the inside out. Yesterday I saw such stories as nonsense. But yesterday I'd have named *you* a villager's fantasy, too." As I speak I continue to work the little legs carefully, to help their circulation. The she-ghoul's sorcery no longer guides my hands, but a physicker's nurturing routines are nearly as compelling. There is weakness here, and I do what I can to help it find strength.

The tiny legs twitch and kick in my hands.

Abdel Jameela's wife howls in my head. *They are drawing on my magic. Something pulls at—*The voice falls silent.

I let go of the legs and, before my eyes, they begin to grow. As they grow, they fill with color, as if blood flowed into them. Then fur starts to sprout upon them.

"There is no strength or safety but in God!" I try to close my eyes and focus on the words I speak but I can't. My head swims and my body swoons.

The spell that I cast on my poor husband to preserve him —these hidden hooves of his nurse on it! O, my surprising, wonderful husband! I hear loud lute music and smell lemongrass and then everything around me goes black.

When I wake I am on my back, looking up at a purple sky. An early morning sky. I am lying on a blanket outside the hovel. I sit up and Abdel Jameela hunches over me with his sour smell. Further away, near the hill-path, I see the black shape of his wife.

"Professor, you are awake! Good!" the hermit says. "We were about to leave."

But we are glad to have the chance to thank you.

My heart skips and my stomach clenches as I hear that voice in my head again. Kitten purrs and a crushed cardamom scent linger beneath the demon's words. I look at Abdel Jameela's legs.

They are sleek and covered in fur the color of almonds. And each leg ends in a perfect cloven hoof. He walks on them with a surprising grace.

Yes, learned one, my beloved husband lives and stands on two hooves. It would not be so if we hadn't had your help. You have our gratitude.

Dazedly clambering to my feet, I nod in the she-ghoul's direction. Abdel Jameela claps me on the back wordlessly and takes a few goat-strides toward the hill-path. His wife makes a slight bow to me. *With my people, learned one, gratitude is more than a word. Look toward the hovel.*

I turn and look. And my breath catches.

A hoard right out of the stories. Gold and spices. Jewels and musks. Silver and silks. Porcelain and punks of aloe.

It is probably ten times the dowry Shireen's father seeks.

We leave you this and wish you well. I have purged the signs of our work in the hovel. And in the language of the donkeys, I have called two wild asses to carry your goods. No troubles left to bother our brave friend!

I manage to smile gratefully with my head high for one long moment. Blood and bits of the old man's bone still stain my hands. But as I look on Abdel Jameela and his wife in the light of the sunrise, all my thoughts are not grim or grisly.

As they set off on the hill-path, the she-ghoul takes Abdel Jameela's arm, and the hooves of husband and wife scrabble against the pebbles of Beit Zujaaj hill. I stand stock-still, watching them walk toward the land of the ghouls.

They cross a bend in the path and disappear behind the hill. And a faint voice, full of mischievous laughter and smelling of early morning love in perfumed sheets, whispers in my head. *No troubles at all, learned one. For last night, your Shireen's husband-to-be lost his battle with the destroyer of delights.*

Can it really be so? The old vulture dead? And me a rich man? I should laugh and dance. Instead I am brought to my knees by the heavy memory of blood-spattered golden hooves. I wonder whether Shireen's suitor died from his illness, or from malicious magic meant to reward me. I fear for my soul. For a long while I kneel there and cry.

But after a while I can cry no longer. Tears give way to hopes I'd thought dead. I stand and thank Beneficent God, hoping it is not wrong to do so. Then I begin to put together an acceptable story about a secretly-wealthy hermit who has rewarded me for saving his wife's life. And I wonder what Shireen and her father will think of the man I have become.

THE CHILDREN OF THE SHARK GOD

~

by Peter S. Beagle

Once there was a village on an island that belonged to the Shark God. Every man in the village was a fisherman, and the women cooked their catch and mended their nets and sails, and painted their little boats. And because that island was sacred to him, the Shark God saw to it that there were always fish to be caught, and seals as well, in the waters beyond the coral reef, and protected the village from the great gray typhoons that came every year to flood other lagoons and blow down the trees and the huts of other islands. Therefore the children of the village grew fat and strong, and the women were beautiful and strong, and the fishermen were strong and high-hearted even when they were old.

In return for his benevolence the Shark God asked little from his people: only tribute of a single goat at the turn of each year. To the accompaniment of music and prayers, and with a wreath of plaited fresh flowers around its neck, it would be tethered in the lagoon at moonrise. Morning would find it gone, flower petals floating on the water, and the Shark God never seen—never in *that* form, anyway.

Now the Shark God could alter his shape as he pleased, like any god, but he never showed himself on land more than once in a generation. When he did, he was most often known to appear as a handsome young man, light-footed and charming. Only one woman ever recognized the divinity hiding behind the human mask. Her name was Mirali, and this tale is what is known about her, and about her children.

Mirali's parents were already aging when she was born, and had long since given up the hope of ever having a child—indeed, her name meant "the long-desired one." Her father had been crippled when the mast of his boat snapped during a storm and crushed his leg, falling on him, and if it had not been for their daughter, the old couple's lives would have been hard indeed. Mirali could not go out with the fishing fleet herself, of course—as she greatly wished to do, having loved the sea from her earliest memory—but she did every kind of work for any number of island families, whether cleaning houses, marketing, minding young children, or even assisting the midwife when a birthing was difficult or there were simply too many babies coming at the same time. She was equally known as a seamstress, and also as a cook for special feasts; nor was there anyone who could mend a pandanus-leaf thatching as quickly as she, though this is generally man's work. No drop of rain ever penetrated any pandanus roof that came under Mirali's hands.

Nor did she complain of her labors, for she was very proud of being able to care for her mother and father as a son would have done. Because of this, she was much admired and respected in the village, and young men came courting just as though she were a great beauty. Which she was not, being small and somewhat square-made, with straight brows—considered unlucky by most—and hips that gave no promise of a large family. But she had kind eyes, deep-set under those regrettable brows, and hair as black and thick as that of any woman on the island. Many, indeed, envied her; but of that Mirali knew nothing. She had no time for envy herself, nor for young men, either.

Now it happened that Mirali was often chosen by the village priest to sweep out the temple of the Shark God. This was not only a grand honor for a child barely turned seventeen but a serious responsibility as well, for sharks are cleanly in their habits, and to leave his spiritual dwelling disorderly would surely be to dishonor and anger the god himself. So Mirali was particularly attentive when she cleaned after the worshippers, making certain that no prayer whistle or burned stick of incense was left behind. And in this manner did the Shark God become aware of Mirali.

But he did not actually see her until a day came when, for a wonder, all her work was done, all her tasks out of the way until tomorrow, when they would begin all over again. At such times, rare as they were, Mirali would always wander down to the water, borrow a dugout or an outrigger canoe, and simply let herself drift in the lagoon—or even beyond the reef—

reading the clouds for coming weather, or the sea for migrating shoals of fish, or her own young mind for dreams. And if she should chance to see a black or gray or brown dorsal fin cutting the water nearby, she was never frightened, but would drowsily hail the great fish in fellowship, and ask it to convey her most respectful good wishes to the Shark God. For in that time children knew what was expected of them, by parents and gods alike.

She was actually asleep in an uncle's outrigger when the Shark God himself came to Mirali—as a mako, of course, since that is the most beautiful and graceful of all sharks. At the first sight of her, he instantly desired to shed his fishy form and climb into the boat to wake and caress her. But he knew that such behavior would terrify her as no shark could; and so, most reluctantly, he swam three times around her boat, which is magic, and then he sounded and disappeared.

When Mirali woke, it was with equal reluctance, for she had dreamed of a young man who longed for her, and who followed at a respectful distance, just at the edge of her dream, not daring to speak to her. She beached the dugout with a sigh, and went home to make dinner for her parents. But that night, and every night thereafter, the same dream came to her, again and again, until she was almost frantic with curiosity to know what it meant.

No priest or wisewoman could offer her any useful counsel, although most suspected that an immortal was concerned in the matter in some way. Some advised praying in a certain way at the temple; others directed her to brew tea out of this or that herb or tree bark to assure herself of a deep, untroubled sleep. But Mirali was not at all sure that she wanted to rid herself of that dream and that shy youth; she only wanted to understand them.

Then one afternoon she heard a man singing in the market, and when she turned to see she knew him immediately as the young man who always followed her in her dream. She went to him, marching straight across the marketplace and facing him boldly to demand, "Who are you? By what right do you come to me as you do?"

The young man smiled at her. He had black eyes, smooth dark-brown skin—with perhaps a touch of blue in it, when he stood in shadow—and fine white teeth, which seemed to Mirali to be just a trifle curved in at the tips. He said gently, "You interrupted my song."

Mirali started to respond, "So? You interrupt my sleep, night on night"—but she never finished saying what she meant to say, because in that moment she knew the Shark God. She bowed her head and bent her right knee, in the respectful manner of the island folk, and she whispered, "*Jalak...jalak*," which means *Lord*.

The young man took her hand and raised her up. "What my own people call me, you could not pronounce," he said to Mirali. "But to you I am no *jalak*, but your own faithful *olohe*," which is the common word for *servant*. "You must only call me by that name, and no other. Say it now."

Mirali was so frightened, first to be in the presence of the Shark God, and then to be asked to call him her servant, that she had to try the word several times before she could make it come clearly out of her mouth. The Shark God said, "Now, if you wish it, we will go down to the sea and be married. But I promise that I will bear no malice, no vengefulness, against your village or this island if you do not care to marry me. Have no fear, then, but tell me your true desire, Mirali."

The market folk were going about their own business, buying and selling, and more chatting than either. Only a few of them looked toward Mirali where she stood talking with the handsome singer; fewer seemed to take any interest in what the two might be saying to each other. Mirali took heart from this and said, more firmly, "I do wish to marry you, dear *jalak*— I mean, my *olohe*—but how can I live with you under the sea? I do not think I would even be able to hold my breath through the wedding, unless it was a very short ceremony."

Then the Shark God laughed aloud, which he had truly never done in all his long life, and the sound was so full and so joyous that flowers fell from the trees and, unbidden, wove themselves into Mirali's hair, and into a wreath around her neck. The waves of the sea echoed his laughter, and the Shark God lifted Mirali in his arms and raced down to the shore, where sharks and dolphins, tuna and black marlin and barracuda, and whole schools of shimmering wrasse and clownfish and angelfish that swim as one had crowded into the lagoon together, until the water itself turned golden as the morning and green as sunset. The great deepwater octopus, whom no one ever sees except the sperm whale, came also; and it has been said—by people who were not present, nor even born then—that there were mermaids and merrows as well, and even the terrible Paikea, vast as an island, the Master of All Sea Monsters, though he prudently stayed far outside the reef. And all these were there for the wedding of Mirali and the Shark God.

The Shark God lifted Mirali high above his head—she was startled, but no longer frightened—and he spoke out, first in the language of Mirali's people, so that she would understand, and then in the tongue known by everything that swims in every sea and every river. "This is Mirali, whom I take now to wife, and whom you will love and protect from this day forth, and honor as you do me, and as you will honor our children, and their children, always." And the sound that came up from the waters in answer is not a sound that can be told.

In time, when the lagoon was at last empty again, and when husband and wife had sworn and proved their love in the shadows of the mangroves, she said to him, very quietly, "Beloved, my own *olohe*, now that we are wed, shall I ever see you again? For I may be only an ignorant island woman, but I know what too often comes of marriages between gods and mortals. Your children will have been born—I can feel this already—by the time you come again for your tribute. I will nurse them, and bring them up to respect their lineage, as is right... but meanwhile you will swim far away, and perhaps father others, and forget us, as is also your right. You are a god, and gods do not raise families. I am not such a fool that I do not know this."

But the Shark God put his finger under Mirali's chin, lifting her face to his and saying, "My wife, I could no more forget that you *are* my wife than forget what I am. Understand that we may not live together on your island, as others do, for my life is in the sea, and of the sea, and this form that you hold in your arms is but a shadow, little more than a dream, compared to my true self. Yet I will come to you every year, without fail, when my tribute is due—every year, here, where we lie together. Remember, Mirali."

Then he closed his eyes, which were black, as all sharks' eyes are, and fell asleep in her arms, and there is no woman who can say what Mirali felt, lying there under the mangroves with her own eyes wide in the moonlight.

When morning came, she walked back to her parents' house alone.

In time it became plain that Mirali was with child, but no one challenged or mocked her to her face, for she was much loved in the village, and her family greatly esteemed. Yet even so it was considered a misfortune by most, and a disgrace by some, as is not the case on certain other islands. If the talk was not public, it was night talk, talk around the cooking fire, talk at the stream over the slapping of wash on stone. Mirali was perfectly aware of this.

She carried herself well and proudly, and it was agreed, even by those who murmured ill of her, that she looked more beautiful every day, even as her belly swelled out like the fishermen's sails. But she shocked the midwife,

21

who was concerned for her narrow hips, and for the chance of twins, by insisting on going off by herself to give birth. Her mother and father were likewise troubled; and the old priest himself took a hand, arguing powerfully that the birth should take place in the very temple of the Shark God. Such a thing had never been allowed, or even considered, but the old priest had his own suspicions about Mirali's unknown lover.

Mirali smiled and nodded respectfully to anyone who had anything to say about the matter, as was always her way. But on the night when her time came she went to the lagoon where she had been wed, as she knew that she must; and in the gentle breath of its shallows her children were born without undue difficulty. For they were indeed twins, a boy and a girl.

Mirali named the boy Keawe, after her father, and the girl Kokinja, which means *born in moonlight*. And as she looked fondly upon the two tiny, noisy, hungry creatures she and the Shark God had made together, she remembered his last words to her and smiled.

Keawe and Kokinja grew up the pets of their family, being not only beautiful but strong and quick and naturally kindly. This was a remarkable thing, considering the barely veiled scorn with which most of the other village children viewed them, taking their cue from the remarks passed between their parents. On the other hand, while there was notice taken of the very slight bluish tinge to Keawe's skin, and the fact that Kokinja's perfect teeth curved just the least bit inward, nothing was ever said concerning these particular traits.

They both swam before they could walk properly; and the creatures of the sea guarded them closely, as they had sworn. More than once little Keawe, who at two and three years regarded the waves and tides as his own servants, was brought safely back to shore clinging to the tail of a dolphin, the flipper of a seal, or even the dorsal fin of a reef shark. Kokinja had an octopus as her favorite playmate, and would fall as trustingly asleep wrapped in its eight arms as in those of her mother. And Mirali herself learned to put her faith in the wildest sea as completely as did her children. That was the gift of her husband.

Her greatest joy lay in seeing them grow into his image (though she always thought that Keawe resembled her father more than his own), and come to their full strength and beauty in a kind of innocence that kept them free of any vanity. Being twins, they understood each other in a wordless way that even Mirali could not share. This pleased her, for she thought, watching them playing silently together, *they will still have one another when I am gone.*

The Shark God saw the children when he came every year for his tribute, but only while they were asleep. In human form he would stand silently between their floor mats, studying them out of his black, expressionless eyes for a long time, before he finally turned away. Once he said quietly to Mirali, "It is good that I see them no more often than this. A good thing." Another time she heard him murmur to himself, *"Simpler for sharks..."*

As for Mirali herself, the love of the Shark God warded off the cruelty of the passing years, so that she continued to appear little older than her own children. They teased her about this, saying that she embarrassed them, but they were proud, and likewise aware that their mother remained attractive to the men of the village. A number of those came shyly courting, but all were turned away with such civility that they hardly knew they had been rejected; and certainly not by a married woman who saw her husband only once in a twelvemonth.

When Keawe and Kokinja were little younger than she had been when she heard a youth singing in the marketplace, she called them from the lagoon, where they spent most of their playtime, and told them simply, "Your father is the Shark God himself. It is time you knew this."

In all the years that she had imagined this moment, she had guessed—so she thought—every possible reaction that her children might have to these words. Wonder... awe... pride... fear (there are many tales of gods eating their children)... even laughing disbelief—she was long prepared for each of these. But it had never occurred to her that both Keawe and Kokinja might be immediately furious at their father for—as they saw it—abandoning his family and graciously condescending to spare a glance over them while passing through the lagoon to gobble his annual goat. Keawe shouted into the wind, "I would rather the lowest palm-wine drunkard on the island had sired us than this...this *god* who cannot be bothered with his wife and children but once a year. Yes, I would prefer that by far!"

"That one day has always lighted my way to the next," his mother said quietly. She turned to Kokinja. "And as for you, child—"

But Kokinja interrupted her, saying firmly, "The Shark God may have a daughter, but I have no more father today than I had yesterday. But if I *am* the Shark God's daughter, then I will set out tomorrow and swim the sea until I find him. And when I find him, I will ask questions—oh, indeed, I will ask him questions. And he *will* answer me." She tossed her black hair, which was the image of Mirali's hair, as her eyes were those of her father's people. Mirali's own eyes filled with tears as she looked at her nearly grown daughter, remembering a small girl stamping one tiny foot and shouting, "Yes, I will! Yes, I will!" *Oh, there is this much truth in what they say*, she thought to her husband. *You have truly no idea what you have sired.*

In the morning, as she had sworn, Kokinja kissed Mirali and Keawe farewell and set forth into the sea to find the Shark God. Her brother, *being* her brother, was astonished to realize that she meant to keep her vow, and actually begged her to reconsider, when he was not ordering her to do so. But Mirali knew that Kokinja was as much at home in the deep as anything with gills and a tail; and she further knew that no harm would come to Kokinja from any sea creature, because of their promise on her own wedding day. So she said nothing to her daughter, except to remind her, "If any creature can tell you exactly where the Shark God will be at any given moment, it will be the great Paikea, who came to our wedding. Go well, then, and keep warm."

Kokinja had swum out many a time beyond the curving coral reef that had created the lagoon a thousand or more years before, and she had no more fear of the open sea than of the stream where she had drawn water all her life. But this time, when she paused among the little scarlet-and-black fish that swarmed about a gap in the reef, and turned to see her brother Keawe waving after her, then a hand seemed to close on her heart, and she could not see anything clearly for a while. All the same, the moment her vision cleared, she waved once to Keawe and plunged on past the reef out to sea. The next time she looked back, both reef and island were long lost to her sight.

Now it must be understood that Kokinja did not swim as humans do, being who she was. From her first day splashing in the shallows of the lagoon, she had truly swum like a fish, or perhaps a dolphin. Swimming in this manner she outsped sailfish, marlin, tunny and tuna alike; even had the barracuda not been bound by his oath to the Shark God, he could never have come within snapping distance of the Shark God's daughter. Only the seagull and the great white wandering albatross, borne on the wind, kept even with the small figure far below, utterly alone between horizon and horizon, racing on and on under the darkening sky.

The favor of the waters applied to Kokinja in other ways. The fish themselves always seemed to know when she grew hungry, for then schools of salmon or mackerel would materialize out of the depths to accompany her, and she would express proper gratitude and devour one or another as she swam, as a shark would do. When she tired, she either curled up in a slow-rocking swell and slept, like a seal, or clung to the first sea turtle she encountered and drowsed peacefully on its shell—the leatherbacks were the most comfortable—while it courteously paddled along on the surface, so that she could breathe. Should she arrive at an island, she would haul out on the beach—again, like a seal—and sleep fully for a day; then bathe as she might, and be on her way once more.

Only a storm could overtake her, and those did frighten her at first, striking from the east or the north to tear fiercely at the sea. Not being a fish herself, she could not stay below the vast waves that played with her, Shark God's daughter or no, tossing her back and forth as an orca will toss its prey, then suddenly dropping out from under her, so that she floundered in their hollows, choking and gasping desperately, aware as she so rarely was of her own human weakness and fragility. But she was determined that she would not die without letting her father know what she thought of him; and by and by she learned to laugh at the lightning overhead, even when it struck the water on every side of her, as though *something* knew she was near and alone. She would laugh, and she would call out, not caring that her voice was lost in wind and thunder, "Missed me again—so sorry, you missed me again!" For if she was the Shark God's daughter, who could swim the sea, she was Mirali's stubborn little girl too.

Keawe, Mirali's son, was of a different nature than his sister. While he shared her anger at the Shark God's neglect, he simply decided to go on living as though he had no father, which was, after all, what he had always believed. And while he feared for Kokinja in the deep sea, and sometimes yearned to follow her, he was even more concerned about their mother. Like most grown children, he believed, despite the evidence of his eyes, that Mirali would dwindle away, starve, pine and die should both he and Kokinja be gone. Therefore he stayed at home and apprenticed himself to Uhila, the master builder of outrigger canoes, telling his mother that he would build the finest boat ever made, and in it he would one day bring Kokinja home. Mirali smiled gently and said nothing.

Uhila was known as a hard, impatient master, but Keawe studied well and swiftly learned everything the old man could teach him, which was not merely about the choosing of woods, nor about the weaving of all manner of sails and ropes, nor about the designing of different boats for different uses; nor how to warp the bamboo float, the *ama*, just so, and bind the long spars, the *iaka*, so that the connection to the hull would hold even in the worst storms. Uhila taught him, more importantly, the understanding of wood, and of water, and of the ancient relationship between them: half alliance, half war. At the end of Keawe's apprenticeship, gruff Uhila blessed him and gave him his own set of tools, which he had never done before in the memory of even the oldest villagers.

But he said also to the boy, "You do not love the boats as I do, for their own sake, for the joy of the making. I could tell that the first day you came to me. You are bound by a purpose—you need a certain boat, and in order to achieve it you needed to achieve every other boat. Tell me, have I spoken truly?"

Then Keawe bowed his head and answered, "I never meant to deceive you, wise Uhila. But my sister is far away, gone farther than an ordinary sailing canoe could find her, and it was on me to build the one boat that could bring her back. For that I needed all your knowledge, and all your wisdom. Forgive me if I have done wrong."

But Uhila looked out at the lagoon, where a new sailing canoe, more beautiful and splendid than any other in the harbor danced like a butterfly at anchor, and he said, "It is too big for any one person to paddle, too big to sail. What will you do for a crew?"

"He will have a crew," a calm voice answered. Both men turned to see Mirali smiling at them. She said to Keawe, "You will not want anyone else. You know that."

And Keawe did know, which was why he had never considered setting out with a crew at all. So he said only, "There is a comfortable seat near the bow for you, and you will be our lookout as you paddle. But I must sit in the rear and take charge of the tiller and the sails."

"For now," replied Mirali gravely, and she winked just a little at Uhila, who was deeply shocked by the notion of a woman steering any boat at all, let alone winking at him.

So Keawe and his mother went searching for Kokinja, and thus—though neither of them spoke of it—for the Shark God. They were, as they had been from Keawe's birth, pleasant company for one another: Keawe often sang the songs Mirali had taught him and his sister as children, and she herself would in turn tell old tales from older times, when all the gods were young, and all was possible. At other times, with a following sea and the handsome yellow sail up, they gave the canoe its head and sat in perfectly companionable silence, thinking thoughts that neither of them ever asked about. When they were hungry, Keawe plunged into the sea and returned swiftly with as much fish as they could eat; when it rained, although they had brought more water than food with them, still they caught the rain in the sail, since one can never have too much fresh water at sea. They slept by turns, warmly, guiding themselves by the stars and the turning of the earth, in the manner of birds, though their only real concern was to keep on straight toward the sunset, as Kokinja had done.

At times, watching his mother regard a couple of flying fish barely missing the sail, or turn her head to laugh at the dolphins accompanying the boat, with her still-black hair blowing across her cheek, Keawe would think, *god or no god, my father was a fool.* But unlike Kokinja, he thought it in pity more than anger. And if a shark should escort them for a little, cruising lazily along with the boat, he would joke with it in his mind—*Are you my aunt? Are you my cousin?*—for he had always had more humor than his sister. Once, when a great blue mako traveled with them for a full day, dawn to dark, now and then circling or sounding, but always near, rolling one black eye back to study them, he whispered, "Father? Is it you?" But it was only once, and the mako vanished at sunset anyway.

On her journey Kokinja met no one who could—or would—tell her where the Shark God might be found. She asked every shark she came upon, sensibly enough; but sharks are a close-mouthed lot, and not one hammerhead, not one whitetip, not one mako or tiger or reef shark ever offered her so much as a hint as to her father's whereabouts. Manta rays and sawfishes were more forthcoming; but mantas, while beautiful, are extremely stupid, and taking a sawfish's advice is always risky: ugly as they know themselves to be, they will say anything to appear wise. As for cod, they travel in great schools and shoals, and think as one, so that to ask a single cod a question is to receive an answer—right or wrong—from a thousand, ten thousand, a hundred thousand. Kokinja found this unnerving.

So she swam on, day after day: a little weary, a little lonely, a good deal older, but as determined as ever not to turn back without confronting the Shark God and demanding the truth of him. *Who are you, that my mother should have accepted you under such terms as you offered? How could you yourself have endured to see her—to see us, your children—only once in every year? Is that a god's idea of love?*

One night, the water having turned warm and silkily calm, she was drifting in a half-dream of her own lagoon when she woke with a soft bump against what she at first thought an island. It loomed darkly over her, hiding the moon and half the stars, yet she saw no trees, even in silhouette, nor did she hear any birds or smell any sort of vegetation. What she did smell awakened her completely and set her scrambling backward into deeper water, like a frightened crab. It was a fish smell, in part, cold and clear and salty, but there was something of the reptilian about it: equally cold, but dry as well, for all that it emanated from an island—or *not* an island?—sitting in the middle of the sea. It was not a smell she knew, and yet somehow she felt that she should.

Kokinja went on backing into moonlight, which calmed her, and had just begun to swim cautiously around the island when it moved. Eyes as big and yellow-white as lighthouse lamps turned slowly to keep her in view, while an enormous, seemingly formless body lost any resemblance to an island, heaving itself over to reveal limbs ending in grotesquely huge claws. Centered between the foremost of them were two moon-white pincers, big enough, clearly, to twist the skull off a sperm whale. The sound it uttered was too low for Kokinja to catch, but she felt it plainly in the sea.

She knew what it was then, and could only hope that her voice would reach whatever the creature used for ears. She said, "Great Paikea, I am Kokinja. I am very small, and I mean no one any harm. Please, can you tell me where I may find my father, the Shark God?"

The lighthouse eyes truly terrified her then, swooping toward her from different directions, with no head or face behind them. She realized that they were on long whiplike stalks, and that Paikea's diamond-shaped head was sheltered under a scarlet carapace studded with scores of small, sharp spines. Kokinja was too frightened to move, which was as well, for Paikea spoke to her in the water, saying against her skin, "Be still, child, that I may see you more clearly, and not bite you in two by mistake. It has happened so." Then Kokinja, who had already swum half an ocean, thought that she might never again move from where she was.

She waited a long time for the great creature to speak again, but was not at all prepared for Paikea's words when they did come. "I could direct you to your father—I could even take you to him—but I will not. You are not ready."

When Kokinja could at last find words to respond, she demanded, "Not *ready*? Who are *you* to say that I am not ready to see my own father?" Mirali and Keawe would have known her best then: she was Kokinja, and anything she feared she challenged.

"What your father has to say to you, you are not yet prepared to hear," came the voice in the sea. "Stay with me a little, Shark God's daughter. I am not what your father is, but I may perhaps be a better teacher for you." When Kokinja hesitated, and clearly seemed about to refuse, Paikea continued, "Child, you have nowhere else to go but home—and I think you are not ready for that, either. Climb on my back now, and come with me." Even for Kokinja, that was an order.

Paikea took her—once she had managed the arduous and tiring journey from claw to leg to mountainside shoulder to a deep, hard hollow in the carapace that might have been made for a frightened rider—to an island (a real one this time, though well smaller than her own) bright with birds and flowers and wild fruit. When the birds' cries and chatter ceased for a moment, she could hear the softer swirl of running water farther inland, and the occasional thump of a falling coconut from one of the palms that dotted the beach. It was a lonely island, being completely uninhabited, but very beautiful.

There Paikea left her to swim ashore, saying only, "Rest," and nothing more. She did as she was bidden, sleeping under bamboo trees, waking to eat and drink, and sleeping again, dreaming always of her mother and brother at home. Each dream seemed more real than the one before, bringing Mirali and Keawe closer to her, until she wept in her sleep, struggling to keep from waking. Yet when Paikea came again, after three days, she demanded audaciously, "What wisdom do you think you have for me that I would not hear if it came from my father? I have no fear of anything he may say to me."

"You have very little fear at all, or you would not be here," Paikea answered her. "You feared me when we first met, I think—but two nights' good sleep, and you are plainly past *that*." Kokinja thought she discerned something like a chuckle in the wavelets lapping against her feet where she sat, but she could not be sure. Paikea said, "But courage and attention are not the same thing. Listening is not the same as hearing. You may be sure I am correct in this, because I know everything."

It was said in such a matter-of-fact manner that Kokinja had to battle back the impulse to laugh. She said, with all the innocence she could muster, "I thought it was my father who was supposed to know everything."

"Oh, no," Paikea replied quite seriously. "The only thing the Shark God has ever known is how to be the Shark God. It is the one thing he is supposed to be—not a teacher, not a wise master, and certainly not a father or a husband. But they *will* take human form, the gods will, and that is where the trouble begins, because they none of them know how to be human—how can they, tell me that?" The eye-stalks abruptly plunged closer, as though Paikea were truly waiting for an enlightening answer. "I have always been grateful for my ugliness; for the fact that there is no way for me to disguise it, no temptation to hide in a more comely shape and pretend to believe that I am what I pretend. Because I am certain I would do just that, if I could. It is lonely sometimes, knowing everything."

Again Kokinja felt the need to laugh; but this time it was somehow easier not to, because Paikea was obviously anxious for her to understand his words. But she fought off sympathy as well, and confronted Paikea defiantly, saying, "You really think that we should never have been born, don't you, my brother and I?"

Paikea appeared to be neither surprised nor offended by her bold words. "Child, what I know is important—what I *think* is not important at all. It is the same way with the Shark God." Kokinja opened her mouth to respond hotly, but the great crab-monster moved slightly closer to shore, and she closed it again. Paikea said, "He is fully aware that he should never have taken a human wife, created a human family in the human world. And he knows also, as he was never meant to know, that when your mother dies— as she will—when you and your brother in time die, his heart will break. No god is supposed to know such a thing; they are simply not equipped to deal with it. Do you understand me, brave and foolish girl?"

Kokinja was not sure whether she understood, and less sure of whether she even wanted to understand. She said slowly, "So he thinks that he should never see us, to preserve his poor heart from injury and grief? Perhaps he thinks it will be for our own good? Parents always say that, don't they, when they really mean for their own convenience. Isn't that what they say, wise Paikea?"

"I never knew my parents," Paikea answered thoughtfully.

"And *I* have never known *him*," snapped Kokinja. "Once a year he comes to lie with his wife, to snap up his goat, to look at his children as we sleep. But what is that to a wife who longs for her husband, to children aching for a real father? God or no god, the very least he could have done would have been to tell us himself what he was, and not leave us to imagine him, telling ourselves stories about why he left our beautiful mother... why he didn't want to be with us..." She realized, to her horror, that she was very close to tears, and gulped them back as she had done with laughter. "I will never forgive him," she said. "Never."

"Then why have you swum the sea to find him?" asked Paikea. It snapped its horrid pale claws as a human will snap his fingers, waiting for her answer with real interest.

"To *tell* him that I will never forgive him," Kokinja answered. "So there is something even Paikea did not know." She felt triumphant, and stopped wanting to cry.

"You are still not ready," said Paikea, and was abruptly gone, slipping beneath the waves without a ripple, as though its vast body had never been there. It did not return for another three days, during which Kokinja explored the island, sampling every fruit that grew there, fishing as she had done at sea when she desired a change of diet, sleeping when she chose, and continuing to nurse her sullen anger at her father.

Finally, she sat on the beach with her feet in the water, and she called out, "Great Paikea, of your kindness, come to me, I have a riddle to ask you." None of the sea creatures among whom she had been raised could ever resist a riddle, and she did not see why it should be any different even for the Master of All Sea Monsters.

Presently she heard the mighty creature's voice saying, "You yourself are as much a riddle to me as any you may ask." Paikea surfaced close enough to shore that Kokinja felt she could have reached out and touched its head. It said, "Here I am, Shark God's daughter."

"This is my riddle," Kokinja said. "If you cannot answer it, you who know everything, will you take me to my father?"

"A most human question," Paikea replied, "since the riddle has nothing to do with the reward. Ask, then."

Kokinja took a long breath. "Why would any god ever choose to sire sons and daughters with a mortal woman? Half-divine, yet we die—half-supreme, yet we are vulnerable, breakable—half-perfect, still we are forever crippled by our human hearts. What cruelty could compel an immortal to desire such unnatural children?"

Paikea considered. It closed its huge, glowing eyes on their stalks; it waved its claws this way and that; it even rumbled thoughtfully to itself, as a man might when pondering serious matters. Finally Paikea's eyes opened, and there was a curious amusement in them as it regarded Kokinja. She did not notice this, being young.

"Well riddled," Paikea said. "For I know the answer, but have not the right to tell you. So I cannot." The great claws snapped shut on the last word, with a grinding clash that hinted to Kokinja how fearsome an enemy Paikea could be.

"Then you will keep your word?" Kokinja asked eagerly. "You *will* take me where my father is?"

"I always keep my word," answered Paikea, and sank from sight. Kokinja never saw him again.

But that evening, as the red sun was melting into the green horizon, and the birds and fish that feed at night were setting about their business, a young man came walking out of the water toward Kokinja. She knew him immediately, and her first instinct was to embrace him. Then her heart surged fiercely within her, and she leaped to her feet, challenging him. "So! At last you have found the courage to face your own daughter. Look well, sea-king, for I have no fear of you, and no worship." She started to add, "Nor any love, either," but that last caught in her throat, just as had happened to her mother Mirali when she scolded a singing boy for invading her dreams.

The Shark God spoke the words for her. "You have no reason in the world to love me." His voice was deep and quiet, and woke strange echoes in her memory of such a voice overheard in candlelight in the sweet, safe place between sleep and waking. "Except, perhaps, that I have loved your mother from the moment I first saw her. That will have to serve as my defense, and my apology as well. I have no other."

"And a pitiful enough defense it is," Kokinja jeered. "I asked Paikea why a god should ever choose to father a child with a mortal, and he would not answer me. Will you?" The Shark God did not reply at once, and Kokinja stormed on. "My mother never once complained of your neglect, but I am not my mother. I am grateful for my half-heritage only in that it enabled me to seek you out, hide as you would. For the rest, I spit on my ancestry, my birthright, and all else that connects me to you. I just came to tell you that."

Having said this, she began to weep, which infuriated her even more, so that she actually clenched her fists and pounded the Shark God's shoulders while he stood still, making no response. Shamed as she was, she ceased both activities soon enough, and stood silently facing her father with her head high and her wet eyes defiant. For his part, the Shark God studied her out of his own unreadable black eyes, moving neither to caress nor to punish her, but only—as it seemed to Kokinja—to understand the whole of what she was. And to do her justice, she stared straight back, trying to do the same.

When the Shark God spoke at last, Mirali herself might not have known his voice, for the weariness and grief in it. He said, "Believe as you will, but until your mother came into my life, I had no smallest desire for children, neither with beings like myself, nor with any mortal, however beautiful she might be. We do find humans dangerously appealing, all of us, as is well-known—perhaps precisely because of their short lives and the delicacy of their construction—and many a deity, unable to resist such haunting vulnerability, has scattered half-divine descendants all over your world. Not I; there was nothing I could imagine more contemptible than deliberately to create such a child, one who would share fully in neither inheritance, and live to curse me for it, as you have done." Kokinja flushed and looked down, but offered no contrition for anything she had said. The Shark God said mildly, "As well you made no apology. Your mother has never once lied to me, nor should you."

"Why should I ever apologize to you?" Kokinja flared up again. "If you had no wish for children, what are my brother and I doing here?" Tears threatened again, but she bit them savagely back. "You are a god—you could always have kept us from being born! *Why are we here?*"

To her horror, her legs gave way under her then, and she sank to her knees, still not weeping, but finding herself shamefully weak with rage and confusion. Yet when she looked up, the Shark God was kneeling beside her, for all the world like a playmate helping her to build a sand castle. It was she who stared at him without expression now, while he regarded her with the terrifying pity that belongs to the gods alone. Kokinja could not bear it for more than a moment; but every time she turned her face away, her father gently turned her toward him once more. He said, "Daughter of mine, do you know how old I am?"

Kokinja shook her head silently. The Shark God said, "I cannot tell you in years, because there were no such things at my beginning. Time was very new then, and Those who were already here had not yet decided whether this was...*suitable*, can you understand me, dear one?" The last two words, heard for the first time in her life, caused Kokinja to shiver like a small animal in the rain. Her father did not appear to notice.

"I had no parents, and no childhood, such as you and your brother have had—I simply *was,* and always had been, beyond all memory, even my own. All true enough, to my knowledge—and then a leaky outrigger canoe bearing a sleeping brown girl drifted across my endless life, and I, who can never change... I changed. Do you hear what I am telling you, daughter of that girl, daughter who hates me?"

The Shark God's voice was soft and uncertain. "I told your mother that it was good that I saw her and you and Keawe only once in a year—that if I allowed myself that wonder even a day more often I might lose myself in you, and never be able to find myself again, nor ever wish to. Was that cowardly of me, Kokinja? Perhaps so, quite likely unforgivably so." It was he who looked away now, rising and turning to face the darkening scarlet sea. He said, after a time, "But one day—one day that *will* come—when you find yourself loving as helplessly, and as certainly wrongly, as I, loving against all you know, against all you are... remember me then."

To this Kokinja made no response; but by and by she rose herself and stood silently beside her father, watching the first stars waken, one with each heartbeat of hers. She could not have said when she at last took his hand.

"I cannot stay," she said. "It is a long way home, and seems longer now."

The Shark God touched her hair lightly. "You will go back more swiftly than you arrived, I promise you that. But if you could remain with me a little time..." He left the words unfinished.

"A little time," Kokinja agreed. "But in return..." She hesitated, and her father did not press her, but only waited for her to continue. She said presently, "I know that my mother never wished to see you in your true form, and for herself she was undoubtedly right. But I... I am not my mother." She had no courage to say more than that.

The Shark God did not reply for some while, and when he did his tone was deep and somber. "Even if I granted it, even if you could bear it, you could never see all of what I am. Human eyes cannot"—he struggled for the exact word—"they do not *bend* in the right way. It was meant as a kindness, I think, just as was the human gift of forgetfulness. You have no idea how the gods envy you that, the forgetting."

"Even so," Kokinja insisted. "Even so, I would not be afraid. If you do not know *that* by now..."

"Well, we will see," answered the Shark God, exactly as all human parents have replied to importunate children at one time or another. And with that, even Kokinja knew to content herself.

In the morning, she plunged into the waves to seek her breakfast, as did her father on the other side of the island. She never knew where he slept—or if he slept at all—but he returned in time to see her emerging from the water with a fish in her mouth and another in her hand. She tore them both to pieces, like any shark, and finished the meal before noticing him. Abashed, she said earnestly, "When I am at home, I cook my food as my mother taught me—but in the sea..."

"Your mother always cooks dinner for me," the Shark God answered quietly. "We wait until you two are asleep, or away, and then she will come down to the water and call. It has been so from the first."

"Then she *has* seen you—"

"No. I take my tribute afterward, when I leave her, and she never follows then." The Shark God smiled and sighed at the same time, studying his daughter's puzzled face. He said, "What is between us is hard to explain, even to you. Especially to you."

The Shark God lifted his head to taste the morning air, which was cool and cloudless over water so still that Kokinja could hear a dolphin breathing too far away for her to see. He frowned slightly, saying, "Storm. Not now, but in three days' time. It will be hard."

Kokinja did not show her alarm. She said grimly, "I came here through storms. I survived those."

"Child," her father said, and it was the first time he had called her that, "you will be with me." But his eyes were troubled, and his voice strangely distant. For the rest of that day, while Kokinja roamed the island, dozed in the sun, and swam for no reason but pleasure, he hardly spoke, but continued watching the horizon, long after both sunset and moonset. When she woke the next morning, he was still pacing the shore, though she could see no change at all in the sky, but only in his face. Now and then he would strike a balled fist against his thigh and whisper to himself through tight pale lips. Kokinja, walking beside him and sharing his silence, could not help noticing how human he seemed in those moments—how mortal, and how mortally afraid. But she could not imagine the reason for it, not until she woke on the following day and felt the sand cold under her.

Since her arrival on the little island, the weather had been so clement that the sand she slept on remained perfectly warm through the night. Now its chill woke her well before dawn, and even in the darkness she could see the mist on the horizon, and the lightning beyond the mist. The sun, orange as the harvest moon, was never more than a sliver between the mounting thunderheads all day. The wind was from the northeast, and there was ice in it.

Kokinja stood alone on the shore, watching the first rain marching toward her across the waves. She had no longer any fear of storms, and was preparing to wait out the tempest in the water, rather than take refuge under the trees. But the Shark God came to her then and led her away to a small cave, where they sat together, listening to the rising wind. When she was hungry, he fished for her, saying, "They seek shelter too, like anyone else in such conditions—but they will come for me." When she became downhearted, he hummed nursery songs that she recalled Mirali singing to her and Keawe very long ago, far away on the other side of any storm. He even sang her oldest favorite, which began:

When a raindrop leaves the sky,
it turns and turns to say good-bye.
"Good-bye, dear clouds, so far away,
I'll come again another day...."

"Keawe never really liked that one," she said softly. "It made him sad. How do you know all our songs?"

"I listened," the Shark God said, and nothing more.

"I wish... I *wish*..." Kokinja's voice was almost lost in the pounding of the rain. She thought she heard her father answer, "I, too," but in that moment he was on his feet, striding out of the cave into the storm, as heedless of the weather as though it were flowers sluicing down his body, summer-morning breezes greeting his face. Kokinja hurried to keep up with him. The wind snatched the breath from her lungs, and knocked her down more than once, but she matched his pace to the shore, even so. It seemed to her that the tranquil island had come malevolently alive with the rain; that the vines slapping at her shoulders and entangling her ankles had not been there yesterday, nor had the harsh branches that caught at her hair. All the same, when he turned at the water's edge, she was beside him.

"*Mirali.*" He said the one word, and pointed out into the flying, whipping spindrift and the solid mass of sea-wrack being driven toward land by the howling grayness beyond. Kokinja strained her eyes and finally made out the tiny flicker that was not water, the broken chip of wood sometimes bobbing helplessly on its side, sometimes hurled forward or sideways from one comber crest to another. Staring through the rain, shaking with cold and fear, it took her a moment to realize that her father was gone. Taller than the wavetops, taller than any ship's masts, taller than the wind, she saw the deep blue dorsal and tail fins, so distant from each other, gliding toward the wreck, on which she could see no hint of life. Then she plunged into the sea—shockingly, almost alarmingly warm, by comparison with the air—and followed the Shark God.

It was the first and only glimpse she ever had of the thing her father was. As he had warned her, she never saw him fully: both her eyesight and the sea itself seemed too small to contain him. Her mind could take in a magnificent and terrible fish; her soul knew that that was the least part of what she was seeing; her body knew that it could bear no more than that smallest vision. The mark of his passage was a ripple of beaten silver across the wild water, and although the storm seethed and roared to left and right of her, she swam in his wake as effortlessly as he made the way for her. And whether he actually uttered it or not, she heard his fearful cry in her head, over and over—"*Mirali! Mirali!*"

The mast was in two pieces, the sail a yellow rag, the rudder split and the tiller broken off altogether. The Shark God regained the human form so swiftly that Kokinja was never entirely sure that she had truly seen what she knew she had seen, and the two of them righted the sailing canoe together. Keawe lay in the bottom of the boat, barely conscious, unable to speak, only to point over the side. There was no sign of Mirali.

"Stay with him," her father ordered Kokinja, and he sounded as a shark would have done, vanishing instantly into the darkness below the ruined keel. Kokinja crouched by Keawe, lifting his head to her lap and noticing a deep gash on his forehead and another on his cheekbone. "Tiller," he whispered. "Snapped... flew straight at me..." His right hand was clenched around some small object; when Kokinja pried it gently open—for he seemed unable to release it himself—she recognized a favorite bangle of their mother's. Keawe began to cry.

"Couldn't hold her... *couldn't hold...*" Kokinja could not hear a word, for the wind, but she read his eyes and she held him to her breast and rocked him, hardly noticing that she was weeping herself.

The Shark God was a long time finding his wife, but he brought her up in his arms at last, her eyes closed and her face as quiet as always. He placed her gently in the canoe with her children, brought the boat safely to shore, and bore Mirali's body to the cave where he had taken Kokinja for shelter.

And while the storm still lashed the island, and his son and daughter sang the proper songs, he dug out a grave and buried her there, with no marker at her head, there being no need. "I will know," he said, "and you will know. And so will Paikea, who knows everything."

Then he mourned.

Kokinja ministered to her brother as she could, and they slept for a long time. When they woke, with the storm passed over and all the sky and sea looking like the first morning of the world, they walked the shore to study the sailing canoe that had been all Keawe's pride. After considering it from all sides, he said at last, "I can make it seaworthy again. Well enough to get us home, at least."

"Father can help," Kokinja said, realizing as she spoke that she had never said the word in that manner before. Keawe shook his head, looking away.

"I can do it myself," he said sharply. "I built it myself."

They did not see the Shark God for three days. When he finally emerged from Mirali's cave—as her children had already begun to call it—he called them to him, saying, "I will see you home, as soon as you will. But I will not come there again."

Keawe, already busy about his boat, looked up but said nothing. Kokinja asked, "Why? You have always been faithfully worshipped there—and it was our mother's home all her life."

The Shark God was slow to answer. "From the harbor to her house, from the market to the beach where the nets are mended, to my own temple, there is no place that does not speak to me of Mirali. Forgive me— I have not the strength to deal with those memories, and I never will."

Kokinja did not reply; but Keawe turned from his boat to face his father openly for the first time since his rescue from the storm. He said, clearly and strongly, "And so, once again, you make a liar out of our mother. As I knew you would."

Kokinja gasped audibly, and the Shark God took a step toward his son without speaking. Keawe said, "She defended you so fiercely, so proudly, when I told her that you were always a coward, god or no god. You abandoned a woman who loved you, a family that belonged to you—and now you will do the same with the island that depends on you for protection and loyalty, that has never failed you, done you no disservice, but only been foolish enough to keep its old bargain with you, and expect you to do the same. And this in our mother's name, because you lack the

38

courage to confront the little handful of memories you two shared. You shame her!"

He never flinched from his father's advance, but stood his ground even when the Shark God loomed above him like a storm in mortal shape, his eyes no longer unreadable but alive with fury. For a moment Kokinja saw human and shark as one, flowing in and out of each other, blurring and bleeding together and separating again, in and out, until she became dazed with it and had to close her eyes. She only opened them again when she heard the Shark God's quiet, toneless voice, "We made fine children, my Mirali and I. It is my loss that I never knew them. My loss alone."

Without speaking further he turned toward the harbor, looking as young as he had on the day Mirali challenged him in the marketplace, but moving now almost like an old human man. He had gone some little way when Keawe spoke again, saying simply, "Not only yours."

The Shark God turned back to look long at his children once again. Keawe did not move, but Kokinja reached out her arms, whispering, "Come back." And the Shark God nodded, and went on to the sea.

MISERY

~

by Heather Brewer

Misery was a strange name for a town, and Alek wasn't at all certain that it was fitting. He had, in the year that he'd called Misery home, experienced nothing worse than a strange sense of loss. An odd, unexplainable grief wafted through its windows and doors at all hours, as if the town's inhabitants had been glazed in a thin film of sorrow, and perhaps, regret. But even with that strange, ever-present gloom, the town's name had never made much sense to Alek at all. No one who lived here was miserable, exactly. They were simply *were*. Nothing more. Nothing less.

And, just as Misery simply was, so too were its citizens. Alek could not recall, no matter how terribly he strained to do so, his life before he had called Misery home. Nor could he recall having moved here. Not exactly. One day, he wasn't here. He was somewhere else—somewhere, he could recall, with many colors. And the next, he was not.

He supposed he should be grateful for remembering the colors of his past. The only colors in Misery were black, white, silver, and a palette of grays. Apart, of course, from the eyes of all who lived here. Alek's eyes were a vibrant green. His best friend, Sara's, were bright blue. He loved looking at his neighbors' eyes. They were a brief reminder of something before Misery. Something which Alek could not recall, and could not identify with any measure of certainty.

Not that he minded being here. Not at all, really. After all, it wasn't exactly a miserable kind of place.

"Morning, Alek." Mr. Whirly passed by on the street, tipping his bowler hat in Alek's direction. He didn't have a smile on his face, but no one ever seemed to smile in Misery. It was, Alek thought, strange that he recalled what smiling was at all.

Mr. Whirly was dressed in a three piece suit of varying grays, his silver cufflinks gleaming in the afternoon sun. He always looked so dapper, and made a point to greet everyone he passed. Except, of course, for Sara, who he still hadn't forgiven for running over his freshly sprouted daisies with a lawn mower last spring. Alek smiled and nodded his hello. "Morning, Mr. Whirly."

It was never a *good* morning in Misery. Just morning. Then afternoon. Then evening. Nothing was good. Or bad, really. So Alek felt rather guilty about questioning the absolute blandness of it all. Like the colors, the actions they all took here seemed so bland. It worried him sometimes, though he'd never had the guts to voice his concerns to anyone but Sara— who was currently waiting for him near the town center.

The town's center was marked by a large, ornate fountain. At its peak stood a large crow. Its shiny glass eyes peered down at passersby. Alek didn't much care for it, for reasons he couldn't quite explain. The statue unsettled him, tying tight knots in his stomach whenever he looked at it. But he couldn't stand to not look at it, either.

"You're late." Sara cocked her head to the side in a way that reminded Alek of someone's mother, rather than their best friend. But then, Sara had been that way since the day they'd met—judgmental and protective of him in only the best ways.

Alek half shrugged. "I was busy."

"You were delaying the inevitable." She cast him a concerned glance, one that said that she hadn't at all forgotten about their conversation the night before. "Still nervous?"

Alek swallowed hard. Nervous? He was actually pretty terrified. So much so that he hadn't slept at all last night, and every moment this morning had been consumed by his absolute fear of what was to come today. Not that he should be worried or anything. He didn't know of one person in the town of Misery who'd received a Gift they hadn't liked. Of course, his subconscious continued to insist on reminding him, there was always the first time. What if that first time belonged to him? "Yeah. Kinda."

"You are the only person I know who gets nervous over receiving your Gift." Sara frowned. It wasn't that she was upset or anything. She was merely concerned for him. Still… Alek could have done with a reassuring smile from her this morning. "It's not like you didn't receive a Gift last year, y'know. Or the year before. And have any of them been bad? No. So what are you worried about, exactly?"

Sara's irritation merely framed the obvious in gilded, extravagant swirls. Alek's nervousness over something so simple, something so very ordinary made her nervous too. And that was precisely why Alek hadn't told anyone else in town about the way his stomach clenched every time he thought about receiving his upcoming Gift. It was better, in a place like Misery, to just go with the flow, and not upset anyone with his strange reluctance. He couldn't explain why, exactly. It was just… *better* this way.

Alek shrugged, trying like hell to keep his attention off of the stone crow perched atop the elaborate fountain, despite the fact that its glass eyes were sparkling brightly in the sun, begging to be examined closer. "Two years ago, my Gift was you. Last year, my Gift was my own room at the boarding house. What if this year doesn't compare?"

She examined his face carefully, narrowing her eyes just a bit in suspicion. When she spoke, her voice had fallen into mere whispers. "That's not it at all, is it, Alek? You're afraid of something. I know you. I can tell. What are you afraid of?"

It amazed him at times how well that Sara knew him, or how she could predict so easily when things weren't sitting so well inside his mind. When it came to predictions, to knowing things that were unknowable, the citizens of Misery turned to a woman by the name of Jordan. Jordan was psychic, or sensitive, or just incredibly gifted when it came to understanding the annual blessings that were bestowed upon the people here. No one knew where the Gifts came from, or who sent them. Like anything else in Misery, people simply accepted the Gifts as the norm, refusing to make waves by questioning the Gifts' origins.

Two years ago, Jordan had told him that a new friend was coming to Misery, and that she and Alek would become very close in a relatively short period of time. Maybe it had been Alek's loneliness talking, but he'd doubted at the time that his Gift of friendship would ever come true. The very next day, Sara had found him at the town center, not so far from the spot they were standing at now. He'd vowed that day that he'd never doubt

Jordan or her abilities ever again. And yet here he was, his stomach all tied in knots, his palms slick with anxious sweat.

"Fine. Don't tell me." Sara folded her arms in front of her and turned, leading Alek down the sidewalk, in the direction of Jordan's house. As they came to a stop at the corner across from [place], she continued her thought. "But I'll bet you just about anything that you're wrong. It's your *Gift*, Alek. How can that be anything to worry about?"

"Morning, you two. Causing trouble early today, are you?" Virginia called to them from where she was kneeling in her flower beds. Beside her was a pile of weeds, as gray and dull as the flowers themselves, but somehow full of much less life. She wore a big floppy hat to block out the sun's rays, and had to hold up the brim just to meet Alek and Sara's eyes.

Sara put on a pleasant smile. "No, ma'am. Just walking over so Alek can receive his Gift."

"Oh, has it been so long already? I swear, after so much time here, every year seems to blend into the next." Virginia stood and brushed dirt from her knees before approaching the white picket fence between she and the sidewalk they were standing on. "Are you looking forward to your Gift, Alek?"

Alek gulped as silently as he could manage, swallowing his hesitancy at receiving something he knew on the surface would be satisfactory. Then he nodded at her. "Every year. When do you receive your next gift, Virginia?"

She wiped a bead of sweat from her forehead with the back of her hand as she considered his question, leaving behind a smudge of soil. "Well, let's see. If you get your Gift today, my next Gift must be in about two months. But, you know, after last year, I don't really need another Gift."

Alek shrugged. "Maybe you'll get some new flowers to put in your garden."

Virginia sighed. "You know what I'd really like? Some color. Maybe some color for my roses. Oh yes, I'd like that very much."

The three of them exchanged looks. Looks that spoke volumes.

Then Virginia stammered, as if she were afraid that someone might overhear them. "Of course, I'm not complaining. I like Misery just the way it is. It's just that you have such beautiful green eyes, Alek. I wish I could see that in my garden too. Anyway, you two should scoot. Don't want to be late to receive your Gift."

"Yeah." Alek's heart felt hollow and heavy. His voice dropped off, into an almost whisper. "I wouldn't want that."

Alek moved down the sidewalk, his steps hesitant. Beside him, in direct contrast, Sara's stride was confident and sure. Lining the street were large oak trees. A strong wind gusted high above the two friends, blowing several leaves in varying shades of gray from the branches. The leaves danced and fluttered on the wind before settling gently on the grass and in the street. High in the sky, tucked half way behind a gray cloud, was a white hot sun. The scene should have been serene, should have settled any upset in Alek's nerves, and calmed the churning of his stomach. But it didn't. The quiet simply added to his stress, though he couldn't exactly point to what was stressing him out or why.

At the end of the street stood a large Victorian house, with three floors and a high peaked, round tower that loomed above the rest of the surrounding homes. The house was painted a charcoal gray. The front porch was wide and inviting, and a mat sat in front of the stark white door which read "welcome all". Under each window was a charming flower box, and planted inside were small blooms that seemed cheerful, despite their lack of color. Its shutters were carved with amazing detail—storybook images on each piece—and painted stark black. Alek's favorite image was carved on the shutters that surrounding the window nearest the front door. One side featured a house made of candy, with two children skipping merrily up to the door. The other showed a woman peering out of the home's window, grinning menacingly. The image had always appealed to Alek, but today, it felt sinister. He tore his gaze away from it and rapped on the front door, ready to receive his Gift. Maybe Sara was right. Maybe he was just being stupid about the whole thing.

Besides, the last two Gifts he'd received had turned out even better than expected. So what was he so worried about?

A sing-songy voice called from within, "Be right there!"

Alek's heart skipped a beat, but he willed it to steady its rhythm, and cast Sara a reassuring glance—not that she was the one who needed any reassuring. He hoped it reassured her, at least. But he was pretty sure she knew he was full of crap. He was scared, and they both knew it. They just didn't know why.

The door opened in, and Jordan poked her head out, all smiles. Her brown eyes were bright and dazzling amidst all of the gray. She wore a floral apron around her waist, over her tasteful dress. Her curly hair was held neatly back from her face with a floral scarf. On any normal day, Alek really liked coming to visit Jordan. She had a motherly quality to everything she said, everything she did. It was comforting. It was nice. But today, it wasn't helping. "Come on in, Alek. Sara, you can wait on the porch swing. I left you some lemonade and cookies to munch on, but this shouldn't take long."

Sara gave Alek's shoulder a comforting squeeze and turned on her heel toward the porch swing. He watched the bounce in her step for a moment before turning back to Jordan and forcing a smile. She held the door open for him and he stepped inside. The table just inside the front door held its usual platter of fresh-baked cookies. As he grabbed a gooey snicker doodle, Jordan closed the front door behind them and said, "Are you excited about your Gift, Alek?"

He really wished people would stop asking him that. He bit into the cookie, which wasn't as sweet as he'd wanted it to be. The cookie he'd had last year had definitely been sweeter. But then, last year he hadn't been nervous at all. He chewed and swallowed, and the bite went down hard. Suddenly, he wished he had some lemonade to wash it down with. "To be honest... not really. I've felt a bit... off all day. Is that weird?"

"Hmmm." That's all she said. Just a thoughtful noise. Not even a word, really. It did little to settle Alek's nerves. She tilted her head, looking him over for a moment, before gesturing to the parlor door behind him.

Alek nodded and sat his unfinished cookie on the table before turning to the parlor. The door to the parlor wasn't really a door at all, but an archway. Grand black velvet drapes separated the space from the foyer, held back by large silver tassels. As he moved inside, a medley of herby smells wafted over his senses. He couldn't identify which herbs had blended together to create the aroma, but he rather liked the way the spicy sweet scent tickled his nose.

At the center of the parlor was a small round table, also draped in velvet, and sitting to either side of it were two small stools, which reminded Alek of mushrooms. On the rounded walls hung several picture frames, containing photos of people that Alek didn't recognize. He'd never dared ask who the subjects were. It wasn't really his business, anyway.

Jordan plopped down on a mushroom stool and gestured for Alek to do the same. Once he had, she held out her hand and said, "Well, let's see what we have here. Close your eyes and hold out your dominant hand."

He lowered himself onto the stool, and slowly held out his right hand. His fingers were trembling slightly, and just as Jordan took his hand in hers, he noticed a small grouping of cookie crumbs on his palm. He thought about mentioning it, but before he could, her fingers had already brushed them away. She squeezed his hand, closed her eyes, and released a cleansing breath.

That's what she called it. A cleansing breath. As if every problem in the world could be lessened by simply taking a deep breath and letting it out slowly.

Alek took a breath and blew it out. If nothing else, it didn't hurt to try.

The room suddenly seemed very quiet, although it was no more silent than it had been just a moment before. After a moment, she frowned, as if he'd done something wrong. "Relax, Alek. You have to relax or I can't sense what your Gift will be. You're so tense, I'm not getting it right now. Just breathe, okay?"

He took a deep breath, and as he released it, he focused on his muscles, relaxing each and every one as well as he was able. Maybe his concerns were baseless. Maybe he was just being stupid, worrying about his Gift. But he'd never know if he didn't chill out and relax.

"Ahh. Hmmm." She opened her eyes then, and averted her gaze from meeting his. She patted him on the hand in a way that was designed to comfort him, an act that sent his heart into a more concerned rhythm. Was something wrong? What was his gift? Last year, she'd smiled brightly right away. The year before, she'd hugged him. But this year, her eyes were wide with concern and darting all around the room. Maybe his gut had been right after all. Maybe his Gift wasn't going to be much of a gift after all. Or maybe he wasn't receiving a Gift at all. It would be a first in Misery, unheard of, but Alek's imagination was running wild.

He gathered up what courage he could and asked, "What... what is it?"

She shook her head, and shrugged, a strange cloud settling over her usually cheerful exterior. "It's... nothing."

Jordan blew out a breath, instantly relaxing. Nothing! It was nothing. He couldn't have felt more relieved. He settled back on the mushroom stool, every bit of tension leaving his body. "Oh, man. That's great. You have no idea what that means to me, Jordan. I was so worried all morning that it would be something bad."

Then Jordan met his eyes at last. She gripped his hand once again, but this time as if to keep him from running away. When she spoke, her voice was tinged with panic. "No, Alek. You're not understanding me. Your gift. It's nothing."

"You mean…" His heart beat twice, hard and hollow inside his chest. A sick feeling filled his pores, seeping deep inside of him. "You mean I don't get a gift this year?"

It was ridiculous and horrible and not anything at all that could possibly happen in Misery. So why was it happening to him?

"That's not what I'm saying." She cupped one hand over the top of his and gave it a squeeze, as if trying desperately to comfort him in a situation where no comfort could be found. "Listen. When I tap into a person, I generally receive a vision of what their Gift will be. And this year, yours was… nothing. I saw nothing. It was a cloudy haze. It was… nothing. For your Gift, you are receiving nothingness. Non-existence."

The last word she spoke sat in his chest like a hot stone. "Non-existence? You mean… I'm going to die?"

Everything in the room suddenly seemed smaller. The table, the mushroom stools, the picture frames, the walls. As well as every molecule of air that was available to breathe.

"No," she said, after a too-long pause. "You won't die. You're just not going to *be* anymore. By the end of this day, you're no longer going to exist."

Alek's heart was pounding in his ears. His breaths came sharp and quick as the panic took hold of him, and it felt very much like something had gripped his lungs and was squeezing them as tightly as it could manage. He shook his head, giving himself over to denial, and met Jordan's eyes. He wanted to see even a hint of a smile in them, like this was all just some sick, cruel joke. But all he found was the truth. He was going to blink out of existence by the day's end.

Tears welled up in Alek's eyes against his will. This couldn't be it, couldn't be the end of him. He was just a kid, just a teenager. he hadn't even kissed a girl yet. When he spoke, his voice shook slightly. "Please, Jordan. You have to help me."

She grew very quiet, brushing a few tears from the tip of her nose and her cheeks. He'd fully expected her to shake her head, to tell him that there was absolutely nothing that they could do to preserve his future. But she didn't. After a moment, she released his hand and sat back in her chair, cradling her arms around her waist, darting her eyes about the room, as if a thought had popped into her head. One that had deeply disturbed her.

Alek sat forward, his eyes locked on her grief-stricken face. "What is it, Jordan? What can I do? There has to be something! And if you know and you don't tell me—"

"There is something." She met his eyes, and then blinked, as if she were shaking off a bad dream. "Maybe. But I can't help you with it. And it might not even work. It probably won't work at all."

"But it might." He wasn't feeling a burst of optimism, but he did know that if they, if he, did nothing to prevent himself from dying, blinking out of existence, whatever you wanted to call it, then that was exactly what was going to happen. "Please?"

She stood, arms still wrapped around her waist, and began pacing the small room slowly. "Have you ever heard of a man by the name of Cameron Boswell, Alek? Probably not. He was here a bit before your time."

But Alek did remember him. Not from memory, but from whispers around town. People said he was a troublemaker. People said that Misery was better off without him here. But people said little else about him.

She didn't wait for an answer. She merely paused for a moment and became lost in thought again, leaving her parlor, Alek, and the entire town of Misery behind for the time being. In her eyes, Alek could tell that she was someplace else. Someplace better. Then worse. A brief smile touched her lips before crumbling away like ashes in the wind. Whatever she had been thinking about had made her happy—incredibly happy—but whatever that was gone now, and all that was left were shadows. "He was a kind man. Outgoing. Generous. But not well liked around town. Maybe it was because he was different than everyone else. Not in any way that you could see just by looking at him. But Cameron... Cameron was different."

Her smile returned long enough to lightly brush the edges of her lips before fluttering away again. "On his fifth anniversary in town, Cameron came to me to receive his Gift. It was the same as yours, Alek. His gift was nothing."

Alek sucked in his breath. He wasn't the first to receive the gift of nothing, and what scared him most about that was that Cameron was nowhere to be found. Blinked out of existence, maybe. He swallowed the lump in his throat and said, "What happened to him?"

She moved to the archway and stared out into the foyer at nothing in particular. Slowly, she raised her right hand and gripped the drapes gently, as if they might help to steady her should she fall. "He came to me with this crazy theory. He thought that if he could manage to leave Misery, he might not cease to exist. If he could somehow get past its borders and head for the next town, then maybe he'd be alright."

Alek's forehead creased as he strained to recall where exactly the border to Misery was located. Had he ever been to the edge of town? *Was* there an edge to town? He wasn't certain. He only knew that ideas were only crazy-sounding to those who had other options. If Cameron had actually left Misery, and was living out his days somewhere else, if he had proven that it could be done, then Alek was totally on board the crazy train, without hesitation. "Where is it? The way out of town, I mean."

"I'm not sure anyone really knows. Cameron thought that you could leave Misery by heading north, and climbing that really big hill there. He said the other side of it was the border. I don't know if he was right or not."

But Cameron had known. And Alek very much wanted to know that too. That there was a way out. That he didn't have to blink out of existence, just because Misery had deemed it so. He stood at last and brushed past her into the foyer, determination driving him forward. "I'm going. I have to try."

But before his fingertips could make contact with the doorknob, she gripped the back of his shirt. "Wait! You can go. You should! But don't tell anyone else. The people who live here... in a way, they are Misery. If they know you're trying to leave... I don't know. It's not safe, Alek. They'll stop you."

Alek paused, letting his hand fall back to his side, before turning back to Jordan. If he didn't ask her now, he might not ever know. "How do you know all of this, Jordan? I mean, I get that the Gift giving is some kind of psychic deal. That's not exactly a secret. But how do you know all about Cameron?"

Her eyes glistened with tears, and when she spoke, her voice cracked slightly. "Cameron and I were engaged."

Engaged. And then Cameron went away forever. It had to be an impossible thing to face—losing your fiancé in one way or another. Either by him disappearing completely or leaving town forever. "I'm sorry."

"The day I gave him his Gift, he told Mr. Whirly and I about his plans to leave. Mr. Whirly used to be a joyous man, full of a bubbly, infectious spirit. But he changed after hearing Cameron's plans. He just seemed... darker." She lifted the corner of her apron and dabbed at her eyes. "Cameron didn't really have a chance after that. He made it to the bottom of the big hill before he disappeared. I was there. I saw the whole thing happen. He simply... ceased to be. It was horrible. I don't want it to happen to anyone else."

Alek watched her for a moment, wishing he could take her pain away. Then he reached out and gave her hand a squeeze. She squeezed his back, and they exchanged nods before putting on pleasantly false smiles. By the time Alek opened the door, all seemed well with the two of them, though it was anything but.

Sara crammed the remainder of a half-eaten cookie in her mouth and chewed fast before swallowing. As she skipped across the porch to Alek, who was closing the door behind him, she said, "So? What's your Gift?"

Alek smiled, remembering what Jordan had said about Mr. Whirly. "I can't tell you just yet. But I know where to go to get it."

"That's weird. Where do you have to go?" She followed him down the steps, a doubtful crease in her forehead.

Alek paused as they reached the next block. He had to get rid of Sara, couldn't risk her changing like Mr. Whirly had with Cameron. What if Jordan was right? What if the townspeople really were the town? He couldn't fully trust anyone. Maybe not even Jordan—something that sent a nervous chill down his spine. Shrugging casually, he couldn't help but notice Virginia toiling in her flowerbeds again. "The north side of town. I can go get it and bring it back."

"Don't be stupid. I'll come with you." The words had no sooner left her mouth than Virginia looked up at them, a burning curiosity in her gaze. On any other day, Alek might not have noticed such blatant curiosity. But today was different. Today was his last day in Misery, one way or the other.

He lowered his voice, trying to keep any sense of nervousness out of his tone. "I'd kinda like to get it on my own, okay?"

Sara threw her arms up in exasperation. "Why are you acting so weird?"

Virginia had stood up then, and approached her picket fence. Mr. Hoffman had stopped on the sidewalk where he was walking his poodle. Both stared at Alek with an intensity that solidified his belief in Jordan's words.

Alek tugged her sleeve and headed north. He had no choice but to take Sara with him. "I'm not. Come on then."

Sara moved up the sidewalk with him, but slowly, almost reluctantly. They'd moved two blocks before Alek felt eyes on him, almost burning their gaze into his back. Glancing as casually as he could manage over his right shoulder, he noticed Mr. Hoffman following from about a block away. He was pulling back on his poodle's leash as it barked and showed its teeth, the way that Alek had never seen it do before. Behind Mr. Hoffman by a matter of steps was Virginia, who had seemed so kind and caring just a few minutes before he'd set foot in Jordan's house. But there was no kindness in her face now, no smile on her lips. Misery had changed, with the mention of a single word: nothing.

"Alek, slow down!"

Sara was jogging beside him now. Alek hadn't even realized that he'd instinctively picked up his pace. But he couldn't slow down, couldn't face whatever it was that Virginia and Mr. Hoffman had planned for him.

As he reached the final street block at the foot of the hill, Sara panting behind him by several feet, he dared a glance over his shoulder again. Several more townspeople were hurrying to his current location, none of them looking happy at all. Mr. Whirly was bringing up the rear. Alek couldn't be sure, but he swore he saw a large gray crow circling overhead. But the hill was right there! He was so close to freedom, so close to being safe. He turned back to the hill with a determined breath. And a familiar hand fell on his left shoulder.

Alek turned to face Sara. She was still his best friend, still the girl he told everything too, and why should this be any different? But as he opened his mouth to explain, his eyes met with hers. Only her eyes were different now. They sparkled like glass in the sun. Her eyes were that of the crow's from the fountain. Because she was a part of Misery as much as it was. Her mouth contorted into a maniacal grin. "You can't leave us, Alek. You can't ever leave us."

A familiar voice—Jordan's voice, though he couldn't see her from where he was standing—shouted, "Run, Alek! Run for your life!"

Alek screamed and bolted up the hill. Behind him, he could hear the townspeople scrambling after him, but he couldn't look back. He didn't want to see what was coming for him, couldn't bear to see what had happened to his friends, his neighbors. He ran, digging his sneakers into the soft earth, and at last, he reached the crest of the enormous hill. He hurried over its peak to the other side.

He was there! He was free!

But as he leaned forward on his knees to catch his breath, his breath caught in his throat in a moment of utter terror.

His hands. His hands, which should have been on his knees, were gone. Invisible. Disappeared. They were nothing, and that nothingness was quickly moving up his arms. He was fading, and fast. Tears poured down his cheeks and he shouted into the sky. "Nooooo!!! I made it! I made it!"

Alek fell to his knees, which he could no longer see, and waited for something to happen—for Misery to consume him, or for his nothingness to be completed. His heart pounded in terror. In the distance, on the side of the hill facing away from town, he saw a flash of something. It was probably the crow's eye, he mused.

Only…it was something purple. Bright purple. A color, unlike anything at all in the town of Misery. Then there was another flash. This time orange. Then pink. Then red.

And then Alek stopped caring that he was disappearing, because a memory slipped back into his mind. A memory of colors and warmth and joy. It was a memory of home, his home before Misery. He recalled his family, his neighbors, and the way that life had been. Life—that's what it had been. Not the place between lives, the way that Misery was. After all, he recalled, that's what Misery was—a place where people went between their actual lives.

And now, he was going home.

SHADOW CHILDREN

~

by Heather Brewer

"Goodnight, Jon." Dax pulled the covers over his little brother's chest. Jon was wearing his favorite pajamas again, despite the hour-long argument that flannel wasn't exactly a summer weight fabric and the buttons were on the verge of falling off. Surrendering with a sigh, Dax walked out of the room, flipping the light switch as he went. Not a second later, Jon's Batman nightlight went out, which instantly sparked whining from the six-year-old.

"Dax, my nightlight! I can't sleep without my nightlight. The shadows will get me!"

Dax sighed again, silently counting the seconds until mom and dad would be home. It was like this every night. John would whine to mom or dad and they'd make sure his nightlight was working or that the hall light was on, anything to placate Jon's irrational fear of things that weren't really lurking in the shadows, waiting to snatch him away. Only tonight, it was Dax who was left to placate him. Bad enough he had to miss out on Janie's party to babysit his little brother, but now he was also expected to cater to Jon's ridiculous fear of the dark. "I'll grab you a flashlight, Jon. Just give me a second."

It was all he could do to block out Jon's blubbering as he walked into the kitchen. He pulled the drawer open and rummaged around. A flashlight had to be in there somewhere.

"Dax, hurry! The shadows!"

Dax found a couple of flashlights and picked one up, tapping it gently against his chin. Maybe it would be better if he did them all a favor and showed Jon that there were no such things as monsters under your bed, nothing at all lurking in the pitch black of night. If he let Jon cry it out just for one night, maybe the kid would grow up and stop being such a baby. Maybe then babysitting him without pay and missing out on the party of the year wouldn't be so bad. Dax mulled this over for a moment, blocking out the whimpers from down the hall. "It's just the dark, Jon. There's nothing in it that isn't there in the day time."

Jon screamed. And it wasn't one of those little brat screams for attention. He sounded terrified. Like his life depended on someone hearing and responding to his terrified shriek.

Dax bolted back to the bedroom and stared in shocked disbelief.

A long, dark, shadow was looming over the bed. But it wasn't an ordinary shadow. It was darker than the rest of the room, and moved of its own free will. It was a creature made of shadows. It was alive. Part of it whipped forward and wrapped around Jon's ankle. Jon cried, "Help me, Dax!"

The shadow monster was pulling Jon off the bed, but Dax was frozen in place, staring at this thing that couldn't possibly exist. Jon was flailing, tears streaming down his cheeks. Breaking free from his trance, Dax clutched his brother's wrist, but he was hit in the chest and thrown against the wall. Pain bolted through Dax's back as he hit and crumpled to the floor. He struggled to sit up again, but a tentacle of the shadow monster stood in front of him, defying him to move. There were no eyes or mouth, but somehow Dax knew that the thing was looking at him. He swore he heard a growl, but it had no mouth, no substance. The shadow monster lurched back and ripped Dax's brother free of his covers.

Dax ran forward and grabbed Jon by the ankle. They both flew through the air and into the closet. The door slammed shut, sealing them in pitch black.

A sound caught his attention, like a large amount of sand falling through a grainy, wooden hourglass. It was coming from the floor. Dax looked down. The floor was moving. It swirled around his feet, the sand-like substance of what had once been a wood floor crashed over the toe of his sock in small, black waves. He pulled his foot back, but the sand clung to it. Beside him, Jon whimpered as the sand closed over his arm. Dax brushed it away, but it seemed to have a life of its own. The sand covered him and all he could do was lay there, feeling the weight of it curl around his feet, his ankles, his legs, knowing he was sinking into it—whatever it was. It moved up his torso and he felt suffocated—there was no air, only sand.

Beside him, Jon screamed, but his screams were cut off as the sand closed over his small head. Dax grabbed desperately for Jon's hand, but there was nothing to grab. His brother was gone.

Strangely, he could feel his legs dangling on the other side, like he was slipping through some hole. It covered his chest, and Dax took a deep breath and held it, not knowing if he would ever breathe again, not knowing what was happening or what to do to stop it. The sand swirled around, tickling his eyelashes, covering his face. He felt the weight of it on top of his head, and wondered if he would ever see Jon again.

Suddenly, the sand compacted tightly around him and, just as quickly, released. Dax fell several feet, landing on the hard ground below. He coughed and drew air into his lungs. His chest burned, but after a few deep breaths, it came easily again. Remembering the flashlight, he turned it on and looked around, gasping at what he saw.

He was in a cavern. An enormous cavern of what must have been obsidian—the walls were shiny and black, the floor smooth and reflective. He shined the flashlight up at where he'd fallen through, but there was no sign of any hole or trapdoor, or even sand. Only hard, black rock. The floor trembled slightly beneath his feet. He noticed the movement less when he stepped forward, but despite the floor's solid appearance, it struck him as fragile.

On the ceiling, just on the edge of the flashlight beam, something moved. Dax chased it with the light, but it remained at the beam's edge. And like that, on the edge of his hearing, Dax detected a sound, like a group of people whispering very softly. "Hello?"

In the distance, a noise. It sounded like his brother crying.

"Jon? Where are you?" But silence answered him. Dax called out again, but the only sound was his voice chasing after itself in an echo.

The last thing he wanted to do was move deeper into the cavernous tunnel, to move away from this spot, which he feared was the closest he would ever be to home again, but Jon had sounded like he was getting further and further away, so he had no choice. He had to find his brother and then, he had to find a way to get them out of here.

Clutching the flashlight in his hand, Dax moved through the cavern. All around him he could hear faint whispers, but couldn't understand what they were saying. He paused several times, shining the light behind him, trying to catch whoever—whatever—was whispering, but each and every time there was no one there. Dax was, despite the nudging of the darkest corners of his imagination, completely alone.

Jon was nowhere to be found. It was as if he'd vanished into thin air.

The large tunnel broke off into three smaller tunnels up ahead. Dax listened, but heard nothing that told him which one Jon might be down. He ran a frustrated hand through his hair and, just as he'd decided to take the middle tunnel, the whispering stopped and a new sound began. A small click as something hit the floor, then an even smaller noise, like something rolling several feet. He pointed the flashlight down, searching, sweeping the floor for any sign of movement. The sound ceased as whatever it was rattled to a stop just in front of his feet. He bent down, focusing on the item with the light. In near disbelief, he plucked it from the ground, turning it over in his hand.

A red, shiny button. Just like the ones on Jon's pajamas.

Dax stood again, shining the flashlight on the tunnels again. "Jon?"

He stepped forward and just as he was about to enter the center tunnel, he saw movement with his peripheral vision. Taking a step back, he shined his light on the right tunnel entrance. At first there was nothing, but after a moment, Dax thought he could hear a small whimper. He hurried down the right tunnel, clutching the button in his hand and calling out for his brother.

Several yards in, the whispers returned, but though they were louder in the smaller space, Dax still couldn't determine where they were coming from or what they were saying. It was unnerving, like he was being followed by someone without a voice, who insisted on making themselves known. His flashlight flickered and went out. The whispers grew louder and felt like they were closing in, but that was crazy. They were just noises... weren't they? Dax knocked the light against his palm. When the flickering subsided and the light returned, the whispers ceased... and someone was standing in the tunnel with him.

He would have recognized that face and those pajamas anywhere. Relieved to see his brother again, he stepped forward. "There you are. I've been looking everywh—"

The child had his arm extended, stroking the walls in a loving manner that sent a chill up Dax's spine. Something about the way he moved seemed unnatural. Suddenly, but calmly, he turned his head toward Dax. Dax's trembling fingers found his open mouth, hushing a gasp. The child had

Jon's mouth, his cheeks, his forehead, his hair, but the eyes... they were filled with shadows.

The thing in front of him might have looked like Jon, but it wasn't his brother. It was something else. Something sinister. Something dark.

Dax backed up, clutching the flashlight tightly to his chest. When he hit the tunnel wall, he expected it to be cool, but it was warm, almost like a living entity. Even though he knew that it wasn't Jon, he swallowed hard and whispered his brother's name.

The Jon-thing turned slowly, without speaking, and disappeared around the bend.

Dax's heart slammed against his ribs. His breath came in quick gasps. Panic overtook him, but he forced himself to move forward, because something inside of him told him that the Jon-thing knew where his real brother was. Dax turned around the bend, reluctantly following wherever it was that the Jon-thing was leading.

By the time he turned the corner, it was already moving around the next bend. Dax picked up the pace, jogging after the thing that looked like his brother.

After several more bends in the tunnel, he turned the corner into a small room. A boy was lying on the floor in the fetal position, shuddering with sobs. Raising every hair on the back of Dax's neck, the Jon-thing bent down and stroked the boy's hair wordlessly with its small, pale fingers. The boy scrambled away from him, terrified, and Dax shot forward, hugging his brother—his actual brother—tightly. At first, Jon screamed and pushed him away, but then, realizing that it was Dax, he clung to his brother's chest, sobbing into his shirt, soaking the fabric. "It's okay," Dax whispered into his hair, not entirely certain he was telling his brother the truth. "It's going to be okay."

The Jon-thing tilted its head. When it spoke its voice mimicked Jon's perfectly, but still something seemed off about it, false. "You shouldn't lie to children."

Dax sneered. "What are you?"

It smiled, its dry, cracking lips stretching back from its Jon-like teeth, which seemed sharper than Jon's, hungrier. "We are shadow children."

Instinctively, Dax looked around, but saw no one else. "We?"

The Jon-thing smiled and looked up, as if exchanging bemused glances with someone that Dax couldn't see. "We tire of the darkness. We want to live as you live."

A small trail of colored dust, shimmering and full of light, floated in the air between Jon and the monster that was mimicking his form. Jon swooned, not at all steady on his feet. He looked pale. He looked weak. The sickening realization hit Dax that the creature was somehow feeding on his brother, sucking his essence from him and stealing his shape. Maybe it was the only way the thing could become solid. Maybe without whatever it was that it was stealing from Jon it couldn't become anything more than the horrible shadow that had snatched Jon from his bed. Maybe it couldn't face the light before and somehow Jon knew that, and when Dax had forced his brother to remain in the darkness...

Dax swallowed the lump in his throat. It didn't go down easily.

It was his fault. Jon knew that these things existed and he knew how to keep them at bay. Dax ignored that, brushing it off as just a stupid little kid fear, and let the monsters in.

It stretched out its hand again, caressing Jon's hair the way someone might pet a puppy. Dax jerked Jon from it and glared. It met his gaze with its shadowy eyes, blinking some like it couldn't possibly understand why he wouldn't want it touching his brother. "You cannot escape."

Dax gripped Jon to him, standing, holding his brother as tightly as he could without hurting him. He looked at the Jon-thing and tightened his jaw. "Watch me."

With Jon in his arms, he bolted back down the tunnel, back the way he'd come. As he ran, the indistinguishable whispers started again, quickly growing louder until they were almost deafening. Jon cried against his chest, so scared of what was happening, and Dax ran as fast as he could, darting around corners with ease. The whispers grew faint as he ran. He was beating them, beating them all. Finally, out of breath and with nowhere else to run, he entered the large cavern that they had first fallen into. Dax sat Jon down on the ground, only then noticing that the trail of shimmering dust still hung in the air, winding its way through the tunnels. Running from the Jon-thing wasn't enough to sever that essence-stealing tie. His brother tugged at his sleeve, still trembling, but Dax was firm. "Hold on, Jon. Let me figure this out."

On the ceiling, just on the edge of the flashlight beam, something moved.

Dax chased it with the light, but it remained at the beam's edge, just as before. Then suddenly, his ears were filled with a thousand whispery, deafening sounds. He waved the flashlight around, and terror filled him.

Strange shadow creatures, like the monster that had grabbed Jon from his bed, peeled from the cave's ceiling, from its walls and floor. One flew dangerously close to Dax and he ducked back, but not before seeing the image of a young girl's face reflected in its shadowy substance. The sight of it startled him. It wasn't just Jon that they were after. They flew from their place in the cave and swirled around the two boys, surrounding them completely, blocking any chance of escape. Each of the shadows wore the face of a child, some Dax knew personally. The Jon-thing had said that they tired of the darkness, that they wanted what Dax and Jon had, what everybody had. The creatures were going to make mirror forms of every kid on earth, and then what? Kill them all? Suck them dry of their essence, leaving them empty, hollow shells? Panic set in and Dax gasped for air. Layers and layers of the cave floor and walls peeled away until Dax could see what they were peeling away from—and it wasn't black rock. With horrified understanding, he realized that there was no cave. The creatures *were* the cave.

Thousands, maybe millions of shadow monsters, out to replace the people of the world. Dax's heart raced. Beside him, Jon screamed as the shadows closed in.

The floor shrank until there was only an island of shadow left. It trembled wildly beneath their feet.

Dax whipped his flashlight around in desperation. On a low part of the cave ceiling, he saw a flash of color, something brown and familiar.

He scooped Jon up in his arms and said, "Hold on tight."

One of the shadows whipped forward, snatching the flashlight from Dax's grip. It threw the light down, smashing it to bits, leaving them all in darkness. The shadow monsters swarmed closer to the boys, and just as a long shadowy tentacle reached for Jon, Dax leapt toward the familiar sight on the low cave ceiling and clung to the hole in the floor of Jon's closet with the tips of his determined fingers. His biceps burned, but he pulled himself up until he was waist-high into the closet. "Jon, get off now! I'm falling!"

Jon scrambled from his brother through his pitch black room to his bed, drenched in sweat and tears, crying for his brother to hurry, hurry before those monsters got him.

Something wrapped around Dax's ankle and pulled hard, but there was no use. It pulled him back down into the cave, the tips of his fingers only barely clinging to the wood.

He was going to fall. And once he did, those things would suck every bit of his essence away.

A beam of light suddenly shined down into the hole and the creatures backed off. Dax looked up. Jon was holding a flashlight he must have retrieved from the kitchen. Dax pulled himself free from the hole, his muscles burning. He collapsed onto the floor of Jon's closet and hugged his brother, trying to quench his tears, but the danger wasn't over. There was still a hole in the closet floor. It was still dark.

Whispers drifted up from the hole until they were filling the room. Jon's flashlight flickered out, as if it couldn't stand up against the growing darkness. Dax picked up his brother and ran for the door. They had to get out of there, away from the darkness, into the light.

The bedroom door opened and their mother flipped the light switch, bathing the room in incandescent light. "Where have you boys been?! Your father and I have been worried sick!"

Dax panted, his heart settling some into a more normal rhythm. He looked at the closet, at the perfect, unbroken floor. Jon ran across the room and jumped into his mother's arms. Dax couldn't help but notice that the trail of dust was gone, the Jon-thing's connection to him broken at last.

Holding Jon, placing kisses on his cheeks, their mom crossed the room and opened the heavy drapes, letting sunlight inside. It was morning. Had they really been gone that long? It had felt like minutes, maybe an hour, but certainly not several hours.

She turned back to Dax with a concerned look on her face. "Dax? Is everything okay? We were so scared that something happened to you both."

Dax slowly nodded his head, even though everything was about as far from okay as it could get, and looked from the closet to the sunny day outside. Out the window, he could see the neighbor kids playing soccer. To any onlooker, it would seem like an ordinary, normal day.

He turned back to his mom and released a relieved sigh. "Yeah, mom. Everything's fine. We just—"

As she turned around, Jon peered over his mother's shoulder at Dax, who froze. Jon smiled and offered a wave.

Shadows lurked in his eyes—the darkest that Dax had ever seen.

EVEN HAND

~

by Jim Butcher

Editor's Note: Fans of Jim Butcher's Dresden Files *know that Harry Dresden's main nemesis is the mobster Johnny Marcone. This short story offers a fun twist in that it's told from Marcone's perspective rather than Dresden's.*

A successful murder is like a successful restaurant: Ninety percent of it is about location, location, location.

Three men in black hoods knelt on the waterfront warehouse floor, their wrists and ankles trussed with heavy plastic quick-ties. There were few lights. They knelt over a large, faded stain on the concrete floor, left behind by the hypocritically-named White Council of Wizards during their last execution.

I nodded to Hendricks, who took the hood off the first man, then stood clear. The man was young and good looking. He wore an expensive, yet ill-fitting suit and even more expensive, yet tasteless jewelry.

"Where are you from?" I asked him.

He sneered at me. "What's it to y—"

I shot him in the head as soon as I heard the bravado in his voice. The body fell heavily to the floor.

The other two jumped and cursed, their voices angry and terrified.

I took the hood off the second man. His suit was a close cousin of the dead man's, and I thought I recognized its cut. "Boston?" I asked him.

"You can't do this to us," he said, more angry than frightened. "Do you know who we are?"

61

Once I heard the nasal quality of the word "are," I shot him.

I took the third man's hood off. He screamed and fell away from me. "Boston," I said, nodding, and put the barrel of my .45 against the third man's forehead. He stared at me, showing the whites of his eyes. "You know who I am. I run drugs in Chicago. I run the numbers, the books. I run the whores. It's my town. Do you understand?"

His body jittered in what might have been a nod. His lips formed the word "yes," though no sound came out.

"I'm glad you can answer a simple question," I told him, and lowered the gun. "I want you to tell Mr. Morelli that I won't be this lenient the next time his people try to clip the edges of my territory." I looked at Hendricks. "Put the three of them in a sealed trailer and rail-freight them back to Boston, care of Mr. Morelli."

Hendricks was a large, trustworthy man, his red hair cropped in a crew cut. He twitched his chin in the slight motion that he used for a nod when he disapproved of my actions, but intended to obey me anyway.

Hendricks and the cleaners on my staff would handle the matter from here.

I passed him the gun and the gloves on my hands. Both would see the bottom of Lake Michigan before I was halfway home, along with the two slugs the cleaners would remove from the site. When they were done, there would be nothing left of the two dead men but a slight variation on the outline of the stain in the old warehouse floor, where no one would look twice in any case.

Location, location, location.

Obviously, I am not Harry Dresden. My name is something I rarely trouble to remember, but for most of my adult life, I have been called John Marcone.

I am a professional monster.

It sounds pretentious. After all, I'm not a flesh-devouring ghoul, hiding behind a human mask until it is time to gorge. I'm no vampire, to drain the blood or soul from my victim, no ogre, no demon, no cursed beast from the spirit world dwelling amidst the unsuspecting sheep of humanity. I'm not even possessed of the mystic abilities of a mortal wizard.

But they will never be what I am. One and all, those beings were born to be what they are.

I made a choice.

I walked outside of the warehouse and was met by my consultant, Gard—a tall blonde woman without makeup whose eyes continually swept her surroundings. She fell into step beside me as we walked to the car. "Two?"

"They couldn't be bothered to answer a question in a civil manner."

She opened the back door for me and I got in. I picked up my personal weapon and slipped it into the holster beneath my left arm while she settled down behind the wheel. She started driving and then said, "No. That wasn't it."

"It was business."

"And the fact that one of them was pushing heroin to thirteen year old girls and the other was pimping them out had nothing to do with it," Gard said.

"It was business," I said, enunciating. "Morelli can find pushers and pimps anywhere. A decent accountant is invaluable. I sent his bookkeeper back as a gesture of respect."

"You don't respect Morelli."

I almost smiled. "Perhaps not."

"Then why?"

I did not answer. She didn't push the issue and we rode in silence back to the office. As she put the car in park I said, "They were in my territory. They broke my rule."

"No children," she said.

"No children," I said. "I do not tolerate challenges, Ms. Gard. They're bad for business."

She looked at me in the mirror, her blue eyes oddly intent, and nodded.

~

There was a knock at my office door and Gard thrust her head in, her phone's earpiece conspicuous. "There's a problem."

Hendricks frowned from his seat at a nearby desk. He was hunched over a laptop that looked too small for him, plugging away at his thesis. "What kind of problem?"

"An Accord matter," Gard said.

Hendricks sat up straight and looked at me.

I didn't look up from one of my lawyer's letters, which I receive too frequently to let slide. "Well," I said. "We knew it would happen eventually. Bring the car."

"I don't have to," Gard said. "The situation came to us."

I set the finished letter aside and looked up, resting my fingertips together. "Interesting."

~

Gard brought the problem in. The problem was young and attractive. In my experience, the latter two frequently lead to the former. In this particular case, it was a young woman holding a child. She was remarkable—thick, rich, silver-white hair, dark eyes, pale skin. She had very little makeup, which was fortunate in her case, since she looked like she had recently been drenched. She wore what was left of a grey business skirt-suit, had a towel from one of my health clubs wrapped around her shoulders, and was shivering.

The child she held was too young to be in school and was also appealing, with rosy features, white-blonde hair and blue eyes. Male or female, it hardly mattered at that age. They're all beautiful. The child clung to the girl as if it would not be separated, and was also wrapped in a towel.

The girl's body language was definitely protective. She had the kind of beauty that looked natural and... true. Her features and her bearing both spoke of gentleness and kindness.

I felt an immediate instinct to protect and comfort her.

I quashed it thoroughly.

I am not made of stone, but I have found it is generally best to behave as if I am.

I looked across the desk at her and said, "My people tell me you have asked for sanctuary under the terms of the Unseelie Accords, but that you have not identified yourself."

"I apologize, sir," she answered. "I was already being indiscreet enough just by coming here."

"Indeed," I said calmly. "I make it a point not to advertise the location of my business headquarters."

"I didn't want to add names to the issue," she said, casting her eyes down in a gesture of submission which did not entirely convince me. "I wasn't sure how many of your people were permitted access to this sort of information."

I glanced past the young woman to Gard, who gave me a slow, cautious nod. Had the girl or the child been other than they appeared, Gard would have indicated in the negative. Gard costs me a fortune, and is worth every penny.

Even so, I didn't signal either her or Hendricks to stand down. Both of them watched the girl, ready to kill her if she made an aggressive move. Trust, but verify—that the person being trusted will be dead if she attempts betrayal.

"That was most considerate of you, Justine."

The girl blinked at me several times. "Y-you know me."

"You are a sometimes-associate of Harry Dresden," I said. "Given his proclivities about those he considers to be held under his aegis, it is sensible to identify as many of them as possible. For the sake of my insurance rates, if nothing else. Gard."

"Justine, no last name you'll admit to," Gard said calmly, "currently employed as Lara Raith's secretary and personal aide. You are the sometimes-lover of Thomas Raith, a frequent ally of Dresden's."

I spread my hands slightly. "I assume the 'j' notation at the bottom of Ms. Raith's typed correspondence refers to you."

"Yes," Justine said. She had regained her composure quickly—not something I would have expected of the servitor of a vampire of the White Court. Many of the... people, I suppose, I'd seen there had made lotus-eaters look self-motivated. "Yes, exactly."

I nodded. "Given your patron, one is curious as to why you have come to me seeking protection."

"Time, sir," she replied quietly. "I lacked any other alternative."

Someone screamed at the front of the building.

My headquarters shifts position irregularly, as I acquire new buildings. Much of my considerable wealth is invested in real estate. I own more of the town than any other single investor. In Chicago, there is always money to be had by purchasing and renovating aging buildings. I do much of my day to day work out of one of my most recent renovation projects, once they have been modified to be suitable places to welcome guests. Then, renovation of the building begins, and the place is generally crowded with contractors who have proven their ability to see and hear nothing.

Gard's head snapped up. She shook it as if to rid herself of a buzzing fly and said, "A presence. A strong one." Her blue eyes snapped to Justine. "Who?"

The young woman shuddered and wrapped the towel more tightly about herself. "Mag. A cantrev lord of the fomor."

Gard spat something in a Scandanavian tongue that was probably a curse.

"Precis, please," I said.

"The fomor are an ancient folk," she said. "Water dwellers, cousins of the jotuns. Extremely formidable. Sorcerers, shape changers, seers."

"And signatories," I noted.

"Yes," she said. She crossed to the other side of the room, opened a closet, and withdrew an athletic bag. She produced a simple, rather crude-looking broadsword from it and tossed it toward Hendricks. The big man caught it by the handle, and took his gun into his left hand. Gard took a broad-bladed axe out of the bag and shouldered the weapon. "But rarely involved in mortal affairs."

"Ms. Raith sent me to the Fomor King with documents," Justine said, her voice coming out quietly and rapidly. Her shivering had increased. "Mag made me his prisoner. I escaped with the child. There wasn't time to reach one of my lady's strongholds. I came to you, sir. I beg your protection, as a favor to Ms. Raith."

"I don't grant favors," I said calmly.

Mag entered in the manner so many of these self-absorbed supernatural cretins seem to adore. He blasted the door into a cloud of flying splinters with what I presumed was magic.

For God's sake.

At least the vampires would call for an appointment.

The blast amounted to little debris. After a few visits from Dresden and his ilk, I had invested in cheap, light doors at dramatic (as opposed to tactical) entry points.

The fomor was a pale, repellent humanoid. Seven feet tall, give or take, and distinctly froglike in appearance. He had a bloated belly, legs several inches too long to be proportionately human, and huge feet and hands. He wore a tunic of something that resembled seaweed beneath a long, flapping blue robe, covered in the most intricate embroidery I had ever seen. A coronet of coral was bound about his head. His right hand was extended dramatically. He carried a twisted length of wood in his left.

His eyes bulged, jaundice-yellow around septic green, and his teeth were rotted and filthy. "You cannot run from me," he said. His wide mouth made the words seem somehow slurred. "You are mine."

Justine looked up at me, evidently too frightened to turn her head, her eyes wide with fear. A sharper contrast would have been hard to manage. "Sir. Please."

I touched a button on the undersurface of my desk, a motion of less than two inches, and then made a steeple of my hands again as I eyed Mag and said, "Excuse me, sir. This is a private office."

Mag surged forward half a step, his eyes focused on the girl. "Hold your tongue, mortal, if you would keep it."

I narrowed my eyes.

Is it so much to ask for civility?

"Justine," I said calmly. "If you would stand aside, please."

Justine quickly, silently moved out from between us.

I focused on Mag and said, "They are under my protection."

Mag gave me a contemptuous look, raised the staff, and darkness lashed at me, as if he had simply reached out into the floorboards and cracks in the wall and drawn it into a sizzling sphere the size of a bowling ball.

It flickered away to nothingness about a foot in front of my steepled hands.

I lifted a finger and Hendricks shot Mag in the back. Repeatedly.

The fomor went down with a sound like a bubbling teakettle, whipped onto his back as if the bullets had been a minor inconvenience, and raised the stick to point at Hendricks.

Gard's axe smashed it out of his grip, swooped back up to guard, and began to descend again.

"Stop," I said.

Gard's muscles froze just before she would have brought the axe down onto Mag's head. Mag had one hand uplifted, surrounded in a kind of negative haze, his long fingers crooked at odd angles—presumably some kind of mystic defense.

"As a freeholding lord of the Unseelie Accords," I said, "it would be considered an act of war if I killed you out of hand, despite your militant intrusion into my territory." I narrowed my eyes. "However, your behavior gives me ample latitude to invoke the defense of property and self clause. I will leave the decision to you. Continue this asinine behavior, and I will kill you and offer a weregild to your lord, King Corb, in accordance with the conflict resolution guidelines of Section Two, Paragraph Four."

As I told you, my lawyers send me endless letters. I speak their language.

Mag seemed to take that in for a moment. He looked at me, then Gard. His eyes narrowed. They tracked back to Hendricks, his head hardly moving, and he seemed to freeze when he saw the sword in Hendricks's hand.

His eyes flicked to Justine and the child and burned for a moment—not with adoration or even simple lust. There was a pure and possessive hunger there, coupled with a need to destroy that which he desired. I have spent my entire life around hard men. I know that form of madness when I see it.

"So," Mag said. His eyes traveled back to me and were suddenly heavy-lidded and calculating. "You are the new mortal lord. We half-believed that you must be imaginary. That no one could be as foolish as that."

"You are incorrect," I said. "Moreover, you can't have them. Get out."

Mag stood up. The movement was slow, liquid. His limbs didn't seem to bend the proper way. "Lord Marcone," he said, "this affair is no concern of yours. I only wish to take the slaves."

"You can't have them. Get out."

"I warn you," Mag said. There was an ugly tone in his voice. "If you make me return for her—for them—you will not enjoy what follows."

"I do not require enjoyment to thrive. Leave my domain. I won't ask again."

Hendricks shuffled his feet a little, settling his balance.

Mag gathered himself up slowly. He extended his hand, and the twisted stick leapt from the floor and into his fingers. He gave Gard a slow and well-practiced sneer, and said, "Anon, mortal lordling. It is time you learned the truth of the world. It will please me to be your instructor." Then he turned, slow and haughty, and walked out, his shoulders hunching in an odd, unsettling motion as he moved.

"Make sure he leaves," I said quietly.

Gard and Hendricks followed Mag from the room.

I turned my eyes to Justine and the child.

"Mag," I said, "is not the sort of man who is used to disappointment."

Justine looked after the vanished fomor, and then back at me, confusion in her eyes. "That was sorcery. How did you...?"

I stood up from behind my desk and stepped out of the copper circle set into the floor around my chair. It was powered by the sorcerous equivalent of a nine volt battery, connected to the control on the underside of my desk. Basic magical defense, Gard said. It had seemed like nonsense to me—it clearly was not.

I took my gun from its holster and set it on my desk.

Justine took note of my reply.

Of course I wouldn't give the personal aide of the most dangerous woman in Chicago information about my magical defenses.

There was something hard and not at all submissive in her eyes. "Thank you, sir, for—"

"For what?" I said, very calmly. "You understand, do you not, what you have done by asking for my help under the Accords?"

"Sir?"

"The Accords govern relations between supernatural powers," I said. "The Signatories of the Accords and their named vassals are granted certain rights and obligations—such as offering a warning to a Signatory who has trespassed upon another's territory unwittingly before killing him."

"I know, sir," Justine said.

"Then you should also know that you are most definitely not a signatory of the Accords. At best, you qualify in the category of 'servitors and chattel.' At worse, you are considered to be a food animal."

She drew in a sharp breath, her eyes widening—not in any sense of outrage or offense, but in realization. Good. She grasped the realities of the situation.

"In either case," I continued, "you are property. You have no rights in the current situation, in the eyes of the Accords—and more to the point, I have no right to withhold another's rightful property. Mag's behavior provided me with an excuse to kill him if he did not depart. He will not give me such an opening a second time."

Justine swallowed and stared at me for a moment. Then she glanced down at the child in her arms. The child clung harder to her, and seemed to lean somewhat away from me.

One must admire such acute instincts.

"You have drawn me into a conflict which has nothing to do with me," I said quietly. "I suggest candor. Otherwise, I will have Mr. Hendricks and Ms. Gard show you to the door."

"You can't..." she began, but her voice trailed off.

"I can," I said. "I am not a humanitarian. When I offer charity it is for tax purposes."

The room became silent. I was content with that. The child began to whimper quietly.

"I was delivering documents to the court of King Corb on behalf of my Lady," Justine said. She stroked the child's hair absently. "It's in the sea. There's a gate there in Lake Michigan, not far from here."

I lifted an eyebrow. "You swam?"

"I was under the protection of their courier, going there," Justine said. "It's like walking in a bubble of air." She hitched the child up a little higher on her hip. "Mag saw me. He drove the courier away as I was leaving and took me to his home. There were many other prisoners there."

"Including the child," I guessed. Though it probably didn't sound that way.

Justine nodded. "I... arranged for several prisoners to flee Mag's home. I took the child when I left. I swam out."

"So you are, in effect, stolen property in possession of stolen property," I said. "Novel."

Gard and Hendricks came back into the office.

I looked at Hendricks. "My people?"

"Tulane's got a broken arm," he said. "Standing in that asshole's way. He's on the way to the doc."

"Thank you. Ms. Gard?"

"Mag is off the property," she said. "He didn't go far. He's summoning support now."

"How much of a threat is he?" I asked. The question was legitimate. Gard and Hendricks had blindsided the inhuman while he was focused upon Justine and the child and while he wasted his leading magical strike against my protective circle. A head-on confrontation against a prepared foe could be a totally different proposition.

Gard tested the edge of her axe with her thumb, and drew a smooth stone from her pocket. "Mag is a fomor sorcerer lord of the first rank. He's deadly—and connected. The fomor could crush you without a serious loss of resources. Confrontation would be unwise."

The stone made a steely, slithery sound as it glided over the axe's blade.

"There seems little profit to be had, then," I said. "It's nothing personal, Justine. Merely business. I am obliged to return stolen property to signatory members of the Accords."

Hendricks looked at me sharply. He didn't say anything. He didn't have to. I already knew the tone of whatever he would say. *Are there no prisons*, perhaps. Or, *No man is an island, entire of itself. It tolls for thee.* On and on.

Hendricks has no head for business.

Gard watched me, waiting.

"Sir," Justine said, her tone measured and oddly formal. "May I speak?"

I nodded.

"She isn't property," Justine said, and her voice was low and intense, her eyes direct. "She was trapped in a den of living nightmares and there was no one to come save her. She would have died there. And I am not letting anyone take her back to that hell hole. I will die first." The young woman set her jaw. "She is not property, Mr. Marcone. She's a child."

I met Justine's eyes for a long moment.

I glanced aside at Hendricks. He waited for my decision.

Gard watched me. As ever, Gard watched me.

I looked down at my hands, my fingertips resting together with my elbows propped on the desk.

Business came first. Always.

But I have rules.

I looked up at Justine.

"She's a child," I said quietly.

~

The air in the room snapped tight with tension.

"Ms. Gard," I said. "Please dismiss the contractors for the day, at pay. Then raise the defenses."

She pocketed the whetstone and strode quickly out, her teeth showing, a bounce in her step.

"Mr. Hendricks, please scramble our troubleshooters. They're to take positions across the street. Suppressed weapons only. I don't need patrolmen stumbling around in this. Then ready the panic room."

Hendricks nodded and got out his cell phone as he left. His huge, stubby fingers flew over its touchscreen as he sent the activation text message. Looking at him, one would not think him capable of such a thing. But that is Hendricks, generally.

I looked at Justine as I rose and walked to my closet. "You will go with the child into the panic room. It is, with the possible exception of Dresden's home, the most secure location in the city."

"Thank you," she said quietly.

I took off my coat and hung it up in the closet. I took off my tie and slipped it over the same hanger. I put my cuff-links in my coat pocket and rolled up my sleeves, and skinned out of my gun's holster. Then I slipped on the armored vest made of heavy scales of composite materials joined to sleeves of quite old-fashioned mail. I pulled an old field jacket, olive drab, over the armor, belted it, holstered my sidearm at my side, opposite a combat knife, and took a military-grade assault shotgun—a weapon every bit as illegal as my pistol in the city of Chicago—from its rack.

"I am not doing it for you, young lady," I said. "Nor am I doing it for the child."

"Then why are you doing it?" she asked.

"Because I have rules," I said.

She shook her head gently. "But you're a criminal. Criminals don't have rules. They break them."

I stopped and looked at her.

Justine blanched and slid a step further away from me, along the wall. The child made a soft, distressed sound. I beckoned curtly for her to follow me as I walked past her. It took her a moment to do so.

Honestly.

Someone in the service of a vampire ought to have a bit more fortitude.

~

This panic room looked like every other one I've had built: Fluorescent lights, plain tile floor, plain drywall. Two double bunks occupied one end of the room. A business desk and several chairs took up the rest. A miniature kitchen nestled into one corner, opposite the miniature medical station in another. There was a door to a half-bath, and a bank of security monitors on the wall between them. I flicked one switch that activated the entire bank, displaying a dozen views from hidden security cameras.

I gestured for Justine to enter the room. She came in and immediately took a seat on the lower bunk of the nearest bed, still holding the child.

"Mag can find her," Gard told me, when we all rendezvoused outside the panic room. "Once he's inside the building and gets past the forward area, he'll be able to track her. He'll head straight for her."

"Then we know which way he'll be moving," I said. "What did you find out about his support?"

"They're creatures," Gard said, "actual mortal beings, though like none you've seen before. The fomor twist flesh to their liking and sell the results for favors and influence. It was probably the fomor who created those cat-things the Knights of the Blackened Denarius used."

I twisted my mouth in displeasure at the name. "If they're mortal we can kill them."

"They'll die hard," Gard warned me.

"What doesn't?" I looked up and down the hallway outside the panic room. "I think the primary defense plan will do."

Gard nodded. She had attired herself in an armored vest not unlike my own over a long mail shirt. Medieval-looking, but then modern armorers haven't aimed their craft at stopping claws of late. Hendricks, standing watch at the end of the hall, had on an armored vest, but was otherwise covered in modified motorcyclist's armor. He carried an assault shotgun like mine, several hand grenades, and that same broadsword.

"Stay here," I said to Justine. "Watch the door. If anyone but one of us comes down the stairs, shut it."

She nodded.

I turned and started walking toward the stairway. I glanced at Gard. "What can we expect from Mag?"

"Pain."

Hendricks grunted. Skeptically.

"He's ancient, devious, and wicked," Gard clarified. "There is an effectively unlimited spectrum of ways in which he might do harm."

I nodded. "Can you offer any specific knowledge?"

"He won't be easy to get to," she said. "The fomor practice entropy magic. They make the anti-technology effect Dresden puts off look like mild sunspot activity. Modern systems are going to experience problems near him."

We started up the stairs. "How long before he arrives?"

From upstairs, there was the crash of breaking plate glass. No alarm went off, but there was a buzzing, sizzling sound, and a scream—Gard's outer defenses. Hendricks hit a button on his cell phone, and then came with me as I rushed up the remaining stairs to the ground floor.

The lights went out as we went, and Hendricks's phone sputtered out a few sparks. Battery-powered emergency lights flicked on an instant later. Only about half of them functioned, and most of those were behind us.

Mag had waited for nightfall to begin his attack, and then crippled our lights. Quite possibly, he assumed that the darkness would give him an overwhelming advantage.

The hubris of some members of the supernatural community is astonishing.

The night vision scopes mounted on my weapon and Hendricks's had been custom made, based off of designs dating back to World War II, before night vision devices had married themselves to the electronics revolution. They were heavy and far inferior to modern systems— but they would function in situations where electronic goggles would be rendered into useless junk.

We raised the weapons to our shoulders, lined an eye up with the scopes, and kept moving. We reached the first defensive position, folded out the reinforced composite barriers mounted there, and knelt behind them. The ambient light from the city outside and the emergency lights below us was enough for the scopes to do their jobs. I could make out the outline of the hallway and the room beyond. Sounds of quiet movement came closer.

My heart rate had gone up, but not alarmingly so. My hands were steady. My mouth felt dry, and my body's reaction to the prospect of mortal danger sent ripples of sensation up and down my spine. I embraced the fear and waited.

The fomor's creatures exploded into the hallway on a storm of frenzied roars. I couldn't make out many details. They seemed to have been put together on the chassis of a gorilla. Their heads were squashed, ugly-looking things, with wide-gaping mouths full of shark-like teeth. The sounds they made were deep, with a frenzied edge of madness, and they piled into the corridor in a wave of massive muscle.

"Steady," I murmured.

The creatures lurched as they moved, like cheap toys that had not been assembled properly, but they were fast, for all of that. More and more of them flooded into the hallway, and their charge was gaining mass and momentum.

"Steady," I murmured.

Hendricks grunted. There were no words in it, but he meant, *I know.*

The wave of fomorian beings got close enough that I could see the patches of mold clumping their fur, and tendrils of mildew growing upon their exposed skin.

"Fire," I said.

Hendricks and I opened up.

The new military AA-12 automatic shotguns are not the hunting weapons I first handled in my patriotically delusional youth. They are fully automatic weapons with large circular drums that rather resembled the old Tommy guns made iconic by my business predecessors in Chicago.

One pulls the trigger and shell after shell slams through the weapon. A steel target hit by bursts from an AA-12 very rapidly comes to resemble a screen door.

And we had two of them.

The slaughter was indescribable. It swept like a great broom down that hallway, tearing and shredding flesh, splattering blood on the walls and painting them most of the way to the ceiling. Behind me, Gard stood ready with a heavy-caliber big-game rifle, calmly gunning down any creature that seemed to be reluctant to die before it could reach our defensive point. We piled the bodies so deep that the corpses formed a barrier to our weapons.

"Hendricks," I said.

The big man was already reaching for the grenades on his belt. He took one, pulled the pin, cooked it for a slow two count, and then flung it down the hall. We all crouched behind the barriers as the grenade went off with a deafening crunch of shockwave-driven air.

Hendricks threw another one. He may disapprove of killing, but he does it thoroughly.

When the ringing began to fade from my ears, I heard a sound like raindrops. It wasn't raining, of course—the gunmen in the building across the street had opened fire with silenced weaponry. Bullets whispered in through the windows and hit the floor and walls of the headquarters with innocuous-sounding thumps. Evidently, Mag's servitors had been routed and were trying to flee.

An object the size of Hendricks's fist appeared from nowhere and arced cleanly through the air. It landed on the floor precisely between the two sheltering panels, a lump of pink and grey coral.

Gard hit me with a shoulder and drove me to the ground, even as she shouted, "Down!"

The piece of coral didn't explode. There was a whispering sound, and hundreds of tiny holes appeared in the bloodstained walls and ceiling. Gard let out a pained grunt. My left calf jerked as something pierced it, and burned as though the wound had been filled with salt.

I checked Hendricks. One side of his face was covered in a sheet of blood. Small tears were visible in his leathers, and he was beginning to bleed through the holes.

"Get him," I said to Gard, rising, as another coral spheroid rose into the air.

Before it could get close enough to be a threat, I blew it to powder with my shotgun. And the next and the next, while Gard dropped her rifle, got a shoulder under one of Hendricks's, and helped him to his feet as if he'd been her weight, instead of two hundred and seventy pounds of muscle. She started down the stairs.

A fourth sphere came accompanied by mocking laughter and when I pulled the trigger again the weapon didn't function. Empty. I slapped the coral device out of the air with the shotgun's barrel and flung myself backward, hoping to clear the level of the floor on the stairwell before the pseudo-grenade detonated. I did not quite make it. Several objects struck my chest and arms, and a hot blade slipped across my unscarred ear, but the armor turned the truly dangerous projectiles.

I broke my arm tumbling backward down the stairs.

More laughter followed me down, but at least the fomor wasn't spouting some kind of ridiculous monologue.

"I did my best," came Mag's voice. "I gave you a chance to return what was mine. But no. You couldn't keep yourself from interfering in my affairs, from stealing my property. And so now you will reap the consequences of your foolishness, little mortal..."

There was more, but there is hardly a need to go into details. Given a choice between that egocentric drivel and a broken arm, I prefer the latter. It's considerably less excruciating.

Gard hauled me to my feet by my coat with her spare hand. I got under the stunned Hendricks's other arm and helped them both down the rest of the stairs. Justine stood in the doorway of the safe room, at the end of the hallway of flickering lights, her face white-lipped but calm.

Gard helped me get Hendricks to the door of the room and turned around. "Close the door. I may be able to discourage him out here."

"Your home office would be annoyed with me if I wasted your life on such a low percentage proposition," I said. "We stick to the plan."

The valkyrie eyed me. "Your arm is broken."

"I was aware, thank you," I said. "Is there any reason the countermeasure shouldn't work?"

Mag was going on about something, coming down the steps one at a time, making a production of every footfall. I ignored the ass.

"None that I know of," Gard admitted. "Which is not the same answer as 'no.'"

"Sir," Justine said.

"We planned for this—or something very like it. We don't split up now. End of discussion. Help me with Hendricks."

"Sir," Justine said.

I looked up to see Mag standing on the landing, cloaked in random shadows, smiling. The emergency lights on the stairwell blew out with a melodramatic shower of dying sparks.

"Ah," I said. I reached inside the safe room door, found the purely mechanical pull-cord wrapped unobtrusively around a nail-head on the wall, and gave it a sharp jerk.

It set off the antipersonnel mines built into the wall of the landing.

There were four of them, which meant that a wash of fire and just under three thousand round shot acquainted themselves with the immediate vicinity of the landing and with Mag. A cloud of flame and flying steel enveloped the fomor, but at the last instant the swirling blackness around him rose up like a living thing, forming a shield between Mag and the oncoming flood of destruction.

The sound of the explosions was so loud that it demolished my hearing for a moment. It began to return to me as the cloud of smoke and dust on the landing began to clear. I could hear a fire alarm going off.

Mag, smudged and blackened with residue, but otherwise untouched, made an irritated gesture and the fire alarm sparked and fizzled—but not before setting off the automatic sprinklers. Water began pouring down from spigots in the ceiling.

Mag looked up at the water and then down at me and his too-wide smile widened even more. "Really?" he asked. "Water? Did you actually think water would be a barrier to the magic of a fomor lord?"

Running water was highly detrimental to mortal magic, or so Gard informed me, whether it was naturally occurring or not. The important element was quantity. Enough water would ground magic just as it could conduct electricity and short-circuit electronics. Evidently, Mag played by different rules.

Mag made a point to continue down the stairs at exactly the same pace. He was somewhat hampered in that several of the stairs had been torn up rather badly in the explosion, but he made it to the hallway. Gard took up a position in the middle of the hallway, her axe held straight up beside her in both arms, like a baseball player's bat.

I helped Hendricks into the saferoom and dumped him on a bunk, out of any line of fire from the hallway. Justine took one look at his face and hurried over to the medical station, grabbing a first aid kit. She rushed back to Hendricks's side. She broke open the kit and started laying out the proper gear for getting a clear look at a bloody wound and getting the bleeding stopped. Her hands flew with precise speed. She'd had some form of training.

From the opposite bunk, the child watched Justine with wide blue eyes. She was naked, and had been crying. The tears were still on her little cheeks. Even now, her lower lip had begun to tremble.

But so far as anyone else knew, I was made of stone.

I turned and crossed the room. I sat down at the desk, a copy of the one in my main office. I put my handgun squarely in front of me. The desk was positioned directly in line with the door to the panic room. From behind the desk, I could see the entire hallway clearly.

Mag stepped forward and moved a hand as though throwing something. I saw nothing, but Gard raised her axe in a blocking movement, and there was a flash of light, and the image of a Norse rune, or something like it, was burned onto my retina. The outer edge of Gard's mail sleeve on her right arm abruptly turned black and fell to dust, so that the sleeve split and dangled open.

Gard took a grim step back as Mag narrowed his jaundiced eyes and lifted the crooked stick. Something that looked like the blend of a lightning bolt and an eel lashed through the air toward Gard, but she caught it on the broad blade of her axe, and there was another flash of light, another eye-searing rune. I heard her cry out, though, and saw that the edges of her fingernails had been burned black.

Step by step, she fell back, while Mag hammered at her with things that made no sense, many of which I could not even see. Each time, the rune-magic of that axe defeated the attack— and each time, it seemed to cost her something. A lightly singed face here. A long, shallow cut upon her newly-bared arm there. And the runes, I saw, were each in different places on the axe, being burned out one by one. Gard had a finite number of them.

As Gard's heels touched the threshold of the saferoom, Mag let out a howl and threw both hands out ahead of him. An unseen force lifted Gard from her feet and flung her violently across the room, over my desk and into the wall. She hit with bone-crushing force and slid limply down.

I faced the inhuman sorcerer alone.

Mag walked slowly and confidently into my safe room, and stared at me across my desk. He was breathing heavily, from exertion or excitement or both. He smiled, slowly, and waved his hand again. An unpleasant shimmer went through the air, and I glanced down to see rust forming on the exposed metal of my gun, while cracking began to spread through the plastic grip.

"Go ahead, mortal," Mag said, drawing the words out. "Pick up the gun. Try it. The crafting of the weapon is fine, mortal, but you are not the masters of the world that you believe yourselves to be. Even today's cleverest smiths are no match for the magic of the fomor."

I inclined my head in agreement. "Then I suppose," I said, "that we'll just have to do this old school."

I drew the 18th century German dragoon pistol from the open drawer beside my left hand, aimed, and fired. The ancient flintlock snapped forward, ignited the powder in the pan, and roared, a wash of unnatural blue-white fire blazing forth from the antique weapon. I almost fancied that I could see the bullet, spinning and tumbling, blazing with its own tiny rune.

Though Mag's shadows leapt up to defend him, he had expended enormous energy moving through the building, hurling attack after attack at us. More energy had to be used to overcome the tremendous force of the claymores that had exploded virtually in his face. Perhaps, at his full strength, at the height of his endurance, his powers would have been enough to turn even the single, potent attack that had been designed to defeat them.

From the beginning, the plan had been to wear him down.

The blue bolt of lead and power from the heavy old flintlock pierced Mag's defenses and body in the same instant and with the same contemptuous energy.

Mag blinked at me. Then lowered his head to goggle at the smoking hole in his chest as wide as my thumb. His mouth moved as he tried to gabble something, but no sound came out.

"Idiot," I said coldly. "It will be well worth the weregild to be rid of you."

Mag lurched toward me for a moment, intent upon saying something, but the fates spared me from having to endure any more of him. He collapsed to the floor before he could finish speaking.

I eyed my modern pistol, crusted with rust and residue, and decided not to try it. I kept a spare .45 in the downstairs desk in any case. I took it from another drawer, checked it awkwardly one-handed, and then emptied the weapon into Mag's head and chest.

I am the one who taught Hendricks to be thorough.

I looked up from Mag's ruined form to find Justine staring at me, frozen in the middle of wrapping a bandage around my second's head.

"How is he?" I asked calmly.

Justine swallowed. She said, "He m-may need stitches for this scalp wound. I think he has a concussion. The other wounds aren't bad. His armor stopped most of the fragments from going in."

"Gard?" I asked, without looking over my shoulder. The valkyrie had an incredible ability to resist and recover from injury.

"Be sore for a while," she said, the words slurred. "Give me a few minutes."

"Justine, perhaps you will set my arm and splint it," I said. "We will need to abandon this renovation, I'm afraid, Gard. Where's the thermite?"

"In your upstairs office closet, right where you left it," she said, in a *very* slightly aggrieved tone.

"Be a dear and burn down the building," I said.

She appeared beside my desk, looking bruised, exhausted, and functional. She lifted both eyebrows. "Was that a joke?"

"Apparently," I said. "Doubtless the result of triumph and adrenaline."

"My word," she said. She looked startled.

"Get moving," I told her. "Make the fire look accidental. I need to contact the young lady's patron so that she can be delivered safely back into her hands. Call Doctor Schulman as well. Tell him that Mr. Hendricks and I will be visiting him shortly." I pursed my lips. "And steak, I think. I could use a good steak. The Pump Room should do for the three of us, eh? Ask them to stay open an extra half an hour."

Gard showed me her teeth in a flash. "Well," she said. "It's no mead hall. But it will do."

~

I put my house in order. In the end, it took less than half an hour. The troubleshooters made sure the formorian creatures were dragged inside, then vanished. Mag's body had been bagged and transferred, to be returned to his watery kin, along with approximately a quarter of a million dollars in bullion, the price required in the Accords for the weregild of a person of Mag's stature.

Justine was ready to meet a car that was coming to pick her up, and Hendricks was already on the way to Schulman's attentions. He'd seemed fine by the time he left, growling at Gard as she fussed over him.

I looked around the office and nodded. "We know the defense plan has some merit," I said. I hefted the dragoon pistol. "I'll need more of those bullets."

"I was unconscious for three weeks after scribing the rune for that one," Gard replied.

"To say nothing of the fact that the bullets themselves are rare. That one killed a man named Nelson at Trafalgar."

"How do you know?"

"I took it out of him," she said. "Men of his caliber are few and far between. I'll see what I can do." She glanced at Justine. "Sir?"

"Not just yet," I said. "I will speak with her alone for a moment, please."

She nodded, giving Justine a look that was equal parts curiosity and warning. Then she departed.

I got up and walked over to the girl. She was holding the child against her against her again. The little girl had dropped into an exhausted sleep.

"So," I said quietly. "Lara Raith sent you to Mag's people. He happened to abduct you. You happened to escape from him—despite the fact that he seemed to be holding other prisoners perfectly adequately—and you left carrying the child. And, upon emerging from Lake Michigan, you happened to be nearby, so you came straight here."

"Yes," Justine said quietly.

"Coincidences, coincidences," I said. "Put the child down."

Her eyes widened in alarm.

I stared at her until she obeyed.

My right arm was splinted and in a sling. With my left hand, I reached out and flipped open her suit jacket, over her left hip, where she'd been clutching the child all evening.

There was an envelope in a plastic baggie protruding from the jacket's interior pocket. I took it.

She made a small sound of protest, and aborted it partway.

I opened the baggie and the envelope and scanned over the paper inside.

"These are account numbers," I said quietly. "Security passwords. Stolen from Mag's home, I suppose?"

She looked up at me with very wide eyes.

"Dear child," I said. "I *am* a criminal. One very good way to cover up one crime is to commit another, more obvious one." I glanced down at the sleeping child again. "Using a child to cover your part of the scheme. Quite cold-blooded, Justine."

"I freed all of Mag's prisoners to cover up the theft of his records at my lady's bidding," she said quietly. "The child was... not part of the plan."

"Children frequently aren't," I said.

"I took her out on my own," she said. "She's free of that place. She will stay that way."

"To be raised among the vampires?" I asked. "Such a lovely child will surely go far."

Justine grimaced and looked away. "She was too small to swim out on her own. I couldn't leave her."

I stared at the young woman for a long moment. Then I said, "You might consider speaking to Father Forthill at St. Mary of the Angels. The Church appears to have some sort of program to place those endangered by the supernatural into hiding. I do not recommend you mention my name as a reference, but perhaps he could be convinced to help the child."

She blinked at me, several times. Then she said, quietly, "You, sir, are not very much like I thought you were."

"Nor are you. Agent Justine." I took a deep breath and regarded the child again. "At least we accomplished something today." I smiled at Justine. "Your ride should be here by now. You may go."

She opened her mouth and reached for the envelope.

I slipped it into my pocket. "Do give Lara my regards. And tell her that the next time she sends you out to steal honey, she should find someone else to kill the bees." I gave her a faint smile. "That will be all."

Justine looked at me. Then her lips quivered up into a tiny, amused smile. She bowed her head to me, collected the child, and walked out, her steps light.

I debated putting a bullet in her head, but decided against it. She had information about my defenses which could leave them vulnerable—and more to the point, she knew that they were effective. If she should speak of today's events to Dresden...

Well. The wizard would immediately recognize that the claymores, the running water and the magic-defense-piercing bullet had not been put into place to counter Mag or his odd folk at all.

They were there to kill Harry Dresden.

And they worked. Mag had proven that. An eventual confrontation with Dresden was inevitable—but murdering Justine would guarantee it happened immediately, and I wasn't ready for that, not until I had rebuilt the defenses in the new location.

Besides. The young woman had rules of her own. I could respect that.

I would test myself against Dresden in earnest, one day—or he against me. Until then, I had to gather as many resources to myself as possible. And when the day of reckoning came, I had to make sure it happened in a place where, despite his powers, he would no longer have the upper hand.

Like everything else.

Location, location, location.

RED RUN

~

by Kami Garcia

No one drove on Red Run at night. People went fifteen miles out of
their way to avoid the narrow stretch of dirt that passed for a road, between
the single stoplight towns of Black Grove and Julette. Red Run was buried
in the Louisiana backwoods, under the gnarled arms of oaks tall enough to
scrape the sky. When Edie's granddaddy was young, bootleggers used it to
run moonshine down to New Orleans. It was easy to hide in the shadows
of the trees, so dense they blocked out even the stars. But there was still a
risk. If they were caught, the sheriff would hang them from those oaks,
leaving their bodies for the gators, which is how the road earned its name.

The days of bootlegging were long gone, but folks had other reasons for
steering clear of Red Run after dark. The road was haunted. A ghost had
claimed eight lives in the last twenty years—Edie's brother's just over a year
ago. No one wanted to risk a run-in with the blue-eyed boy. No one except
Edie.

She was looking for him.

Tonight she was going to kill a ghost.

~

Edie didn't realize how long she had been driving until her favorite
Jane's Addiction song looped for the third time. Edie was beginning to
wonder if she was going to find him at all, as she passed the rotted twin
pines that marked the halfway point between the two nothing little towns,
when she saw him. He was standing in the middle of the road, on the

84

wavering yellow carpet of her headlights. His eyes reflected the light like a frightened animal, but he looked as real as any boy she'd ever seen. Even if he was dead.

She slammed on the brakes instinctively, and dust flew up around the Jeep and into the open windows. When it skidded to a stop, he was standing in front of the bumper, tiny particles of dirt floating in the air around him.

For a second, neither one of them moved. Edie was holding her breath, staring out beyond the headlights at the tall boy whose skin was too pale and eyes too blue.

"I'm okay, if you're worried," he called out, squinting into the light.

Edie clutched the vinyl steering wheel, her hands sweaty and hot. She knew she should back up—throw the car into reverse until he was out of sight—but even with her heart thudding in her ears, she couldn't do it.

He half-smiled awkwardly, brushing the dirt off his jeans. He had the broad shoulders of a swimmer, and curly dark hair that was too long in places and too short in others, like he had cut it himself. "I'm not from around here."

She already knew that.

He walked toward her dented red Jeep, tentatively. "You aren't hurt, are you?"

It was a question no one ever asked her. In elementary school, Edie was the kid with the tangled blond braids. The one whose overalls were too big and too worn at the knees. Her parents never paid much attention to her. They were busy working double shifts at the refinery. Her brother was the one who wove her hair into those braids, tangled or not.

"I'm fine." Edie shook her head, black bobbed hair swinging back and forth against her jaw.

He put his hand on the hood and bent down next to her open window. "Is there any way I could get a ride into town?"

Edie knew the right answer. Just like she knew she shouldn't be driving on Red Run in the middle of the night. But she hadn't cared about what was right, or anything at all, for a long time. A year and six days exactly— since the night her brother died. People had called it an accident, as if somehow that made it easier to live with. But everyone knew there were no accidents on Red Run.

That was the night Edie cut her hair with her mother's craft scissors, the ones with the orange plastic handles. It was also the night she hung out with Wes and Trip behind the Gas & Go for the first time, drinking Easy Jesus and warm Bud Light until her brother's death felt like a dream she would forget in the morning. The three of them had been in the same class since kindergarten, but they didn't run in the same crowd.

When Wes and Trip weren't smoking behind the school or hanging out in the cemetery, they were holed up in Wes's garage, building weird junk they never let anyone see. Edie's mom thought they were building pipe bombs.

But they were building something else.

~

The blue-eyed boy was still leaning into the window. "So can I get a ride?" He was watching her from under his long, straight lashes. They almost touched his cheeks when he blinked.

She leaned back into the sticky seat, trying to create some space between them. "What are you doing out here, anyway?"

Would he admit he was out here to kill her?

"My parents kicked me out, and I'm headed for Baton Rouge. I've got family down there." He watched her, waiting for a reaction.

Was this part of the game?

"Get in," was all she said, before she could change her mind.

The boy walked around the car and opened the door. The rusty hinges creaked, and it reminded Edie of the first time Wes opened the garage door and invited her inside.

~

The garage was humid and dark, palmetto bugs scurrying across the concrete floor for the corners. Two crooked pine tables were outfitted with vises and tools Edie didn't recognize. Wire and scrap metal littered the floor, attached to homemade-looking machines that resembled leaky car batteries. There were other salvaged and tricked-out contraptions—dials that looked like speedometers, a portable sonar from a boat, and a long needle resting on a spool of paper that reminded her of those lie detectors you saw on television.

"What is all this stuff?"

Wes and Trip glanced at each other before Wes answered, "Promise you won't tell anyone?"

Edie took another swig of vodka, the clear liquid burning its way down her throat. She liked the way it felt going down, knowing it would burn through her memories just as fast.

86

"Cross my heart and hope I die," she slurred.

"It's hope *to* die," Trip said, kicking an empty beer can out of the way. "You said it wrong."

Edie stared back at him, her eyes glassy. "No, I didn't." She tossed the empty bottle at a green plastic trash can in the corner, but she missed and it hit the concrete, shattering. "So are you gonna tell me what you're doing with all this crap?"

Wes picked up a hunk of metal with long yellow wires dangling from the sides like the legs of a mechanical spider. "You won't believe us."

He was right. The only thing she believed in now was Easy Jesus. Remembering every day to forget. "Try me."

Wes looked her straight in the eye, sober and serious. He flicked a switch on the machine and it whirred to life. "We're hunting ghosts."

~

Edie didn't have time to think about hanging out with Wes and Trip in the garage. She needed to focus on the things they had taught her.

She was driving slower than usual, her hands glued to the wheel so the blue-eyed boy wouldn't notice how badly they were shaking. "Where are you from?"

"You know, you really shouldn't pick up strangers." His voice was light and teasing, but Edie noticed he didn't answer the question.

"You shouldn't get in the car with strangers either," she countered. "Especially not around here."

He shifted his body toward her, his white ribbed tank sliding over his skin instead of sticking to it the way Edie's clung to hers. The cracked leather seat didn't make a sound. "What do you mean?"

She felt a wave of satisfaction. "You've never heard the stories about Red Run? You must live pretty far from here."

"What kind of stories?"

Edie stared out at the wall of trees closing in around them. It wasn't an easy story to tell, especially if you were sitting a foot from the boy who died at the end of it. "About twenty years ago, someone died out here. He was about your age—"

"How do you know how old I am?" His voice was thick and sweet, all honey and molasses.

"Eighteen?"

He lifted an eyebrow. "Good guess. So what happened to him?"

Edie knew the story by heart. "It was graduation night. There was a party in Black Grove and everyone went, even Tommy Hansen. He was quiet and always kept to himself. My mom says he was good-looking, but none of the girls were interested in him because his family was dirt-poor. His dad ran off and his mother worked at the funeral home, dressing the bodies for viewings."

Edie saw him cringe in the seat beside her, but she kept going. "Tommy worked at the gas station to help out and spent the rest of his time alone, playing a beat-up guitar. He wanted to be a songwriter, and was planning to leave for Nashville that weekend. If the party had been a few days later, he might have made it."

And her brother would still be alive.

Edie remember the night her brother died, his body stretched out in the middle of the road. She had stepped too close, and a pool of blood had gathered around the toes of her sneakers. She had stared down at the thick liquid, wondering why they called the road Red Run. The blood was as black as ink.

"Are you going to tell me how that kid Tommy died?" The boy was watching her from under those long eyelashes.

Edie's heart started racing. "They had a keg in the woods, and everyone was wasted. Especially Katherine Day, the prettiest girl in school. People who remember say that Katherine drank her weight in cheap beer and wandered into the trees to puke. Tommy saw her stumbling around and followed her. This is the part where folks disagree; in one version of the story, Tommy stat with Katherine while she threw up all over her fancy white sundress. In the other version, Katherine forgot about how poor Tommy was—or noticed how good-looking he was—and kissed him. Either way, the end is the same." Edie paused, measuring his reaction. At this point in the story, people were usually on pins and needles.

But the blue-eyed boy was staring back at her evenly from the passenger seat, as if he already knew the way it ended.

"Don't you want to know what happened next?"

He smiled, but there was something wrong about it. His eyes were vacant and far away. Was he remembering? He sensed Edie watching him, and the faraway look was gone. "Yeah. How did he go from making out with the prettiest girl in school to getting killed?"

"I didn't say he was killed." Edie tried to hide the fear in her voice. She didn't want him to know she was afraid.

"You said he died, right?"

She didn't point out that dying and being killed weren't the same thing. If Edie hadn't known she was in over her head the minute he got in the car, she knew now. But it was too late. "Katherine was dating a guy on the wrestling team, or maybe it was the football team, I can't remember. But he caught them together—kissing or talking or whatever they were doing— and dragged Tommy out of the woods with a bunch of his friends."

The boy's blue eyes were fixed on her now. "Then what happened?" His voice was so quiet she had trouble hearing him over the crickets calling out in the darkness.

"They beat him to death. Right here on Red Run. Some guy who lived out in the woods saw the whole thing."

The boy nodded, staring out the window as the white bark of the pines blurred alongside the car. "So that's why no one drives on this road at night?"

Edie laughed, but the sound was bitter and cold. About as far away from happy as it could be. "This is the Bayou. If you avoided every road where someone died, there wouldn't be any roads left. Folks don't drive on Red Run at night because Tommy Hansen's ghost has killed six people around our age. They say he kills the boys because they remind him of the guys who beat him to death, and the girls because they remind him of Katherine."

Edie pictured her brother lying in the glow of the police cruiser's spotlight, bathed in red. She had knelt down in the sticky dirt, pressing her face against his chest. Will's heart was beating, the rhythm uneven and faint.

"Edie?" She felt his chest rise as he whispered her name.

She cradled his face in her hands, but he was staring blankly beyond her. "I'm here, Will," she choked. "What happened?"

Will strained to focus on Edie's tear-stained face. "Don't worry. I'm gonna be okay." But his eyes told a different story.

"I should have listened…"

Will never finished. But she didn't need to hear the rest.

~

Edie could feel the blue-eyed boy watching her. She bit the inside of her cheek to keep from crying. She had to hold it together a little while longer.

"You really believe a ghost is out here killing people?" He sounded disappointed. "You look smarter than that."

Edie gripped the steering wheel tighter. He had no idea how smart. "I take it you don't?"

He looked away. "Ghosts are apparitions. They can't actually hurt anyone."

"Sounds like you know a lot about ghosts."

~

It was the same thing Edie said the second time she hung out with Wes and Trip in the filthy garage. Wes was adjusting some kind of gadget that looked like a giant calculator, with a meter and needle where the display would normally have been. "We know enough."

"Enough for what?" She imagined the two of them wandering around with their oversized calculators, searching for ghosts the way people troll the beach for loose change and jewelry with metal detectors.

"I told you, we hunt ghosts." Wes tossed the calculator thing to Trip, who opened the back with a screwdriver and changed the batteries.

Edie settled into the cushions on the ratty plaid couch. "So you hang out in haunted houses and take pictures, like those guys on TV?"

Trip laughed. "Hardly. Those guys aren't ghost hunters. They're glorified photographers. We don't stand around taking pictures." Trip tossed the screwdriver onto the rotting workbench. "We send the ghosts back where they belong."

Wes and Trip weren't as stupid as Edie had assumed. In fact, if the two of them had ever bothered to enter the science fair, they would've won. They knew more about science, physics mainly—energy, electromagnetism, frequency, and matter—than any of the teachers at school. And they were practically engineers, capable of building almost anything with some wires and scrap metal. Wes explained that the human body was made up of electricity—electrical impulses that keep you alive. When a person died, those impulses changed form, resulting in ghosts.

Edie only understood about half of what he was saying. "How do you know? Maybe it just disappears."

Trip shook his head. "Impossible. Energy can't be destroyed. Physics 101. Those electrical impulses have to go somewhere."

"So they change into ghosts, just like that?"

"I wouldn't say 'just like that.' I gave you the simplified version," Trip said, attaching another wire to his tricked-out calculator.

"What is that thing?" she asked.

"This," Trip held it up proudly, "is an EMF meter. It picks up electromagnetic fields and frequencies, movement we can't detect. The kind created by ghosts."

"That's how we find them," Wes said, taking a swig from an old can of Mountain Dew. "Then we kill them."

~

Edie was still thinking about that day in the garage when she smelled something horrible coming from outside. It was suffocating—heavy and chemical, like burning plastic. She rolled up her window, even though the air inside the Jeep immediately became stifling.

"Don't you want to let some air in?" the blue-eyed boy ventured.

"I'm more concerned about letting something out."

He waited for Edie to explain, but she didn't. "Can I ask you a question?"

"Shoot," she said.

"If you believe there's a ghost on this road, why are you driving out here all alone at night?"

Edie took a deep breath and said the words she had rehearsed in her mind since the moment he climbed into the car. "The ghost that haunts Red Run killed my brother, and I'm going to destroy it."

Edie watched as the fear swept over him.

The realization.

"What are you talking about? How do you kill a ghost?"

He didn't know.

Edie took her time answering. She had waited a long time for this. "Ghosts are made of energy like everything else. Scatter the energy, you destroy the ghost."

"How do you plan to do that?"

Edie knocked on the black plastic paneling on her door. It was the same paneling that covered every inch of the Jeep's interior. "Ghosts absorb the electrical impulse around them—from power lines, machines, cars—even people. I have these two friends who are pretty smart. They made this stuff. Some compounds conduct electricity," She ran her palm over the black paneling. "Others block it."

"So you're going to trap a ghost in the car with you and—what? Wait till it shorts out like a light bulb?"

"It's not that simple," Edie said, without taking her eyes off the road. "Energy can't be destroyed. You have to disperse it, sort of like blowing up a bomb. My friends know how to do it. I just have to keep the ghost contained until I get to their place. They'll do the rest."

Tommy glanced at the black paneling. "You're crazy, you know that?"

His arm wasn't draped casually over the seat anymore, and his hands were balled up in his lap.

"Maybe," she answered. "Maybe not."

He reached for the handle to roll down his window, but it wouldn't turn. "Your window's—" He paused, working it out in his mind. "It isn't broken, is it?"

Edie took her foot off the gas and let the car roll to a stop. "You didn't really think I'd pick up a hitchhiker on a deserted road in the middle of nowhere?" She turned toward the blue-eyed boy, a boy she knew was a ghost. "Did you, Tommy?"

His eyes widened at the sound of his name.

Edie's heart felt like it was trying to punch its way out of her chest. There was no way to predict how Tommy's ghost was going to react. Wes had warned her that ghosts could psychically attack the living by moving objects or causing hallucinations, even madness. His mom had walked off the second-story balcony of their house when Wes was in fourth grade. It was only a few weeks after she had started hearing strange noises and seeing shadows in the house. Wes's father wanted to move, but his mom said she wasn't going to be driven out of her house by swamp-water superstition. She didn't believe in ghosts. Not until one killed her.

Now Edie was sitting only inches away from a ghost that had already murdered six people.

But he didn't look murderous. There was something else lingering in his blue eyes. Panic. "You can't stop here."

"What?"

"There's something I need to tell you, Edie. But you have to keep driving. It's not safe." He was turning around in his seat, scanning the woods through the windows.

Edie bit the inside of her cheek again. "What are you talking about?"

Before he had time to respond, the light outside flickered as a shadow cut through the path of the car's headlights.

Edie jumped, jerking her eyes back toward the road.

There was a man a few yards away, waving his arms wildly. "Get outta the car now!"

"It's too late," Tommy whispered. "He's already here."

"Who?"

"The man who killed me."

Edie didn't have a chance to ask him to explain. The man in the road was still yelling as he moved closer to the car. "Hurry up! Before that blue-eyed devil skins you alive alike the rest a them!"

Tommy's ghost grabbed her arm, but she couldn't feel his touch. "Don't listen to him, Edie. He wants to hurt you, the same way he hurt me. And your brother."

"What did you say?" The words tore at Edie's throat like razor blades.

"I didn't kill any of those kids that died out here. He did." Tommy pointed at the man in the road. "I watch the road. I try to make sure no one stops near his cabin. I tried to warn all of them, but they wouldn't listen."

Edie remembered her brother's last words.

I should have listened...

She had assumed he was referring to the stories—the constant warnings to stay off Red Run after dark. What if she was wrong? What if he had been talking about a different warning altogether?

"No." Edie shook her head. "Those guys beat you to death—"

Tommy cut her off before she could finish. "They didn't. That's the story he told the police. And no one believed a bunch of drunk kids when they denied it."

The voice outside was getting louder and more frantic. "Whatever that spirit's telling you is a lie! He's trying to keep you in there with him so he can kill you! Come on out, sweetheart."

It was easier to see the man now that he was just a few feet away. He was about her dad's age, but worse for the wear. His green John Deere cap was pulled low over his eyes, and he was wearing an old hunting jacket over his broad shoulders despite the heat.

He was shifting from side to side nervously, his eyes flitting back and forth between the woods and the car.

"He's lying. I swear," Tommy—it was becoming harder to remember that he was a ghost, not a regular boy—pleaded. "Why do you think I got in the car? I wanted to make sure you didn't stop. He doesn't like it when people get this close to his place. Especially teenagers."

"You expect me to believe some old guy is killing people because they're coming too close to his house?" Her voice was rising, a dangerous combination of fear and anger burning through her veins.

"He's crazy, Edie. He cooks meth back there at night, and he's convinced people can smell it. He's always been paranoid, but after being cooped up in a tiny cabin with those fumes for years, it's gotten worse."

Edie remember the nauseating stench of melted plastic. She never would have recognized it. Still. The man was pacing in front of the car, wringing his hands nervously. There was something off about him. But then again, he was facing off against a ghost.

Tommy was still talking. "That's what he was doing the night I got lost in the woods, only back then it was something else. He's been cooking up drugs in his cabin for years, supplying dealers in the city. I was looking for this girl who wandered off, and I got all turned around. I didn't realize how far I'd walked. There was a cabin…" He paused, looking out at the man in the green cap. "Let's just say, I knocked on the wrong door."

The man stopped in the path of one of the headlights, a beam of light creating shadows across his face. "You can't trust the dead. No matter what they say, sweetheart."

Edie reached for the door handle.

Tommy—the boy-ghost—grabbed her other hand. For a second, Edie thought she felt the weight of his hand on hers. It was impossible, but it gave her goose bumps all the same. "He beat me to death, Edie. Then he dragged my body all the way back to the party and left me in the middle of Red Run."

Edie didn't know who to believe. One of them was lying. And if she made the wrong choice, she was going to die tonight.

Tommy's blue eyes were searching hers. "I would never hurt you, Edie. I swear."

She thought about everything Wes and Trip had taught her, which boiled down to one thing: You can't trust a ghost. She thought about her brother lying in the road. *I should have listened.* He could've been talking about the man in the green cap—the one begging her to get out of the car right now.

What was she thinking? She couldn't trust a ghost.

Edie threw the door open before she could change her mind. The smell of burnt plastic flooded into the Jeep.

"Edie, no!" Tommy's eyes were terrified, darting back and forth between Edie and the man in the road. In that moment, she knew he was telling the truth.

She reached for the door to pull it shut again as the man in the green cap rushed toward the driver's side of the car. When he passed through the headlights, Edie saw him grab the buck knife from his waistband.

Edie tried to close the door, but it felt like she was wading through syrup. She wasn't fast enough. But the man in the green cap was, his arm coming around the edge of the door. His knife was in his hand, reddish-brown lines streaking the dull blade.

"Oh, no you don't, you little bitch!" The man grabbed the metal frame before she could close the door, the blade of the knife waving dangerously close to her face.

Tommy appeared just outside the open car door, only inches from the man wielding the knife. Before the man had a chance to react, Tommy rushed forward and stepped right through him.

Edie saw the man's eyes go wide for a second, and he shivered.

"Back up!" Tommy shouted.

Edie didn't think about anything but Tommy's voice as she turned the key, grinding the ignition. She threw the car into reverse, slamming her foot on the gas.

The man swore, his hand uncurling from the handle of the knife. He tried to hold onto the doorframe, his filthy nails clawing at the metal.

Then his fingers slide away, and Edie saw him hit the ground.

She heard the scream as the Jeep bucked and the front tire rolled over his body. Edie didn't stop until she could see him lying facedown in the dust. She could see the crushed bones, forced into awkward angles. He wasn't moving.

Edie didn't notice Tommy standing next to the car. He pulled the door open, bent metal scraping through the silence, and knelt down next to her. "Are you okay?"

"I think I killed him." Her voice was shaking uncontrollably.

"Edie, look at me." Tommy's was calm. She leaned her head against the seat, turning her fact toward his. "You didn't have a choice. He was going to kill you."

She knew Tommy was right. But it didn't change the fact that she had just killed a man, even if that man was a monster.

Tommy's blue eyes were searching her brown ones, their faces only inches apart. "What made you trust me?"

"Your eyes," Edie answered. "The eyes don't lie."

"Even if you're a ghost?"

Edie smiled weakly. "Especially if you're a ghost."

She looked out at the road. For the first time in forever, it was just a road—dirt and rocks and trees. She tried to imagine what it would be like to spend every night out here, so close to the place where you died.

"You're the first person who ever believed me," Tommy said. "The first person I saved."

"Then why did you stay here for so long?"

Tommy looked away. "I didn't have a choice."

Edie remembered Wes telling her that most ghosts couldn't leave a place where they had died traumatically. They were chained to that spot, trying to find a way to right the wrong.

When he turned back to face her, Edie noticed the sadness lingering in his eyes. And something else…

Tommy was fading, flickering like static on an old TV set. He stared down at his hands, turning them slowly as if seeing them for the first time.

"I think you can move on now," Edie said gently. "You know, to wherever you're supposed to be. Red Run doesn't need protecting anymore."

"I don't know where I'm supposed to be. But wherever it is, I'm not ready to go." Tommy was still fading. "There are so many things I never had a chance to do."

Edie ran her hand along the black paneling inside the jeep, and looked at him. "Get in."

Tommy hesitated for a second, smiling. "Just don't take me to meet the friends who made that stuff."

Edie smiled back at him. "You can trust me."

As she drove away, Red Run disappearing into the darkness, Edie felt the weight of this place disappear along with it. "So where do you want to go?"

Tommy was still watching her.

The girl who wasn't afraid to hunt a ghost.

"Maybe I'll hang out with you for a while." Tommy put his hand on top of hers, and she didn't need to feel the weight of it to know it was there. "There are always things that need protecting."

PALE RIDER

~

by Nancy Holder

Shards, ashes, and a freaking *carton* of batteries. Inside the dusty box, there were dozens of double-A six packs.

Dana whooped, victorious. Lowering herself to a squat on the balls of her feet, she pushed back her dreads and caressed the treasure with her flashlight beam. Then she set her flashlight upended so that the light bounced off the ceiling, picked up one of the packs, and wiped off the dust. She turned it over, examining it for an expiration date. The printing was too faded. She grabbed the flashlight, and was just about to unscrew the head so she could test a sample when she heard the creak of a floorboard. She wasn't alone.

"Shit," she whispered. As quietly as she could, she clicked off her flashlight and stuck it in the pocket of her hoodie. Then she grabbed the heavy carton and stood, listening. Her heart pounded.

Nothing. Maybe she had imagined it. Or the poor old house was settling some more.

She quietly shuffled out of the room. This was the third time in two weeks that she'd found batteries in places they'd already searched. She had just known to go inside the ramshackle house and step through the filth and the trash to what appeared to be a home office. Even though she and Jordan had been there before, and carted off anything useable. But this time, she could see the floorboards in her mind, and she'd pried them up.

In the disintegrating world, change was not usually your friend, but life had made an exception.

There was another creak, and then a growl, and something charged at her. She screamed and tore out of the room with her carton. It followed her into the hall, kicking up years of dust and trash while she banged into the walls from side to side with the huge box. She kept yelling, barreling around a fallen door, into pitch-black darkness.

My gun is in my other pocket, she thought.

She whirled around and tried to throw the carton at her attacker—where she thought it might be—but the box was too heavy and it just tumbled through the darkness to the floor. Stumbling backwards, seeing nothing, she got the gun out of her other pocket and fired. The thing howled. Dog. Coyote. She fired a couple more shots and ran out of the house. The wooden porch gave way and she crashed downward through the rotted waist to her waist.

Bathed in amber moonlight, a mangy dog leaped out of the shadows. Dana was trapped. She let out a bellow as it launched itself at her.

It howled; then its limp body smacked against her right arm and it crumbled in a heap beside her. It didn't move. Panting with fear, she planted her palms on either side of her body, fingertips brushing its dirty, matted fur. She pushed up and out of the hole, propelling herself to freedom as she flopped onto her front, then threaded her legs free.

The dog was twitching and panting. *Oh, God, rabies.* Had it bitten her? With a shaking hand, she felt around for her gun, unsure when and where she'd lost it.

No luck.

She tested her footing. Nothing sprained or broken. She stepped back into the house, listening hard, feeling along the floor with the soles of her sneakers for the gun. She still couldn't find it. She could come back for it later, but there was no way she was going to leave the batteries. They were just too precious.

Ear cocked, she groped around for the carton, found it, and picked it up again. She was trembling. She didn't feel any pain. No bites, then. Hopefully.

A creak.

She turned back around to leave. Her knees gave way and she almost slid to the floor.

Silhouetted by moonlight, a man stood in the doorway. Spiky hair, long coat, boots. Her heartbeat went into overdrive.

His dog, she thought, cold and terrified. *He set it on me.*

They faced each other without speaking. She kept it together. You didn't live as long as she had—she was seventeen—by losing your cool. But she was very scared.

"I have a gun," she said.

He raised his hand. "This one?" he said in some kind of accent.

Oh, God. Oh, God, oh, God, she thought. This was what she got. Jordan had told her not to scavenge alone. But she had just *known* they had to get the batteries tonight. Jordan was down with a bug, and no else had felt like going.

She licked her lips and raised her chin. "I have another gun."

"You can have this one back," he said. The accent was German. He sounded like a movie villain. He looked like one in his long coat. She felt naked in her sweatshirt, sneakers and board shorts.

"Stay away from me. I'll call my guard dog on you," she said, but her voice cracked and she realized she was losing her grip on the carton. Icy sweat was streaming down her body.

"I mean you no harm, Delaney."

She jerked, even more afraid. That was her given name, and no one at the house knew it.

He raised his hands above his head, and she saw the outline of her gun. She didn't know what to do. Rush him? Run back into the darkness? Where there might be another dog?

Then suddenly, there was no carton in her arms. It was in his. And they were on the sidewalk outside the house.

"What the heck?" she said.

"*Es geht.*"

He was very tall, not as old as she had thought—maybe five years older than her—and in the moonlight, she saw that his hair was blond. His eyes were light and he had a superhero face—flared cheekbones, square chin. Pierced eyebrow. Maybe that was a tat on his thumb. He was muscular, his long black wool coat stretching across big broad shoulders. These days, most people were a little too thin. Like her. She was all crazy black hair, brown eyes, and bones. "I got your name from your aunt. Well, from her things. I haven't actually met her."

"What aunt?" she asked him cautiously. She and her mom had kept to themselves until her death three years ago. She didn't know any of her relatives.

"Aunt Meg." He waited for her reaction. The name meant nothing to her.

"She's white," he added.

Her stomach did a flip. Maybe this Aunt Meg was from her father's side. Dana didn't even know his name. Dana's mom had never told her white ex-boyfriend that she had gotten pregnant.

"What things?" she asked, catching her sneaker toe on a crack in the sidewalk. Their neighborhood looked like a bomb had gone off. Things fell apart all the time. She caught her toe again. Despite the heaviness of the box against his chest, he reached out a hand to steady her. His fingers were very warm and pale against her dark skin.

"Where is she?" she asked. "Aunt Meg?"

"She used to work for my family. In a way." He took his hand away. "My distant relatives."

She stopped walking. "It was nice of you to taser that dog and all, but just, you know, get to the point."

He stopped, too, and faced her. "It's a sad world when someone who knows a family member of yours is greeted with such hostility."

"This world is more than sad. I don't know that you know her," she countered. "You're just a name-dropper in a coat." When he kept looking at her as if that didn't compute, she said, "I need more proof."

He nodded. "Fair enough."

She looked to the right, at a boarded-up building, and had a funny feeling. His face came into her mind and then there was something black and rectangular. She squinted as she walked, trying to make sense of it.

"Hey," said a voice, and she jerked her head up. She and the guy were standing in front of her house, which she shared with Jordan, Lucy, Mike, and Anny. The strays that had become family. Wrapped in his bathrobe and plaid pajama bottoms, Jordan was standing on the porch, shotgun pointed in their direction. "What's up?"

"We have a rule," she told the guy. "No strangers in the house. Ever."

He looked from her to Jordan and back again. "My name is Alex Ritter. There. I'm not a stranger. It's okay to let me in."

Jordan hesitated. "What?" he said fuzzily.

"It's okay," the guy—Alex said again.

"Cool." Jordan nodded calmly and lowered the shotgun.

Dana was stunned. *"Jordan?"*

"It's really all right, Delaney," the man—Alex said. "I swear it to you."

"It's not," she insisted. Too late, she remembered that he still had her gun. She bounded onto the porch beside Jordan and reached for the shotgun. "We don't know this guy. And he is *weird.*"

Jordan kept hold of the rifle and opened the front door. "Come on in."

"Lucy!" Dana shouted. "Anny! Mike!"

Then they were in the house, and her four roommates were oohing and aahing over the carton of batteries, which Alex was doling out to them like Santa Claus with his bag of presents. Dana looked around wildly. She had lost more time. And this creepy man in black was inside her house.

"These things are over fifteen years old," Jordan marveled as he popped a couple of batteries in her flashlight, twisted the head back on, and gave it a flick. Light poured forth. She didn't remember giving it to him. "Awesome."

"They're warm," Lucy said, holding one between her hands. She leaned over and kissed Dana on the cheek. "You're made of fabulous."

"She chased away some dogs, too," Alex offered. Dana glared at him. Everyone else was taking his sudden appearance in stride. Or maybe she had simply fast-forwarded through the introductions.

She held out a shaking hand. "Give me back my gun."

He did so, willingly, and she stuffed it into her pocket again. Then she turned her back and walked into the kitchen. Out of his line of sight, she slipped through the back door and flew down all the wooden stairs to the cool sand of the beach.

He followed, as she had expected him to, and she pulled out the gun. He looked from it to her face and sighed.

"If you shoot, you shoot," he said.

Then he walked to the water's edge and lifted his chin. "No seaweed," he said. "No seagulls."

But there was something on the beach, next to his boot. She spotted it at the same time that he looked down. He picked it up—tats all over that hand—and his palm blossomed with a pale bluish glow. Her eyes widened as he put the object in his pocket.

"Sea glass," he said, as if that should satisfy her.

He turned his face back to the black water. "I was out here earlier. One good thing about the end of the world. The sunsets are fantastic."

"This is Southern California. Our sunsets are always fantastic." She kept a good grip on the gun. "You'd better tell me what's going on."

"I'm Alex Ritter. From Germany. Berlin."

Despite herself, she was impressed. Eight years ago, people traveled all over the place. But fuel was getting scarce. Her house didn't even have a car.

"I flew here," he added, as if reading her mind. "I have a plane."

"Holy shit," she blurted. There were still planes in the world. And they cost... she didn't even know what they cost. Too much to even think about.

He smiled faintly. His profile was sharply etched against the night. It didn't make any sense that Jordan had let him in, just like that, and everyone had behaved as if it was no big deal. It was a huge deal. He was scary.

"Dana, please, I'm sorry," he said abruptly, turning his face toward her. "There is no good way to have the talk I need to have with you. Let me show you."

Before she could reply, he wiped his face with both his hands and rubbed them together. He moved his head from side to side, as if working out the kinks; then he turned to the sea and opened his arms like an orchestra conductor.

Something hummed against the soles of her feet. A couple of her braids bobbed in a freshet of wind.

Shimmering blue crackles of energy crackled from his fingertips. Then the crackles traveled to the water, and hit it with a sizzle. The waves rippled and flared blue, pink, gold like the Aurora Borealis.

Dana jumped backwards so hard she landed on her butt, and she spastically lifted her sneakers as the water swirled toward her. It took her a moment to realize that he'd clasped her wrist and was pulling her to her feet.

"Don't touch me," she said as she tried to yank her hand away. He was bending over her; there were rings under his eyes and the pupils were dilated. He was jittery and shaky, like he was on something.

She looked from his eyes to the water. The colors were gone. Her mind started spinning rationalizations and denials. She was spooked by the way he cocked his head and gazed at her with an odd, confused expression, like he was trying to remember what to say.

"I don't know how else to tell you this," he said. "But I think it was your Aunt Meg who made all this happen." He waved his hand. "All the chaos. The... ending."

"What?" she blurted. "How?" She backed away from him, holding the gun in both her hands; behind him, the black, colorless surf rolled into the night.

"I don't know how," he said, so softly she barely heard him. "But please, for the love of God, help me fix it."

Then he advanced on her and pushed down her arms. She tried to raise them again but she couldn't. He cupped her face in his hands. Dizziness swept through her and she dropped the gun. He held her still and she could feel him falling right into her, inside her mind. There was nothing but his blue eyes.

Then warmth raced through her, zinging through her bloodstream, and she began to sweat again. The soles on her sneakers made hissing sounds against the damp sand. Sparks skittered through her veins and arteries.

Then she shot like a comet into the air, into space, among the stars, away from the messed-up world. Suspending above the night, she gazed down and saw Los Angeles in ruins, the way it was, and a huge bloom of red surging toward the shore.

Toward her beach, just below her house.

And then saw, in that house, two tiny dots of light. She looked at the dot in the kitchen. It was behind the refrigerator, and as it magnified in her mind, she saw Anny's missing house key. She moved on, and found Jordan's reading glasses between the couch cushions.

She jerked to consciousness, to find that she was she was sprawled in the sand. He was on his hands and knees, his face close to hers, and when he saw that her eyes were opening, he leaned back on his heels with a deep sigh of relief.

"What did you do to me?" she shouted, trying to get up. But her muscles were strangely flaccid.

"I think I activated your gift," he replied. She could hear how freaked out he was.

"*You think you what?*" She felt in the sand for the gun.

"What happened?" he asked.

"You know what happened." He just looked at her, and she huffed. "I saw things. First the world, and the mess." She thought of the mass headed for the beach. "Garbage, or something. And lost things."

She told him about the keys and the glasses. He nodded, looking thoughtful. Then she saw a faint glow around him.

She said, "Did you make those things glow so I could find them?"

"No. I can use energy, in some ways," he said. "Like on the dog."

"And on me."

"I'm sorry," he said.

"And you can make people like you."

"Only when they should," he replied.

"*I* don't like you," she said.

And suddenly she was overcome with weariness. She couldn't keep her eyes open. As they drifted shut, she said, "I think you left your wallet in a building on my street."

He was quiet for a moment.

"Thank you," he said finally, into the muzziness of her sleep.

~

When she woke up just before dawn, she liked him a little more, which was terrifying, because she didn't want to like him at all. He had explained that he'd just found out some unbelievable things—that some kind of supernatural power ran in his family and apparently in hers, too. All his people were missing or dead, but some of them had lived in a castle in the Black Forest. And as soon as he'd gotten inside the castle, he'd turned into Mr. Electric.

Then they were in the house, and he was helping Jordan pull out the refrigerator—a useless appliance except for keeping rats out of boxed food—so Anny could find her house key. Jordan was overjoyed to find his glasses again. There was no one around to make him new ones.

She put all her own valuables in boxes and Jordan promised to keep an eye on them. Then, with shaking hands, she packed a suitcase. He was making her be okay with all this. She could tell. She wanted to make him stop, but she was doing it.

And then she was saying goodbye.

They got his wallet and then he walked her into an alley where a vehicle sat beneath a protective covering. He pulled it off, revealing a beautiful candy-apple red Corvette. She hadn't ridden in a car in years. Something loosened in her chest as she slid in on the passenger's side. The car smelled of old leather and dust. When they climbed in, he pressed his finger against the ignition, and the engine purred.

"I couldn't find the keys," he said. "Do you see them?"

She narrowed her eyes at him. "Is this some kind of test?"

He shook his head, watching her.

Settling back, she let her lids fall shut. A blur of light passed through her mind's eye; then she felt a stab of sorrow, deep and penetrating. It hurt almost like a physical wound. She opened her eyes and looked at Alex.

"There's something about the keys that's sad," she said.

"The keys are sad?" he repeatedly slowly. As they glided out of the alley, he knit his brows. "In the sense of...?"

"I don't know I just felt sadness." She crossed her arms over her chest. "Did you put some kind of double whammy on me?"

"I don't really know what I did to you," he replied.

~

His jet was bigger than she'd pictured it. It was parked in what had once been a parking lot for the beach. Fueled up, ready to go. It could cross the Atlantic nonstop. She sat to his right in the cockpit. He took off his coat, revealing lots of muscles and a black T-shirt. His right arm was completely tattooed. Tats on the left went up to his elbow. It didn't make sense that a guy who looked like him would have access to a Corvette and a plane, and that she was flying to Germany with him.

But it didn't make sense that in eight short years, the world had fallen completely apart. First everyone talked about fuel reserves and no TV, no grid, no net, and very few people. It was as if things were melting. Evaporating. As if the world itself was losing time—or running out of it.

They climbed. She looked down at the coastline. The ocean and sky were the same color. Skyscrapers had collapsed. Streets were broken up. There were no birds. Her mother was buried somewhere below her, in a grave not far from their house because without transportation, they couldn't get her to a graveyard.

Her throat tightening, she brushed tears from her eyes and focused, trying to see her mother's grave in her mind. What she saw was her mother's face, deep black, her lips, so brown, pulled back from white teeth in a smile.

Her throat tightened. She gripped the armrest so hard the beds of her fingernails stung.

"Why did I come with you?" she asked him through tears.

He was quiet for a moment. Then he said, "Why did I come get you?"

~

Hours later, they began their descent through a sky the color of old copper. The sun was beginning to set. Snow was falling onto skeletons of trees and vast deadfalls. Anticipation skittered through her as his castle came into view. It sat on a hill, as he had said. Half of it had been destroyed; the other half rose into the aged, metallic sky.

They landed and rolled to a stop. Alex had explained that he'd been adopted by a wealthy couple named Aaron and Maria Cohen. His parents had been on a trip to Greece when the Collapse had occurred. That was what he called it. Explosions, earthquakes, riots. Eight years of looking for them. Finally he'd found a key, and then a bank safe deposit box. There were his adoption papers, saying that he had been born in town called Ritterburg, in the heart of the Black Forest. He'd lived in the castle for three months before he'd come to get her.

"Here we are," he said, sounding nervous.

Alex had brought a little foldable ladder. She didn't really need it. As she climbed down, he retrieved her suitcase and his black duffel. A gritty brown wind brushed over her. Strips of faded blue cloth dangled from flagpoles at the top of the castle, and somewhere a hinge squeaked back and forth in the bitter wind.

Neither one of them spoke as he led the way to the castle. With his long coat and boots, he looked like Neo from *The Matrix*. There were patches of snow on the ground. They were gray and they kind of smelled, but they were the first snow she had ever seen.

Alex put his hand on the small wooden door, cut into the larger, older door, to push it open. The rectangle of wood hung in the air for a second, then disintegrated, falling to the snow in a heap of fine ash. He pulled back his hand and stared at the space where the door had been.

"Shit," he said in English. "Things are getting worse."

"No kidding," she murmured.

He crossed the threshold and she reluctantly—so very reluctantly— followed him in. There wasn't much left. No roof, piles of stone and rubble, blackened walls stretching up hundreds of feet.

"I've got all the stuff in my room," he said.

Her cheeks warmed. "Do I have a room?"

"*Ja.*" He smiled stretched into a grin. "Just across the hall from mine."

"You were pretty sure of yourself when you came to find me," she muttered, crossing her arms over her chest. She didn't like this place.

Things were tapping for her attention just beneath her consciousness. Whispering just a little too softly for her to hear.

He looked over at her. "I cast a lot of magics to find you, Dana. I didn' t know if you would come, but I wanted to make sure you would feel welcome."

"You could just work a spell on me," she said. "The way you did back in LA."

"I'm sorry about that," he said. "I wasn't proud of it."

His manga-man black coat billowed around his legs as he crossed the marble floor. Most of the black and white squares had been smashed. He led her down a narrow passage bordered on either side by piles of wood and stone. There was more roof there, blocking out the light. Flicking on a flashlight, he led the way. It was icy, and she wrapped one hand around the other. She became aware that a low-level sadness, no, it was despair tinged with anger, crept up the backs of her legs like a needy, starving dog. Freaked out, she glanced over her shoulder, seeing nothing.

"Something's here," she announced. "I feel it."

"What? What do you feel?" he asked, sounding excited. He painted the walls with the beam from his flashlight.

She told him.

"Maybe it's a ghost?" he said.

"*Maybe?*" she echoed, alarmed. "Damn it, Alex."

He opened a door, pulling back his hand quickly as if he expected it to fall apart the way the front door had. His flashlight passed over a stone floor, swept clean. He moved to table and lit a trio of candles, except that she didn't see a lighter or a match.

He handed a candle to her. In the soft glow, she saw him open his palm, and a small ball of light appeared.

"I'm not clear what your 'gift' is," she said.

"One of them is light," he replied. "At least, I think it is. I'm on my own figuring all this out."

They moved toward a bed dressed in a thick, furry coverlet and topped with a stack of pillows. Unhappiness rose around her like a mist.

"This place is bad," she said. "Let's get out of here."

"Bad," he said. "How—"

She pushed past him, not willing to stay inside. He joined her in the hall.

"Better?" he asked.

"Not really." She looked left and right. "What happened here?"

"Like I said at the beach. They were attacked, as far as I can tell." He made a face. "There are a lot of bones. And cages." He pointed to an open door. "That's my room."

"*Bones?* I think we should leave," she said. "We'll get the stuff you need from here and go somewhere else."

"Hmm," he answered noncommittally.

There was a sleeping bag on the floor of his room, and a heavy wooden table. Stacks and stacks of leather-bound books balanced on a heavy wooden table and several open boxes. Candles, crystals, and herbs were spilling out of them.

"Oh, my God," she said. It would take them days to cart all of it out of the castle.

"*Ja*, you see," he replied.

Then he walked to the table and placed his palm on a black book with scrolled gold writing that she couldn't read.

"I don't know what it says, either," he told her as he flipped it open. There was a loose photograph of a woman with red hair, red eyebrows, and big blue eyes. She was wearing a cat suit and body armor strapped over that. She had a black helmet on her hip with ZECHERLE in white. He tapped his finger on the lettering. "That's her last name. Maybe it's your father's, too."

Delaney Zecherle. Her mom's last name was Martin. Her mom's name had been Tenaya.

He turned the page, edged a small photograph from the crease with his thumbnail, and handed it to her.

She caught her breath at the sight of herself as a little girl in a school picture, grinning away, with no notion of what was to come. She was missing her two front teeth.

"I was six," she said.

She turned over the picture. The handwriting was careful; she read, *Delaney Martin (Dana.)* And the address of their house, the one she had still been living in, with Jordan and the others. Then, (*YOUR NIECE!*)

"Is that your mother's handwriting?" Alex asked her.

She shook her head. "I don't know. We never wrote anything down."

Feelings she couldn't describe swept upward, making her feel out of kilter. She stared at the handwriting, then at the picture. Her heart tugged.

"This was... before," she said.

"*Ja*," he said. They stood shoulder to shoulder, looking down at the Delaney that had been. Stuffed animals and Disneyland, those had been her hopes and dreams. She felt the heat of his skin and wondered what his life had been like with the Cohens. Jets and flying lessons?"

"From what I can tell, your aunt was only here for a couple of weeks before everything went crazy," he said.

There were some burned fragments of lined paper. She put down the picture and carefully sorted through them. She looked a piece of paper.

THINGS TO DO

LEARN GERMAN

On another, she read;

I think something's going on downstairs. Something wrong.

She turned another page of the book, to see photographs of other people dressed like Meg Zecherle. They looked like riot police.

"Those were her teammates," Alex said. "They were some kind of security guards. They patrolled along a place called the Pale."

"What's that?" she asked.

"A border. They had to keep something out. I think it got in."

She looked at the massive volumes. "All this, and that's all you've got?""Most of this is written in Latin. I think. I think some was very old German." He opened a book at random. "Here or there I found something I could read. Spells." He looked abashed. "Imagine if you came here. Would you know what to do?"

They shared a grim smile.

"There's nothing more about... us?" she asked, not sure which "us" she meant.

"Maybe you can find something," he said. "There *is* something," he went on, reaching for another book. Bound in maroon leather, it was enormous.

He opened it to the first page. There was a black-and-white woodblock print of a man in a three-cornered hat on a horse, and a small child clasped against his chest. The horse was cantering the night. Clouds billowed in the background, and in the largest of them, a shadowy face smiled wickedly down at them.

Alex pointed to lines of text beneath the picture. It was organized in stanzas like a poem, and he began to read aloud, in German. She listened to his voice.

"It's *Der Erlkönig*," he said. "'The Erl King.' Do you know it? 'Who rides so late, through night and wind'?" When she shook her head, he said, "I keep coming back to this picture. I keep reading the poem. I don't know why."

"What is it about?"

"The child is sick. The father is riding with him through the forest, and the Erl King wants him. The boy can see him. The father can't. He begs his father to save him from the Erl King. But he doesn't."

"Cheery," she said.

The despair tugged at her again, almost like someone pulling on her hand. Anger skittered ratlike up her spine and she stepped away from the table.

"Delaney?" he asked.

Freaked, she looked around the room. "Is this place haunted?"

"I don't know. His expression told her he had come to a decision. "The town's deserted. We can look for a place—"

A sharp stab of light replaced his face. She saw a circular stone stairway. Saw herself walking down it behind Alex.

She brushed past him and went into the hall. Her thought was to go back out the front door, but instead, she turned in the opposite direction, into the pitch blackness.

Light flared behind her. She heard the thudding of his boots, and then he was beside her. He had a flashlight. He said something to her in German, gave his head an impatient shake.

"English, English," he said to himself. "What is happening?" he asked her."There's something down there," she said, halting before a hole in the floor at the end of the hall. "I saw it. It's a cage."

He was quiet for a moment. Then he said, "There are a lot of cages down there. But you wanted to leave, and I think we should. We can come back."

She nodded. He was right.

But then it happened again: the flash of light. The cage.

And the horrible, horrible despair. Cold, miserable, alone. Dying. Pleading.

"I think I have to go down there," she said hesitantly.

"Okay, here," he said, turning and aiming the flashlight at a curved stone wall, then downward at a circular flight of stone stairs. "I'll go first."

He started down, taking the flashlight beam with him. She followed for a couple of steps, but then she froze. There was no banister and she pushed herself against the wall, afraid she'd fall off the edge of the staircase and never stop falling. She was no Alice, and this was no Wonderland. Grief wafted up from the depths below and twisted around her, like people drowning on the *Titanic*. She recoiled and crossed her arms.

She headed back up.

Then suddenly, rage poured right in, crashing over her head.

Just go down and kick him. Kick him hard, and he'll fall down the stairs and break his neck. It was as if someone else inside her was whispering commands. Raging because he was the enemy, and the end of the world was his fault.

"Alex," she said, swallowing hard.

Oblivious, he kept going.

She took another step up.

Kill him. They lied. They told us we were doing a great thing. But we were not.

She teetered and on the step and went back down. The rage ebbed. Another step down. It faded.

Another.

It was gone.

"Alex, wait," she said. "There's something bad. Really bad."

He was standing at the bottom of the stairs. She got to him and to her surprise, he put his arm around her protectively.

"There's something that's angry. It told me to..." she began. And then realized that she didn't really know this guy, and she had watched him charm his way into her home.

"To what?" he asked.

What the hell am I doing? she thought. She felt as if she were waking up after a long, strange dream.

"It told me to leave," she lied. "And I think—"

And then she felt the sorrow, and the terror. It was longing, and keening, and fear. She thought she heard a moan, and caught her breath. Was someone down here? Someone alive?

"I think we should hurry," she said.

"You're okay, though?" he asked.

"Does it matter?" she snapped, because she was afraid of him. "Why don't you just zap me so I'll do your bidding, master?"

He knit his brows and took his arm away, exhaled and ran his hand across his forehead. She saw how tired he was. He'd just flown halfway across the world, for God's sake. But she hadn't asked him to. She hadn't asked for any of this.

He reached out a hand toward her, then lowered it. The flashlight beam glinted off the piercing in his eyebrow. No, not the beam. There was light around him, as if he were glowing from the inside. His eyes were almost luminescent.

"I feel like you're supposed to be here. And *ja*, I pushed to make that happen. If things were different I would *never* have invaded you..." He shrugged. "But they're not."

"*Invaded?*" she repeated.

He walked on. She walked behind him, staring at the back of his head, at his shoulders. She could almost see tendrils connecting her to him. She didn't feel like she was supposed to be in the castle, but she did feel like she was supposed to be with him. Was that his doing? Was he leading her down there to do something to her?

No, she thought, but how did she know that?

At the bottom of the next landing, a white strip gleamed. Luminous paint. There was a sign in German. EINTRITT VERBOTEN. She knew Verboten meant "forbidden."

The sorrow came back. A silver trickle of strange sounds, like wind chimes, breathed against her ear.

"** **.*"

Twinkling like starlight.

"** **.*"

And she knew they meant "Mama."

"Hello?" she called out.

"Delaney?" Alex said.

"Ssh," she ordered. She listened hard.

"** **.*"

Mama.

"Where are you?" she whispered.

Silence. And...... weeping, and then a kind of gasping, like strangling. And another voice, higher-pitched:

"*** **** **.*"

Help.

She ran forward, past Alex, who tried to reach out a hand to her. Then she stood at the beginning of a double row of cubes, or boxes, that stretched far into the darkness. The sounds were all around her now, coming from the boxes. Whispers, cries for help. Help that never came.

She ran to the closest one and stood facing it. There were bars across the front, and what appeared to be shattered glass in a semicircle on the floor. The moan again:

"*......*".

She felt emotions: Loneliness, misery. Shock. They hadn't expected this to happen to them. Something else was supposed to have happened. Someone else was supposed to be waiting for them. Whatever had been in here had been abandoned, dumped into cells.

"It's evil. So evil," she said.

Then her knees buckled. She felt her eyes roll back in her head. Light blossomed in front of her, reaching to the ceiling in ribbons of color, like the Aurora Borealis Alex had conjured on the ocean. Shadows appeared, then snapped into sharp silhouettes. Misshapen figures rode huge black horses whose hooves sparked as they galloped six inches about the ground. Tiny, gibbering *things* crouched on the saddles. Dogs, breathing fire, wove in and out between the horses' legs as they cantered along a hill. At the head of the parade, a tall figure wearing a helmet decorated with two enormous antlers turns to look at her.

The deepest fear she had ever felt shot through her soul.

Then everything vanished.

Wordlessly, Alex picked her up and carried her out of the room. Up all the flights of stairs, to the main floor of the castle; and there she felt the rage again. *Kick him. Stab him. Kill him.* He raced across the marble floor and through the rubble; the ash of the doorway. Out to the leveled forest, in the gray, smelly snow.

He set her down on a rock and bent down in front of her. He took both her hands in his. They were cold.

"Are you all right now?" he asked her.

She blinked at him. "What was in there?" she asked him. "And what were the things with the horses?"

"Horses?" He looked bewildered. "What did you see?"

She told him. Then, still not sure it was the right thing to do, she told him about the rage.

"It told you to kill me?" he repeated, the blood draining from his face. "That I was a liar?"

She nodded.

He made a face and muttered in German. Then he said, "I guess it's haunted, then." His shoulders rounded and he patted her hand as he got up and plopped down beside her. He gestured to the castle. "I don't think the answer is there." He clicked his teeth and scratched his chin. "I thought you would find it."

She was quiet a moment. Then she said, "You glowed. When I looked at you, I saw light."

"I'm Mr. Electric," he said. He opened his arms. Blue crackles shot from his fingertips. "We can go back to your home. I can make your refrigerator work."

She heard the disappointment in his voice. "But Alex, something was going on with your family. They did something bad. And maybe we're here to fix it."

"You can't go back in there," he said.

"I think I have to," she replied, feeling sick to her stomach at the thought.

"But not tonight." He sighed. "I have a car. We can go to the village."

It was a Mercedes; why was she surprised? They didn't even go back for their stuff. They drove into the deserted village. Some shops were still filled with goods; they got toothbrushes and food, and changes of clothes. Sheets in packages. They broke into an inn and commandeered two rooms. She wasn't sure which would make her feel better, to sleep in the same room or apart. She wasn't sure of anything. She remembered how great it had felt to find that carton of batteries. It felt like that had happened to someone else. Not here, any way.

~

"What did you want out of life, before I came for you?" he asked her, as they shared a bottle of wine—she really wasn't much of a drinker—and ate some canned baba ganoush. They were sitting on his bed. He was wearing a pair of black draw-string pajama bottoms and a gray T-shirt. She had on an oversized T-shirt and leggings. Not very glamorous, but in a way, that was better.

"Batteries," she said. "Endless quantities of them."

He smiled crookedly. "I'm older than you. I was laying plans for my adult life. We were really rich."

"Did you, um, have a girl friend?"

"I always had a girl friend." He wagged his eyebrows and sipped from their bottle. "I was going to follow in my father's footsteps, be rich, then save the rainforest."

"I think you added that last part to make yourself sound more noble." She thought about the voice in the castle telling her that he was a liar. Maybe it had lied.

He handed her the bottle and she cradled it in her lap. "I wanted my mom not to die. And I wanted to meet my father." Her voice dropped. "And I wanted to be safe."

"I think you need your own bottle of wine," he drawled. "Because you got nothing on the list."

"Are you saying I'm not safe with you?" she asked. She meant to tease him, but her voice shook.

He blew the air out of his cheeks. She wanted to take it back, but she decided to let it hang there, and see how he responded.

"I think," he said, "that we should go to sleep."

~

But she was too afraid to sleep. She went to her own room and lay down, but she felt too vulnerable that way. She paced, wondering if Alex was awake.

From her window, she could see the castle, and she made a face at it, like a little kid. She never wanted to go in there again. But her purse was in there. Her clothes. Everything. She hoped Jordan remembered to take good care of her stuff. She had her mom's jewelry, meager as it was, and some souvenirs from the days before—report cards, birthday cards, a Barbie doll and her favorite stuffy, Clown Bear.

Sighing, she leaned her head on the glass. Coolness pressed against her cheek and then the sky exploded into colors. Blue, pink, purple, shimmering and flaring; she stared, transfixed, as gray clouds billowed into being. The moon rose and became the face in the book Alex had shown her. Staring at her. Whispering to her, in words she didn't understand. In a rising and falling voice, like someone reciting a poem. She put her hand on the glass and felt such a *pull*.

"Alex!" she shouted.

She heard him spring out of his bed and race across the hall. Within seconds, he was standing beside her.

"I see it," he cried. "That's the Pale. I know it. I can feel it."

"The face is the Pale?" she asked.

He cocked his head. "What face?"

She pointed. It was staring at them both.

No, it wasn't.

It was staring at Alex.

She looked at him. He was bathed in moonlight, every inch of him. His skin, his hair, his eyes.

She told him, and he held out his arms. "I don't see it," he said. He gazed back through the window. "Delaney, what if *I'm* the lost thing that you were supposed to find?"

And she didn't know why—maybe because he was afraid—but she put her arms around him. His body was very solid. He was staring out the window; now he gave her his attention. She raised on her tiptoes and brushed his lips with hers. Cautiously, he kissed her back. Just the one kiss, chaste, and then she unloosened her arms.

"Just when it couldn't get any weirder," she said, and he chuckled. Then his smile faded.

"I think we should drive toward those lights. Now," he said.

~

As soon as they got in car, it began to rain. Wind blew. Alex turned on the windshield wipers as he drove back through the town, to the castle, then past it too, as the lights intensified.

Nothing whispered to her.

"Did I mention that you're very pretty?" he said. "I like your dark skin."

The raindrops painted shadowy tattoos on his face, and she wondered if he had them in other places, too.

"I like your tats."

"*Danke,*" he said.

The rain came down, and she thought about her mom, and as she often did, the faceless man who had been her father.

The lights filled the sky; it seemed that if they drove forward any farther, they would drive into them. Alex stopped the car and she opened her door.

He came around to her side of the car and laced his fingers through his. As if on cue, it stopped raining. The earth rumbled beneath her feet. Shadows billowed against the colors, gauzy and diffuse. They started to coalesce and thicken, taking on the shapes she had seen in the castle, by the cages.

"Oh, God," she whispered, and he took her hand. Squeezed it. She couldn't squeeze back. She was too terrified.

116

The flares of color vanished, and a figure on a massive horse faced them. It was dressed in ebony chain mail covered with a black chest plate. Its black helmet was smooth, with no eyeholes and topped with curved antlers that flared with smoky flames; fastened at the shoulders, a cloak furled behind like the wake of an obsidian river. In its right chain-mail gauntlet, it held the reins of the horse. Its left arm was raised, and another hand in a gauntlet rested on its fist.

The rider beside it was smaller, dressed much like the other, except that red hair hung over its shoulders. Then it reached up its free hand and pushed back a face plate. It was the woman in the picture. Meg Zecherle.

Her aunt.

She stared at Dana, sweeping her gaze up and down. "Delaney?" she said softly. "Dana? Is that you?"

Alex stepped in front of Dana, placing himself between her and Meg.

"Honey, I have so much to tell you," Meg said, ignoring him. "I was so glad when your mom found me. I was going to come for you. But then…" She exhaled. "Then it all happened."

Tears welled in Dana's eyes and she opened her mouth, but Meg held up her hand and turned to the black figure. It inclined its head. Meg seemed to be listening to it. Then she turned her attention back to Dana.

"I'm sorry, but we'll have to save that for later. But we will talk. I promise."

"Just tell me who my father is," Dana said.

"He was a good man," Meg replied. "But, honey, he passed away before you were born."

"Oh." Her voice was tiny. Tears welled, and she knew right then that that was what she had wanted her life to be like, before. She'd wanted to have a dad. That would have been her magic.

"I'm sorry," Alex murmured. She nodded, a tear spilling down her cheek.

"You're going to have to believe a lot of things that will sound pretty crazy," Meg said.

Dana wiped her cheek. "I think you can skip ahead."

"Okay, but if you need me to slow down, just tell me."

"We will," Alex said.

Meg leaned forward in her saddle. "There was a war. A terrible war, between two magical races. What we might call fairies are known as the fair folk. And the other side are the goblins."

Dana pressed her fingertips over her eyes. She could feel herself tensing, as if bracing herself to hear things she was incapable of handling. She began to shake. Alex put his arm around her waist and pulled her protectively against his side. She did the same. She needed someone to hang onto.

"Hostages were taken on both sides. Infant children, since their code of war demanded that children could never be harmed.

"Finally, it was over. A truce was declared. They agreed to exchange hostages. One baby of the fair folk for one goblin, every Midsummer's Eve, until there were no more. That way, peace would be kept until both sides were made whole.

"For years, my lord faithfully brought a captive goblin baby and laid it in the cradle in the forest," she said, inclining her head in the direction of the tall, black figure. "From the other cradle beside it, he would take the fair child left by his goblin counterpart, and bring it home."

Her lord? Dana thought, with a sudden rush of panic. The stranger who was her aunt called the thing beside her such an archaic name.

"One Midsummer's Night, the local nobleman was riding through the forest. From a hiding place, he saw the exchange. Months later, his wife gave birth to a tiny, sickly girl. The nobleman remembered the swap, and the next Midsummer Night's Eve, he replaced the fair child with his own. What he didn't know was that his baby carried a plague."

"Your... lord... took the plague back with him to the faeries," Dana ventured, and Meg nodded.

"The humanness of the child went undetected because it was so sick. Nearly all the fair folk died, but the goblin babies in their care seemed to be immune. War threatened to break out again, but the goblins were able to prove that they had had nothing to do with what had happened. But they used the plague as leverage. They demanded the immediate release of all their children. The fair folk couldn't care for them anyway, and asked the goblins to keep their own children safe as well, until the plague was gone."

Dana pictured the cages. "But the humans took the goblin babies instead."

"The noble and his lackeys trapped some of them before the goblins arrived to collect them," Meg said. "In all the confusion, the count was off, and neither side realized it."

"But that happened, when?" Alex said.

"Eight hundred years ago," Meg replied.

Alex's arm tightened around Dana.

"But if they were in those cages all that time," Dana said, "wouldn't they grow up?"

"They only age in their own realm. On this plane, they stayed babies. Miserable. Lonely. Unloved. For centuries."

"*Scheiss*," Alex murmured.

"Alex didn't know," Dana said quickly, and she knew that to be true. She knew he was good. And that she was safe with him. "About any of it."

Meg nodded. "I believe you. I was recruited by the Ritters to guard the place where we're standing. The Pale. The border between magic and non-magic worlds. They said it was flimsy. Things were getting across that shouldn't."

She looked over at the figure beside her. "What they were worried about was the Erl King. They were afraid that he'd find out about the goblins in the castle dungeon."

"*The Erl King?* Holy shit, Alex," Dana blurted.

"*Ja,*" he said, and uttered a string of German.

Meg looked a little confused, but she continued. "The Ritter elders never told anyone the truth. But I found out. I saw the cages. And I busted their lie wide open."

"It was *revenge?*" Alex's voice shook. "The goblins destroyed the whole world because of something my family did hundreds of years ago?"

"It was a rescue mission. Fair folk and goblin. *Your* people fought back," she said to Alex. "During the battle, some of them found out and joined our side. But by then, the Pale had fallen. Magic poured into this world and overwhelmed it."

For a moment no one spoke. Dana found Alex's hand and held it.

Meg's features softened. "Magic made our world sick. The fair folk baby that was stolen was the first domino. The goblins toppled next. What happened would have happened eventually. But not for a long time."

"And the fair folk baby survived," Alex said.

"And had children. And they had children. And that means..." Meg's voice trailed off.

"There is still magic in the world." Dana looked at her trembling hands. "As long as we're here."

Alex twined his fingers with hers. "But even if we leave, how many will be left?"

Meg sighed. "We don't know. We don't even know how to find them."

Dana raised her head. The flames on the Erl King's helmet flickered in the night wind. A flake of ash fluttered away, and as she thought about all that he must have lost, too, it began to glow.

She whispered so quietly it seemed as if the wind took her words away, "I find lost things."

FROST CHILD
~

by Gillian Philip

Editor's Note: Sithe captain Griogair MacLorcan is his queen's fighter of choice, skilled and ruthless at clearing her glens of the vile Lammyr. When the Lammyr defiantly return, holding a young Sithe girl captive, Griogair routs them and frees the child. But the girl Lilith has been a long time with Lammyr, and keeps secrets of her own. The most vulnerable of creatures can be the most deadly.

This prequel to Gillian Philip's acclaimed novel Firebrand *tells how Seth's parents Griogair and Lilith met - and the first deadly consequences.*

If I'd had my way, I wouldn't have been up to my knees in pond-muck with my eyes full of sweat and my nostrils full of gods-knew-what stench from below, but if I'd had my way, there wouldn't have been any need.

I'd told my queen ten years back that Lammyr were nesting in this glen. It wasn't like her to be complacent but the dark hollow in the hills was many miles from her caverns, and besides, she knew they were afraid of me. And her indifference had infected me, and I'd put off the work, unwilling to argue my case when there were other tasks to be handled, more congenial quarrels to settle. She'd left it too long, and so had I, and now the creatures would be all the harder to prise from their hole.

It was a good day for it: by which I mean it was silent and still and as grey as death. I should say, it was an appropriate day. As far as approaching the Lammyr unheard and unseen, it was the worst we could have picked.

~*Griogair*, said Niall Mor MacIain.

121

I glanced across to where he crouched, silent, at one of the cavern entrances. It was no more than a slit in the rock, black and dank, the cold breath of underground seeping from it like marsh gas. The gods knew how deep it was, or where it led, but Niall's sword blade was bare and he couldn't repress half a smile; he'd been longing for this. He was rash, was Niall, and he loved a fight, and though I often disapproved, I'd liked him enough to make him my lieutenant.

And after all, I could understand his attitude. Peace and quiet were all very well, but we were getting bored, and fat, and lazy, and so were our fighters. And nobody ever pitied a Lammyr.

~*Quietly, then*, I told him. ~*On three.*

~*Onetwothree*, said Niall, and jumped.

~

There was one advantage to leaving it this long: the Lammyr were every bit as sluggish as we'd been. The first of them turned on me in the gloom with a grinning snarl, but I had the advantage of it, and it went down fast. But they were all over the tunnels, quiet and fast and deadly, slinking into their holes like angry snakes. And it was hard to know where those tunnels ended, so we had to dive after them and engage them in the darkness.

I caught the glinting light of yellow eyes to my right; lunged for it. My blow was glancing and I ended up on the rocky floor, grunting as the air was knocked out of my lungs. The Lammyr pattered out of reach and I breathed hard in the silence, listening for its next move.

"They'll try to run," murmured Donal behind me, his sword raised. "They always do."

"They should have tried already." I frowned. The Lammyr always had an escape route; much as they loved death and a battle, they didn't see the point of losing fighters unnecessarily. I fully expected them to turn tail, to try and squirm out of some back entrance when they realised we meant business.

Usually I didn't care where they went; the idea was to kill enough of them to encourage the rest to relocate their foul nest. But these had been here too long, and worse, they'd slunk back after the first time I routed them. Who knew why? I wasn't asking; I was here to wipe them out. I didn't give Lammyr a second chance. I valued my throat.

I hated this work. I hated being separated from most of my fighters, with just one man at my back to guard it.

And I hated that my backup wasn't Leonora.

It wasn't as if she was handy with a blade; it was only that with Lammyr, there was no more useful fighting partner than a witch. And while I'd never intended to fall for anyone as dangerous and capricious as a witch, I had, and I'd never regretted it.

Ahead of me, wounded, the Lammyr hissed. "Missing your bondmate, Griogair?"

"No," I said, annoyed at myself for leaving my block down. Quickly I shuttered my mind.

It giggled. "Shouldn't think so loud."

"Shouldn't goad me." I went still, aware that the pinprick light of its eyes had vanished again. To my left there was a faint rustle, a skittering slither, and the man behind me gave a yelp of shock and rage. I felt his blood spatter my arm, and then he was cursing to beat the pain.

"Donal?" I said.

"Fine," he snarled.

He wasn't, but he'd have to wait. And I wasn't about to drop my block again to ask him properly.

The Lammyr giggled again, but I ducked as a thrown blade sliced the air above my head, then rolled back. I caught its bony ankle more by chance than skill, yanked it down hard as it leaped for the unseen ceiling, and snatched for its wrist before it could reach for another blade.

Gods, it was a strong one. We rolled and struggled in a silent death-grip, and I couldn't swing my sword arm, and Donal was evidently out of action. Dropping my sword, I found the Lammyr's skinny neck with my hands.

There was mucal blood on its dry papery skin, and I wanted to recoil, but I only shuddered and crushed its throat. I was used to the touch of Lammyr blood after all this time, and it wouldn't burn me, but it wasn't pleasant. One of its flailing hands grabbed my own neck, but it was wounded and I wasn't, and I had the better angle and the better grip. It died with an exasperated rattling sigh.

They lived to kill, but when it came to the end, they didn't mind dying. That was always the trouble with Lammyr.

I stumbled back off it, wiping my hands, then turned to seek out the light of Donal's eyes. They still glinted in the darkness, though dully.

~So how fine are you really?

~I'd like to see Grian fairly fast. His teeth showed in whatever light seeped from the cavern walls.

I gripped his arm and hauled him to his feet. Yes, he needed the healer; I could tell from the quantity of blood. I didn't want to follow this tunnel further anyway. Distant sounds and energetic shouts told me my men were having better luck than Donal and me, and I wanted to rendezvous with them in the deeper heart of this nest. The plan had been to drive the Lammyr from the narrow passageways and into their central quarters. Lammyr, armed and forewarned and lurking in tunnels, were at their most lethal. Herd them to a hall for a fair fight, and you always had a chance of fewer casualties.

I was eager to get Donal out of the way. I didn't think he was mortally wounded – not that I'm an expert – but the sooner he got to the healer the happier I'd be, and besides, I wanted to keep an eye on Niall Mor's back. If he was overenthusiastic he could easily get himself killed.

I found three of my fighters guarding the entrance I'd used, so I left Donal with them; then I was running down the cleared passageways in the direction of the battle-howls.

The remaining Lammyr were backed together in a cavern lower down the tunnel system where the air was cold and dank, unwarmed by the feeble light of flames in wall recesses. Each had a blade in its hand but while Niall Mor and his men circled them warily, the leader watched me enter, licking its dry lips and half-smiling.

"Crickspleen," I said. "Been a while."

"Hello, Griogair." It tossed its curved blade lightly from bony hand to bony hand. No hilts for these creatures; it simply bled where the steel caught its skin, and the colourless drops hissed on the stones at its feet. "Safe passage, and we'll stay away?"

"Oh come on, Crickspleen. We had that deal forty years ago, and here you are again."

It shrugged, amused. "You were softer forty years ago. Over the Veil, then. We'll go to the otherworld."

I rolled my eyes. "You know that isn't allowed."

"Oh, of course. That's why you'll never find a Lammyr in the otherworld." It smirked.

I bit my lip, eyeing it, while Niall Mor fidgeted beside me.

~*Come on, Griogair. Let's get it done.*

~*Don't be in such a rush.* "What are you defending?" I asked it abruptly.

It was a wild shot in the dark, but I saw wariness flicker in its eyes. My hunch was right, then. They hadn't run because they owned something worth keeping.

"Nothing," said Crickspleen at last.

Despite my mind-shield, it knew that I knew it was lying. Its mouth quirked.

"You'd have my word," it crooned. "You know my word is binding."

"I don't want it. If I let you go again, Kate would have my guts for a hat."

"It was worth a try." It gave a bleakly contented sigh. 'No deal then."

It flew at me; an arc of blade-light cut the air, but I hit the cavern floor, feeling the breath of the blade-edge on my scalp. The speed of the damn things could still catch me by surprise, but I wasn't much slower.

I swore as I rolled, dodged, sprang back up. It was nothing but a moving shadow but I'd fought them before. Anticipating its moves was the trick. I bent backwards to avoid the next blow, then came at it low and brought my sword blade with me as I spun.

They look so fragile, so ephemeral. It feels almost wrong as the blade strikes. You'd think the impact in its flesh would be barely discernible, but you have to keep control to finish the blow. Like slicing metal wire.

But I had a good blade. Crickspleen toppled in two halves, the rattle of satisfaction escaping its yellow lips and leaving it lifeless.

The others hadn't been idle, either Lammyr or Sithe. As I rebalanced and lifted my sword again, the chaos and carnage around me was in full-throated roar. I wiped sticky Lammyr-blood from my face and sought another, but we'd had them outmanoeuvred from the start, and in here they hadn't the space to use their speed to full advantage. There was nothing for me to do but finish a few scraps my fighters had started.

When the last blade had fallen we stood in the silence, alert for a stirring hand or limb or a sucked breath, hearing nothing but the slow oozing drip of blood.

I was glad to be able to drop my block and communicate properly. And, of course, scan the caves. ~*Any of us wounded?*

Niall Mor raised a questioning eyebrow at a fighter whose blood streamed from her scalp down the side of her face and neck. She shook her head, angry but not weakened.

~*Nothing serious.*

I narrowed my eyes at the woman, half-blinded by her own blood. *~Dobhran, go back to Grian. The rest of you, follow me.* I frowned as I peered into the darkest corners. *~And block again.*

"We took them all, Griogair," said Niall Mor, though he kept his voice low.

"Maybe. I want to know what else is here. Search the whole warren."

If anybody grumbled, they kept it behind their own blocks, but they went to the task without enthusiasm. This was no place for a Sithe, or not for my Sithe anyway. If someone liked living underground he could go to be the queen's bondsman, and even Kate's lair felt like the sweet open air next to this place. It was as if the rocks above us were pressing down slowly, shrinking the spaces between, reluctant to let us leave. I suppressed a shiver.

There were faint lights in the lower tunnels, muted by iron sconces that were surprisingly beautifully made. The Lammyr could still astonish me. There were times I could almost like them. But it never got beyond *almost*.

The air was cold and stale, but the rankness that accompanied Lammyr occupation was mostly absent. There were only the scents of earth and water and small squirming creatures. I made my way with care, and I kept my blade unsheathed, and so did Niall Mor at my back.

All the same, I might easily have missed her. She was only a shadow, small and dark, huddled in the corner of a side room. It was Niall's intake of breath that alerted me, since his eyesight was so much sharper than anyone's.

I went still, watching for movement. The child might have been a corpse, so stiff was she, but her eyes were wide, unblinking, and lit with the silver glow of a Sithe. No full-mortal girl, then, brought from the otherworld on one of their illicit forays, but a captured Sithe child. Their brazenness was breathtaking, but even this didn't explain their reluctance to leave.

I stretched out my hand to the child, made a beckoning motion. If anything, she pressed even closer against the wall.

Niall stepped cautiously past me. *~Come, child. It's safe.*

I didn't have time to swear at him for dropping his block. He reeled back with a short scream, clawing at his forehead, and the Lammyr came down on him like a falling demon, its leather coat swirling around it.

I lashed with my sword, hacking its wrist more by accident than skill, and it was only by that outrageous chance that Niall avoided having his throat opened. Its hand spun and bumped to the stone floor, and I had to duck to dodge the squirt of blood. Niall rolled out of its way too, reaching out for the girl in the corner. But instead of taking his hand, she scuffled along the wall towards the wounded Lammyr. It gave me a twisted smile.

Still rubbing his head, Niall glanced up to ensure there were no more Lammyr skulking in the roof; I could only stare at the girl, huddling behind her captor, more afraid of us than she was of it. The Lammyr shook the stump of its wrist at me, mockingly, scattering thick clotting droplets. "She's ours, Griogair," it hissed.

I shook my head. "How young did you get her?"

"Young enough."

"You might as well give her back." Niall Mor lifted his sword with a snarl, as angry with himself as he was with the Lammyr. "The rest are dead."

"It was worth a try," said the Lammyr, and sprang at us.

I felt its second blade whisper past my skull, and an instant later the sting of pain, but I'd dodged in the right direction and Niall had leaped high to come down on it. His first strike missed as the creature twisted sideways, but his backslash caught its belly, making it slump with a groan to the ground. I finished it with a thrust to its back.

The girl did not look at us, but at the Lammyr. Not with grief exactly, but perhaps regret. She did not move from her dark nook, keeping her arms wrapped round her knees. When she finally did catch my eye, through a straggling curtain of black hair, I didn't know what I saw there. The strongest impression was of nothing. Her mind-block was astonishing in its thoroughness, its smooth glassy impenetrability.

Niall was quicker than I was to break the strange deadlock. Sheathing his sword on his back, he crouched in front of her, his fingers linked so that she could see them.

"Child, you'll have to come with us. You don't belong here."

She looked from him to the corpse of the Lammyr and back, then got to her feet. For a moment she looked terribly old, but then she nodded quite meekly.

"Where am I going?" she asked.

It was almost a shock to hear her speak. "To be with your own kind," Niall said.

Again she glanced at the Lammyr before studying the two of us. Her reply was almost indifferent. "All right."

It wasn't Niall she approached; she sidled close against me. Niall might have put a reassuring arm round her thin shoulders; I refrained, though, and I suspected, then and now, it was why she chose me. And she stayed close enough to touch me—though she didn't—as I led the way out of the tortuous caverns.

We didn't think to ask her if she had any possessions; we must have assumed she had none, and in that at least our instincts were right. At least, she had none but the thin dress she wore, and the leather belt and pouch around her waist, and the silver collar on her neck. She drew the stares of every one of my fighters as we emerged from the cavern mouth, but she walked on beside me with her head straight and unbowed, her expression once again not so much insouciant as indifferent. She waited only for me to mount my own horse, and didn't hesitate to be pulled up onto its back after me. So small and skinny was she, I couldn't even be sure she was still there till I urged the horse forward, and I felt her bony arms go round my waist.

There was no point racing home; our wounded had already gone with Grian to the dun. This meant he wasn't there to mend the slash in my ear, but for all its copious bleeding the wound was superficial and I made do with a strip of cloth wrapped round my head. At any rate we could afford to take it easy, to revel in the faint sunlight breaking through the earlier mist. Eventually the heavy sense of ill-omen lifted even from me.

It had not gone badly, after all. The Lammyr were cleared from this particular nest, and our casualties had been surprisingly light, and the job I'd been dreading was done. Whatever Crickspleen had wanted with the unnerving girl at my back, he was thwarted. I even felt light-hearted enough to make conversation with her.

Not that the conversation itself was exactly light. "Where are your parents?"

"They're dead. Ever so long ago." Her tone was matter-of-fact.

"Did the Lammyr kill them?"

"I don't remember."

She might have been blocking like a three-hundred-year-old veteran, but I could still tell that was a lie. I glanced over my shoulder, but she seemed untroubled, watching the light flow over the landscape. I wondered how long it had been since she'd last seen the sunlight. It depended on how closely she was kept prisoner, and given how calmly she seemed to have accepted her captivity—as calmly as she'd greeted her release, in fact—I suspected she'd had a certain amount of freedom.

"What's your name?" I suddenly remembered to ask.

She paused again, barely perceptibly. "Lilith. I think."

"You think?"

I felt the slightest of shrugs in her body behind me. "They called me Lilith."

Why did I get the feeling that everything she said was not quite a lie, but not quite the truth either?

I stopped worrying about it when we came in sight of the dun, its stone walls gilded by sunlight and dappled in sea-reflections. My heart never failed to lighten when I rode home, especially on a morning like this: the mist had cleared altogether and sparks of light glittered across the water, and the air smelt of sea-grass. Unthreatened for now, life in the fortress was raucously cheerful, and the gates were thrown wide. Falaire was leading five horses across the machair and the dunes for their swim; the black cattle cropped lazily; the guards on the rampart gave us a yell of welcome. So none of our wounded could be too badly hurt, and the news must have spread that the raid on the Lammyr had been as straightforward as it ever could be.

I left the reins loose, let my horse pick his own way up the rock-and-peat slope to the dun gates. Niall was joking and flirting with one of the other fighters, and I was half-listening and laughing under my breath at her retorts, and I'd almost forgotten the thin creature at my back when she leaned forward, showing eagerness for the first time.

"It's beautiful," she said. Her tone was still noncommittal, but there was no mistaking the way her body tensed with interest.

"Yes," I said.

She said no more, but as we clattered into the courtyard she didn't shrink under the stares of my clann; she returned them with a frank curiosity. All the same I felt a little protective of her, so when my fighters halted I rode on to the door of the forge, and dismounted into the force of its blasting heat. The child slid down into my arms and I set her on the ground.

For the first time she hesitated, and gripped my arm. Her cheekbones were flushed with the heat, and the darkness within seemed very deep compared to the sunlit courtyard, but with my hand on her back, she stepped inside at last.

"Griogair?" Wiping sweat from her forehead, Lann straightened and stared at the girl. "What's this?"

"Her name's Lilith," I said.

Warily Lann laid down the half-made sword and stepped forward. She slipped a finger under the carved circlet round the child's neck. It was slender, delicate and strong, and exceptionally beautiful.

"That's not silver. That's Lammyr steel."

Lann had an annoying habit of telling me what I knew. "Of course it is," I said sharply. "Get it off her."

"Yes, Griogair. And do what with it?"

I shrugged. "Melt it down."

For the first time the child shot me a look of hostility, and her hand went to her throat. "It's mine."

"No. It was theirs, and so were you. Now you aren't."

She frowned, studying my eyes. I wanted to blink and look away.

"All right," she said at last. "If I'm yours instead."

~

"Where the hell did they get her?" I asked Niall Mor as we leaned on the rampart watching the sun set.

"You're not expecting an answer from me," he pointed out dryly.

"Just thinking aloud." I took a long swig of ale. "Either she doesn't remember or she isn't telling."

The last of the light lay green on the sea, so that it glowed like liquid tourmaline. The child Lilith sat on the rocks down by the shore, perfectly alone and perfectly content. She was just as she'd been all day: quiet, self-contained, but not remotely shy. She had made no complaint about the scratches and grazes Lann had left on her neck as she cut the Lammyr collar away; in fact Lann had seemed unnerved by her.

So was I.

"It's not surprising she's strange," said Niall. "She must have been years with the Lammyr. I'd be bloody strange."

"Who says you aren't? And you make Lann nervous."

He grinned. "Not as nervous as she makes me."

I rolled my eyes. "Do something about it, then. Don't be so damn indecisive."

"Yes, boss. And speaking of bound lovers, when does Leonora come back?"

"A week." I felt the usual ripping stab of longing in my gut. Gods, binding hurt sometimes. But I wasn't about to say anything that might dissuade Niall. He'd been pissing about for quite long enough, and he wasn't the only man in the dun who was sniffing around Lann like an

130

enthusiastic hound. Not to mention at least one woman: my best sharpshot archer who'd taken a sudden interest in the creation of swords.

"It's not as if we have to bind," he said unconvincingly.

"Uh-huh. Wait till she's bound to Falaire, and you don't get to sleep with her whenever you like."

Niall fell silent. I hoped he felt bad. And jealous. Binding would make offspring a little more likely, after all, and I couldn't wait to see the warrior he and Lann would come up with.

That only made me think of Leonora again. Abruptly I stood up.

"Either go and flirt with her, or get a detachment together and do something about that broken wall on the south boundary."

"It's dark." My lieutenant yawned and stretched, and grinned as he got to his feet. "Can't see the stones at this hour."

Shaking my head, I watched him jog down the stone steps towards the forge. About to follow him, I turned back to call to Lilith. The sun had lowered beyond the sea horizon and the landscape was darkening fast to charcoal and indigo.

My shout of summons stayed in my throat. She was standing at the edge of the water now, balanced delicately on a slab of basalt, arms outstretched and head thrown back, like a little girl about to spin into a dance. She looked blissful but she looked rapt, too, and in a way that sent tremors down my spine. Falaire was leading two horses up the path through the rocks and back towards the dun, but she took no notice of him, simply swayed back and forth on her tiptoes, singing softly.

I shuddered. As far as I could tell she was singing to the empty air and the ocean. I had no grounds for suspicion, no reason to rebuke her: only the solid certainty that she was calling, over and over again, to someone—something—beneath the water's opalescent skin.

~

She seemed happy to be solitary, haunting the dun like a small quick shadow, and I admit I didn't take enough interest in her: not then. Of course that was a mistake, and of course I regretted it, but I had much on my mind, and more to do. There were patrols to coordinate, quarrels to settle, a whole winter to prepare for; and that winter was already drawing near, hauling itself across the land like a sluggish giant, shadowing the broad blue skies and crushing the sun tight against the horizon.

The clann gave her a place to live with her own people; we provided her with warmer clothes and furs now that the darkness fell earlier; and then we let her slip from our conscious minds. I knew she wasn't exactly gregarious, but I saw the other children try to make friends; I saw her sit peacefully watching their games even when she didn't join in, and—it seemed to be all she required—they were distantly kind to her, and didn't persecute her for her strangeness.

All of them but one, that is.

Ramasg MacRaonull: never my favourite child of the clann, but he had the makings of a sturdy fighter. He had a head of wiry black curls, impenetrable hazel eyes, and quick violent fists. He also had a tendency to sulk at criticism, and an inclination to laziness, but I knew he'd grow out of both. I didn't take him for a bully till the day I found him tormenting Lilith; I'd certainly never thought him capable of actual malevolence.

I wasn't accustomed to taking notice of the clann children; at least, not till they were old enough to begin proper fight training. I found Lilith harder to ignore, largely because I'd often scratch an itch on my neck and turn to find her watching me. I suppose I was just more aware of her than of the others, and that was why I noticed that evening when she wasn't around.

There had been some name-calling, but that was hardly surprising; she'd lived with Lammyr for the gods knew how long and even the children who liked her were properly wary of her. I thought a few insults and insinuations harmless, under the circumstances, and it wasn't as if they seemed to affect her. Lilith was fearless. I'd seen her eyes linger on Ramasg when he threw taunts. She never flinched and she never responded, just looked; I tell you, I would not have wanted that gaze on me.

Niall said the trouble with Ramasg was that his tongue was faster than his brain. I knew otherwise: that his mouth was a true reflection of his mindset. It wasn't pleasant, but as I said, I knew he'd grow out of it.

I wish I'd been right about that.

Niall only went into the stables that evening because he wanted to check on a horse that was lame. Falaire was anxious about the animal, and since she was one of Lann's favourites, Niall wanted to check her before nightfall. No doubted he wanted to the excuse to convey any news to Lann, still occupied in the forge.

It was quiet and musty in the stalls, with the low snuffling snorts of contented horses, the shift of a hoof, the slow tug-and-crunch of teeth on hay. Niall comforted Lann's mare, gave her an extra treat, prepared to leave. He told me he almost missed the girl, cowering there in the furthest stall beneath the hooves of my grey hunting stallion. And when he did see her, he almost failed to recognise her.

She'd managed to free herself from the post she'd been tied to; the rope's frayed remains hung there. But she was still gnawing at the length of it around her wrists, though she stopped when she saw Niall, and stared at him in silence. She didn't say a word, though her glaring eyes were stained and swollen with tears. Her long black hair no longer straggled across her face; it had been hacked back to a rough dirty crop.

She didn't flinch when he crouched and sawed through her wrist-bonds with his hunting knife, but she did at least manage to spit a name.

"Ramasg."

~

Ramasg was unrepentant, even in the face of a hard strike from me.

"She should have had it off long ago," he snarled, putting a hand to his bruised cheek. "She never cut it when her parents died. I asked her."

"That's not your business, you little shit," said Niall Mor. "And she's half your size."

"Makes up for it in other ways," he muttered.

"You'd better explain that," I said, pacing to the window and staring out at the machair. I was simmering with rage, and I didn't trust myself not to hit him again.

"She's a witch, isn't she? You don't need to worry about her."

Niall and I looked at each other, then at him.

Niall had to take two breaths before he could speak. "Gods' sake, boy. This is Griogair you're insulting."

Ramasg swallowed and shot me a nervous look. "Leonora's different."

"Really?" I asked silkily. "How?"

He'd got his nerve back. "Lilith's evil, that's how. You can tell from her eyes. And she stares."

Niall rolled his eyes. "I'm going to slap you myself in a minute."

"She stares at you because she can't believe what an arse you are," I told Ramasg. "And neither can I."

"You'll see," he muttered.

"I'll see the ditch in the lower field cleared," I said. "Niall, take him down there."

Niall took hold of his arm, but he pulled back to give me a sullen glare. "She's trying to summon a kelpie."

That took me aback. "What?"

"A kelpie. There's been one off the shoreline for days. She's trying to bond with it."

There was a triumph in the twitch of his mouth as Niall yanked him out of the room. He was a vindictive little bastard, but he'd unsettled me and he knew it. I could see no reason for him to lie, because it was such an outlandish accusation, and besides, I remembered shivering as I watched her singing to the ocean.

I rubbed my hands across my face, wishing for a straightforward problem: a caveful of Lammyr, or a full-scale war. Sighing, I slung my sword down on the table and went out of the dun to look for her.

She was in her usual place on the rocks, sitting with her arms wrapped round her knees and humming to herself. Maybe, I thought, she was humming to something else. Her newly-chopped hair blustered in the cold breeze; she'd done nothing to improve the rough mess Ramasg had made of it, but I couldn't help thinking it suited her in a strange way.

I sat down at her side, nearly unbalancing when she promptly huddled against me. She hadn't struck me as a girl who was much affected by the cold.

"He won't do it again," I told her. "He's out clearing the ditches."

She nodded contentedly.

"He came up with some excuses." I took a breath to broach the subject.

"Oh. Did he mention the horse?"

The breath stayed stuck in my throat. At last I managed to say, "It's a waterhorse?"

She threw a pebble idly into the waves. "It'll come to me in the end."

"Lilith," I said. "Lilith, that's not wise."

She shrugged. "It doesn't have to be wise. They're lovely."

"They're deadly. And unpredictable." I was finding it stupidly difficult to argue with her. "You could lose your life."

She gave a dismissive snort. "Or I could gain the best warhorse in your stables."

"It's not worth the risk. For you or anyone else in the dun."

"Yes. It is."

I shook my head in irritation. "If you want a familiar, find a cat or a raven or a wolf-pup. Put waterhorses out of your head. They can't be trusted."

"You'll see," she said simply. "It wouldn't be my familiar anyway. It would be my warhorse."

"Lilith!" I barked. "This should not be done! It hasn't been done in centuries, and it ended badly the last time."

She tilted her head to give me an endearing smile. "All the more reason to do it. For me it'll end just fine."

I would have talked sense into her, I'm sure of that. And I should have waited to do it, and spent the time well, but I was unnerved by her candid innocent grin and her closeness. It was clear she held a particular and pointless affection for me, and I wanted to do nothing to encourage it. And besides, at that precise moment, I heard the call in my mind that I couldn't resist, and would never want to.

I sprang to my feet, and this time it was Lilith who nearly slipped sideways. I steadied her with a hand on her fragile shoulder and said, "Sorry—"

"What is it?" Her eyes were quizzical and hurt.

I gave her a grin of pure happiness. And that was probably a mistake as well.

"It's Leonora," I told her. "It's my lover. She's coming back to the dun."

~

If I thought Leonora would have any special sympathy for the lost witch-child, I'd misjudged both her mood and her inclinations. Still, like the diplomat she could always be, she didn't raise the subject till later that night, till we were both in bed and the coverlet thrown aside in our untidy haste.

She'd caught her first sight of Lilith when the child trailed after me into the courtyard on the afternoon of her return. Leonora had taken no notice of her; but then Leonora had ignored everyone but me. She'd slipped lightly from her horse and walked straight into my arms, laughing with a combination of happiness and anticipation.

She'd studied Lilith in the Great Hall that evening, though. The child had settled herself in a dark corner, eating and drinking quietly, watching rather than participating. There was nothing new in that behaviour. At least she'd wasted no time in following my advice about a familiar: a young crow hopped at her feet, cocking its head for the shreds of meat she offered. Laughing, she stroked its black neck with a fingertip, and it dipped its head as if in a mock-bow.

Crows were smart and crows were watchful. Crows, principally, were not a danger to anyone they met, unless you counted the dead. I was relieved; the bird would take her mind off waterhorses. I told myself that had been a temporary infatuation, much like her fondness for me. And that would pass, too.

Leonora was not convinced.

She lay across my body, head close against mine, languid with the aftermath of love as I drew an idle line down her spine with one finger. Appearance, as always with Leonora, was deceptive: her mind was in constant fascinated motion, picking at puzzles, decoding other minds, weaving intricate political schemes. I lifted her hair and kissed the prominent tendon on her neck, and she murmured happily.

"The queen was well?" It was a formal question in a strikingly informal situation; I knew Kate was always well.

Leonora gave a low laugh. "She'd like to be better. Still playing with that risible idea of hers."

"Getting rid of her name?" I shivered. Raidseach. Kate's true name unnerved me, the very sound of it, but it was better than the alternative.

"Indeed. She won't do it. She knows the consequence. The idea's a plaything, that's all. Her trouble is, she's bored." Leonora propped herself up on one elbow and kissed my forehead. "She was pleased about Crickspleen."

"Mm." That seemed long ago now.

Leonora traced her finger down my ribs, and I felt her take a light breath. "You should send Lilith to her."

Shadows played on the ceiling as the flames in the fireplace flickered and jumped. I watched them, thinking.

"Why?" I asked at last.

Leonora kissed me. "Because she's tremendously strong and tremendously vulnerable. Kate would know how to manage her. She'd be safe there, and so would everyone else."

"You don't like her."

She smiled. "What makes you think that? I barely know the child."

I grinned up at her. "You've been home nearly a full day, Rochoill. You know her well enough."

Leonora made a motion that might have been a shrug. "She's hard to See. But yes, I've Seen her well enough to know she ought to be with Kate."

Absently I stroked her hair. "She does flirt with kelpies," I said.

Leonora gave a dry laugh. "That's not all she flirts with."

"Leonora, she's eleven years old."

"And daily growing, as they say."

"Is that why you want her to leave?"

"Now, now." She nipped my ear quite hard. "I'm only thinking of what's best for her."

"All the same." I rolled over and put my finger between her teeth to stop her biting me again, and she looked amused. "I'll give her a chance. She's happy here."

"As you wish. And on your own head be it."

~

And so Lilith became an unspoken gamble between me and Leonora, albeit a good-tempered one. Surprisingly, Leonora didn't seem to mind the kelpie business, and I grew a little suspicious that she was encouraging Lilith's interest—or perhaps not discouraging it—so that I'd be proved wrong in the end.

"I've seen the creature," she told me as we rode along the beach one evening. "It's no more than a colt."

"Aye, and daily growing." I threw her own words back at her, and she laughed.

"Oh, don't worry, Griogair. It wouldn't be the first time a witch has tamed a kelpie."

"You've never been tempted."

She shrugged. "I've no interest in them, but then I don't need a warhorse. I'm surprised you've never fancied taming one. Just because it hasn't been done in centuries…"

"They're trouble," I said flatly.

"So are you, my dear." She reached out a hand to take mine, kissed it, then let her horse spring forward into a gallop, sending spray flying from the small shoreline waves. For a moment I reined in my own horse, dazzled to watch them, the low winter sun glittering in the spindrift, Leonora's tawny hair and the mare's white mane bannering in the wind of their own speed.

She glanced back over her shoulder. *~Do keep up, Fitheach, my love.*

I laughed, and took the challenge.

~

The crow Lilith had tamed was a clever thing, nimble and cunning, and she'd grown impossibly fond of it. It was a true familiar: she never went anywhere without it, whether perched on her shoulder or hopping at her feet or ducking and diving in the air above her. The pouch she wore at her waist was now exclusively devoted to its favourite treats, so that the girl always smelt faintly of dead pigeon.

All the same, she hadn't forgotten her first ambition, as I discovered when Niall and I were out on the machair one frosty morning, debating whether to bring the cattle back inside the dun. Despite the crystal blue of the sky, a new onslaught of winter lay heavy on the horizon, and hardy though the beasts were, the wolf packs had grown more desperate as the months wore on. I hated to imagine having to kill one, and I'd deserve the bad luck such a deed would bring me.

We'd walked up to the top of the dunes to study the dark menacing cloud that lay on the far line between ocean and sky, but the oncoming weather was suddenly secondary.

"Gods above and gods below," said Niall, and drew the sword off his back.

I'd got my breath back, so I murmured, "Put it away. You'll look a bit damn silly if you're more scared of it than she is."

Lilith sat on one of her favourite rocks, wrapped in a goatskin cloak, looking utterly contented as she fed scraps of pigeon to the crow and the kelpie. The crow took them greedily straight from her hand; the kelpie seemed more skittish, but it strained its head curiously towards her, flaring its nostrils and pawing the sand, snatching a shred of bloody pigeon-meat from her just as the crow reached for it. The bird's indignant caw and Lilith's laughter drifted to us on the breeze.

Cautiously I walked along to the rocks and clambered down, Niall at my heels, his sword sheathed, his fingers still twitching for it. Leonora had been right: it was barely more than a first-year colt, nothing like fully grown. That didn't mean it didn't have a deadly look. As it caught sight of us it jerked up its head, and bared its teeth, a tendril of pigeon-flesh caught on one lower fang. Its black eye fixed on us and it flattened its ears, screaming a baby-stallion warning.

Lilith turned her head and smiled at us, giving a little wave. "Isn't he beautiful?"

"Very," I murmured, because he was. Niall said nothing at all, just stared at the creature.

"Oh, don't be scared of him," she said. "He's only a foal really. He won't come out of the sea yet. I'm just getting to know him. I haven't even made a bridle."

"You can't bring that into the dun," Niall managed to say.

"Of course not. Not yet." She jerked her head at the opposite end of the beach and said contemptuously, "That's what Ramasg's scared of, too."

I followed her gesture. Sure enough, a shadow darted behind the rocks, too late: a shadow with straggly black hair. I frowned.

"Has he been bothering you again?"

"A bit. But I can handle him." She flicked her fingers dismissively, and the kelpie colt snuffled eagerly at them. The crow must have been jealous, because it hopped onto Lilith's arm and glared at the creature.

I could barely take my eyes off it myself. It was a lovely thing, its coat pale grey enough to be nearly white, its still-damp mane and tail tangled with weed. As I watched, its demonic eyes seemed to soften, a green light kindling in their depths, and it nickered to me, tossing its head. I smiled.

"Griogair!"

Niall had lunged for my arm, but Lilith had already taken my hand and gently removed it from the kelpie's neck, where I did not remember putting it. My fingers slipped free of the writhing fronds of its mane, and it whickered with disappointment as I blinked myself back to full consciousness.

"You sneaky little bastard!" I exploded.

Lilith laughed. "It's only doing what comes naturally. You could soon tame it."

Strange, but she was right. I couldn't resent the thing, any more than I could resent a wolf for wanting to eat. And for its sheer beauty and grace, you could forgive it anything. I knew that was its trick, but I suddenly didn't care.

"You could ride one," added Lilith, gazing at me with worshipful eyes. "I could bring you one, and you could bond with it."

"Maybe later," I said gruffly. "Give me a century or two to get used to the idea."

"You'd be mad," growled Niall, earning a frown of dislike from Lilith.

"Anyway, Niall's right for now," I added. "Don't bring it near the dun."

'Of course not. None of them could deal with it.' There was a proud gleam in her eyes. "I've got Dornadair to keep me company, anyway." She puckered her lips, which the crow nudged with its beak as if kissing her.

I laughed and shook my head.

"Don't be late back," I said. "There's snow on the way."

~

I was more aware of Ramasg after seeing him spying on Lilith down on the shore. There was still something I disliked about the boy, something I distrusted, and if anything he seemed to have grown worse: more underhand, more vicious. I saw him spit in her food when her back was turned; I saw him spill pitch deliberately on her cloak, or drop something suddenly to trip her.

She was right, though; she could handle him now. If she ever retaliated I didn't know about it, but I don't think she did. Or rather, she retaliated in the most wounding way possible, which was to pretend Ramasg did not exist. He was so clearly jealous of her, as well as afraid and contemptuous, that her complete failure to see him must have been like a fishhook in his gullet. Nor did it help his prestige even among his own friends, which duly plummeted, especially since Lilith was always careful to acknowledge them, to smile shyly and nod at them as they passed her in the courtyard. She'd be a clever politician when she was older.

And as she said, she had the crow Dornadair. It might go off hunting alone now and then, but mostly they were together, out on the moor or down on the rocks. When she called it, with a strange guttural cry, it would come to her; she would spend hours with her undersized bow and arrow, hunting pigeons and grouse for it simply because it disliked the taste of seabird. It had even reached an amicable coexistence with the kelpie-colt, which surfaced and trotted out of the waves for Lilith almost on command now.

"You've got to admit," I told Leonora smugly, "she's happy here."

"I do admit it, freely." And Leonora gave me that smile that told me: Just wait.

Lilith was contented, then, and she had never been the kind of child to shriek or throw tantrums or even to laugh too loud. Her easy, low-pitched happiness lasted the whole of that late spring as the air grew mild and the flowers crept in a wild rash of colour across the machair, and the grass began to smell once more of warmth and summer instead of frost and death.

That was why, when she came running to me in the Great Hall, I waved Niall aside and opened my arms to her, shocked by her demented grief. That was why I knew immediately that her despair was real, and heartshredding, and terribly, violently dangerous.

~

Dornadair, she gasped through her tears, was gone. He had not responded to her call; she could not locate his disordered, playful mind with her own. He had been gone for three hours; twice as long as they had ever been apart before.

Dornadair, she said, was dead.

The clann members near to us shook their heads and sympathised in their matter-of-fact way, and Leonora became surprisingly sad and quiet, kissing the girl's face and begging her not to worry till the worst was known. Even Niall tried to console Lilith, stroking her hair and shushing her, but she would not be shushed, and I knew she would not be consoled till the bird was found.

There were three hours of daylight left to us, and we had no choice. Niall sighed and made for the stables to ready our horses while I squeezed the girl's shoulders and promised to find Dornadair. I doubted very much that we'd find him alive; I trusted Lilith to know that. But still we had to ride out, and it didn't matter how much I cajoled and warned; she had to come with us.

Lilith rode at my back, clasping my waist like a drowning child, her breath coming in short gasps. There was no point in speed; we simply had to cover the moor at a walk, searching the uneven ground and the heather knolls till our eyes ached. None of us, tellingly, looked to the sky.

As the shadows lengthened I began to despair of finding the bird, and the thought of dragging Lilith back to the dun without it was more than I could face. Niall, thirty yards away, gestured to a high outcrop of stone that breached the moor like the fin of a basking shark, and headed his horse towards its sloping flank; Lilith and I took the further and more gentle rise.

The sun, too brilliant to look at, was sunk halfway beneath the horizon when Lilith gave a cry that made my blood cold.

I hoped it was Dornadair; I hoped it wasn't. But as my horse picked its way across the smooth rocks towards the untidy mess of limp black feathers, it was obvious what lay there. Lilith slipped from my horse's back before I had even reined it in, and was running across the plateau towards the crow's corpse.

Niall rode across at my shout, and dismounted to hold my horse's reins; I made myself go to Lilith's side and crouch down. I didn't dare touch the sleek black feathers, twitching and blustering in the wind, but she reached out and gathered up the crow's pathetic remains, hugging him against her as if she could warm life back into his bones. But even her hot tears dripping into his feathers couldn't do that.

I squeezed her shoulder, and got to my feet, finding it difficult to take a breath through the pity in my throat. I was about to speak to her again when I noticed the other, smaller dead thing, a slab of rock and a small crevice away.

I went over to it, and lifted it by one wing. The carcass was ripped open at the breastbone, but otherwise barely touched.

Besides, even when it's stripped to the bone, I know what a pigeon looks like.

Leonora sniffed, wrinkling her nose in distaste. "Poison, certainly. Quite a lot of it." She laid the pigeon down on the bench. "At least it must have been relatively quick."

If that was meant to calm me, it had the opposite effect. "I'll kill the little bastard," I snarled.

"You think it was Ramasg? You ought to be sure, Griogair."

"I'm more than sure. Fionnaghal says a pigeon was stolen from the kitchens, and the other children say it was Ramasg who took it. I didn't even have to threaten them. Lilith isn't the only one who's upset."

Niall poked gloomily at the pigeon's gizzard. "I never thought he'd go so far."

"If I'd ever thought it myself, I'd have strung him up by the balls. Too late now. We should have known."

"Offer Lilith a whipping. When you catch up with him."

"I doubt she'll settle for that. Did you see the state of her?"

"And it's if you catch up with him," added Leonora. "Has anyone seen the boy?"

Niall shook his head. "Lying low. The first smart thing he's done in a year, not that it'll help him. He has to come back to the dun sooner or later."

Leonora slipped an arm round my waist and hugged me. "It wasn't your fault, Fitheach. And grief-stricken as she is, she'll find another familiar."

"True," said Niall. "It's terrible, but it isn't like losing a bound lover."

He spoke very lightly—more lightly than he would have done if he'd actually bound himself to Lann by that point—but I think he was wrong, anyway. Perhaps Lilith wasn't joined to Dornadair at the soul, but she was not quite twelve years old and she loved him more than I think she'd loved anything in her brief life. That wasn't a bond you could dismiss; and love came hard to Lilith under any circumstance.

All the same, after a few days she had recovered her composure enough to return to the life of the dun—quietly, and making eye contact with no one, but she was there among the clann, and her eyes were dry. Her quick recovery surprised and pleased me, though her underlying grief remained tangibly raw. I had the feeling some of the clann children wanted to sympathise with her, to apologise for Ramasg, but one flinty stare and they'd back swiftly off. So much for my hopes, so high in the early spring, for her full integration into clann life.

Ramasg was still skulking. At least, I thought, the last of the harsh winter had been driven off by what promised to be a fine summer. He wouldn't freeze out there—though in my harsher moments I thought he fully deserved to—and he was as familiar with caves and shelter stones as any clann child would be after fourteen years running wild on the moor. Besides, Lilith was already back to her habit of roaming—more mournfully now that she had no companion—and I had no doubt that if she saw so much as Ramasg's broken fingernail in a rockface, she'd tell me.

~

He'd been gone a week when my uneasiness grew too great to ignore. He might not freeze, and he might not starve, and wolves wouldn't touch him, but he was just stupid enough to get stuck in a cave or run into a wandering rogue Lammyr. My rage still burned hot in my chest, but I was afraid that with time it might subside to an ember and that I wouldn't have the heart for any punishment he'd deserve.

And the blunt fact is, I was worried.

I chose a warm bright morning to go out looking for him, the kind of morning no one could resist. On a day like this, anyone in his right mind would long for home and for happiness; anyone would swallow his fear and his pride and bow to the inevitable, get the worst of his homecoming over with. Or at least, he would be tempted to. If I could meet him halfway, drawn from whatever cave he was hiding in by the smell of new wildflowers and the glittering sea, I could bring him home to face us all. The world never looks so bad on such a day.

I left my sword behind as well as my coat; a rare thing for me to do, but that was the atmosphere in the sky and the breeze. The closest caverns of any depth were about two miles to the north of the dun; however the seas raged, however hard the storms whipped the waves against the cliff, in the blackest depths of those rock-holes there was always dry sand and safety. It seemed the obvious place to begin my hunt; and only after I'd checked them thoroughly would I search the bleakest furthest edges of the moor. I didn't see the point of prolonging this, and I was confident I'd find the boy.

Instead, I found Lilith.

I called her name, and rode down the narrow gully in the rocks onto the hard sand. She waved, but didn't get to her feet to greet me. The reason was quickly obvious: the kelpie-colt lay on the sand beside her, its forelegs tucked beneath it, its newly-bridled head resting peacefully in her lap. When I dismounted and walked the last few yards—my horse refused to go a single step closer to its oh-so-distant cousin—Lilith glanced up, her grin impish, her face flushed with delight.

"Look!" she whispered. "I've tamed him!"

"Yes," I marveled. "You have."

For all I knew of kelpies and for all I knew of witches, there was something innocent and delightful about the scene. She was a ragged little wild thing, dark and intense; it was a crafty brute with a relentless thirst for flesh; but all I could think of as I watched them was old paintings of maidens and unicorns.

She stroked its head in wonder, tugging at its ears, combing its silky forelock with her fingers. And suddenly I was more than accepting; I was glad that after the terrible end of Dornadair, and her inconsolable desolation in the days afterwards, she'd found another companion.

"He's very beautiful," I smiled. "Make sure he's fully tame before you bring him near the dun."

"Of course I will. Thank you, Griogair!" She bent her head to the kelpie again, crooning, and reached for her pouch, drawing out a small chunk of meat. The creature shifted its head to take it delicately from her hand, gulping it down before taking her second offering. She stroked it as she fed it, caressing its cheekbone, its neck, its gills.

I don't know why the first shiver of cold certainty rippled across my skin; perhaps it was her contentment, the utter obliteration of her grief; perhaps it was the realisation that she and her little bow had graduated to bigger game. The chunks of flesh she fed it were torn from something far larger than a pigeon, and as the kelpie nickered, peeling back its upper lip to sniff for more treats, I saw tiny threads of woven fabric caught on its canine teeth.

I snatched for the next morsel as Lilith took it from her pouch, but she held it away from me, shaking her head solemnly, and gave it to the creature. I was certain there were strands of wiry black hair stuck to the meat.

"It's better if I feed him," she said. "For now."

"Lilith." The blood in my veins was snow-water. "Have you seen anything of Ramasg? I thought he might be in the caves."

She looked over her shoulder, very calmly, at the slit of darkness that was the first cave mouth. I almost thought I could hear the cliff breathing; I shook off the fancy.

"No," she said. "I think he was here. But he isn't now."

Everything she said was not quite a lie, and not quite the truth. That was what I'd thought the day I first met her; that was what I thought again the day I said goodbye to her, lifting her onto the bay pony's back.

At least, I tried to lift her; but she clung to me, her eyes wide and tearless but her grip tight enough to crush my spine. I turned helplessly to Leonora, who reached out a hand to the child.

"Come along, now. You'll like Kate, I promise."

Lilith wouldn't look at her.

With a sigh, Kate herself dismounted, signaling her two escorts to stay on their horses. She came over to Lilith, who remained pressed to me, and she crouched close beside her, making the girl meet her eyes.

"You'll be happy with me," she promised. "I'll make sure of it."

Her pale hand stroked the child's cheek gently, rhythmically, till at last Lilith's eyes seemed to focus, staring hard into the queen's. Many a grown Sithe had flinched under that gaze, but Kate didn't.

And when she wanted or needed to be, Kate was simply enchanting. I'd seen my monarch many times; I had spoken to her, laughed with her, argued with her, carried out her wishes; and still, every time I saw her my gaze could only linger. Her tall paleness; her intense amber eyes; the summer sunlight striking flakes of gold from her chestnut hair. I did not love her, except as my queen, but more than enough people did; and the adoration she inspired had kept her on the throne for centuries. There was no one her equal, no one to compete with her; or no one, I thought with a glance at Leonora, who had the desire to do so.

"Give her to me, Griogair." Kate smiled at Lilith, running a hand through her hair.

145

"Not me that's holding onto her," I muttered dryly. But even as I said it, I felt the child's grip loosen very slightly.

"You know well I'll take care of you," said Kate. "Don't you, Lilith?"

The girl hesitated, then nodded.

"And you know you can't stay here. You know that, after what you did."

She nodded again, silent, though her expression was without shame or remorse.

"Griogair doesn't want you to go." Kate slipped her fingers into Lilith's behind my back. "But he has no choice. He can't keep you here. I'm sure you can come back when you're grown. In fact, I promise you can. I'll bring you back to Griogair in a few years. Yes?"

Lilith looked up at me, studying my face for the longest time. And then, at last, her arms slipped reluctantly from around me, and Kate brought her hand forward, their fingers entwined.

"I'll miss you," I said truthfully, as Kate stood up and put an arm round Lilith's shoulders.

The girl only nodded. Niall Mor brought the pony around once more, and this time I lifted Lilith onto it with no effort. Kate sprang lightly onto her own dappled mare.

"It's for the best, Fitheach," murmured Leonora, clasping my hand in hers. "It's all we can do. The clann won't tolerate the child now."

Lilith had turned back to watch us as the escorts led the way out of the gate, and her unnerving gaze met Leonora's. I can't say for certain that anything passed between them, but I'd swear they Saw each other properly for the first time, and that words were exchanged.

Something twitched at the corner of Leonora's mouth as we watched them ride away, something that might have been a smile.

"And the kelpie?" she asked, as the gates swung shut behind Lilith and the queen.

"Gone," put in Niall. "Nobody's seen it since... Well. Since that."

"It'll come back to her." Leonora sounded not entirely unsatisfied.

"So long as it doesn't come back here," muttered Niall as he walked away.

"He's right." I put an arm round Leonora. "So I don't like the look in your eye."

She shook her head thoughtfully. "The child went about things in a bad way, but she wasn't wrong. She's a witch but she's also a Sithe. We were closer to the waterhorses, once."

I rubbed my temple. "I knew I didn't like the look in your eye."

"Then don't ask me questions." She smiled and kissed me. "And you needn't be so regretful, Griogair. It's true; she'll return when she's older. And I'll bring you news of her when I go to Kate's dun in the autumn."

"The autumn?" I frowned. "If you're leaving me again so soon, you owe me some time." I tightened my arm around her waist, suddenly longing for her. Leonora, Rochoill, destroyer of all my sadness.

"I know I do." Her smile was a touch smug, making me laugh. "I'll see you at sunset."

"So long?" I was hungrily disappointed, but I knew there was no point arguing. It would be all the sweeter for a delay, anyway. "Where are you going now?" ~*Rochoill?*

But she had already shuttered her mind as she flicked me a last amused glance.

"To the shoreline, Griogair, my love," and her voice was already a bewitching lilt. "Down to the sea to sing."

SOUTH

~

by Gillian Philip

Ice lies in a thin slick across the bay, but he's in the water anyway. The boy always is. Just like his grandmother.

It might as well be the other side of the earth: her side of it. A late and overcast day in monochrome, so there's only white, and spikes of grass and tree, and the hills drawn in charcoal streaks with scribbles of gully in between. Not so much snow, now.

The world's only colour lies in the beam of the Land Rover headlights—sick yellow of winter grass, a few dull pink yards of road. I switch off the engine and the lights too. Creak the door open into silence, and walk down to the shore, tightening my scarf round my neck. Cold burns my throat when I call to him.

"Culley. Time to come home now."

I wait, used to it now, the tight slow thump of my heart as I wait for him to not-come-back. One day he'll be gone. One day, like his mother.

Not today.

He hauls himself from the water, nostrils flaring open, cropped hair stiff with salt against his long skull, bits of ice still glittering in it. He towels his scalp with one hand, pulls on jeans with the other, tugging denim over damp skin.

He smiles at me. "Grandpappy."

"Culley. Your father is worried. It's late."

He looks at the sky, surprised. "I was just coming."

Like a boy hauled from the slides in the play park, he's sheepish, apologetic, a little resentful.

The relief chokes my throat, so to pass the embarrassing moment I bend to retrieve his jumper from the black rocks, and hand it to him. Unhurried, he pulls it over his head; big as it is, it stretches across his overdeveloped shoulders. He smiles at me again, his dark hair stiff with salt and frost but already drying.

"I'll take you back," I say.

"Thanks. I'm sorry. It's hard to know the time." He scratches his scalp nervously, and the frost-light makes the slight membrane between his fingers look thinner than ever.

He's a gentle boy. He doesn't like to cause hurt, regrets it when he so often does. I don't worry for him. Not much.

I keep the rifle in the Land Rover, but I know I won't need it.

~

His grandmother looked much the same, first time I saw her. Half-naked, that is, not gentle. In that climate I thought she was mad, with nothing but a silky-fur blanket clasped round her like a cloak.

I'd gone to watch the penguins because I had some time off, and watching the penguins was a hobby for me, not work like it was for Mal. He watched penguins and fur seals and sometimes leopard seals, when there were any, when there was ice in the bay. They didn't come in the warmer weather. He watched them and counted them and made records, and because those were the days before the internet, he sent data back home on the Inmarsat. I helped him, when I wasn't fixing things. He loved his job, and I loved mine. You had to, or you wouldn't be out on this lonely outcrop of a godforsaken island.

The unexpected woman sat on a rock, watching the penguins too, and they seemed more nervous of her than of me, but I wasn't watching emperors any more. I laid my binoculars down because I didn't need them; she was that close.

When they say blood runs cold it's a cliché, but there's no other way to describe it. She wasn't supposed to be there. I'd thought Mal and I were alone at this end of the island, and I thought for a ridiculous moment she'd missed her cruise ship and been left behind. Except that people off the cruise ships didn't dress like that – half-naked under a silky-fur wrap.

She turned her head and looked at me.

"Are you all right?" I asked.

My gut had tightened with the fear of madness. It was well below zero but her pale skin didn't prickle with gooseflesh and she didn't shiver, not once. Her hair was sleek and black and wet, and for a crazy moment I thought she must have been in the water. But that wasn't possible. Not in her skin.

"I'm fine," she smiled, "I'm grand. Hello yourself."

To step away from a near-naked woman, and one so beautiful: that would have been the mad thing. And when Malcolm found out, as he certainly would the next time we got garrulous with homesickness and rum, he'd never let me forget it.

So I took a step closer instead, and saw that her hair wasn't black at all but an odd iron-grey, with a hint of what might have been dappling. And though she was so tall and straight and slender, and her face was a long reptilian oval – which isn't to say it wasn't beautiful – her shoulders looked disproportionately powerful. She smelt of the sea: of grease-ice and salt and tussac grass, and quite possibly penguin-shit. I fell in love.

I said, "You'll have to come back to the base. You'll have to come back with me."

~

I'm a practical man. I'm not a scientist like Mal; I'm an engineer. I fix things. I fix plumbing and generators and wireless masts and chemical toilets, when they need fixing. So I'm practical, and I'm rational, but where I come from they do have the seal stories. I thought the superstitions and the myths and the legends all came from the same place I did. It never occurred to me there could be others. I didn't know there'd be an equivalence, a balance in the round globe, a mirror image of the north, if you like, which was the south.

I thought they made the seal stories because common seals look so human: gentle and intelligent and empathetic. But those seals of the south don't look human. Or if they do, it's another kind of human altogether.

I should have thought. But I didn't think. I didn't think at all in the months, turning into years, when Elin was mine.

~

Mal counted the leopard seals and studied them, and he loved them and respected them, but he feared them properly too. He stayed out of the water when the ice was in the bay, and he stayed away from the land's edge when the penguins flocked like a black-and-white buffet. He didn't want to be mistaken for one, he said, laughing.

Elin liked Mal. She laughed when he laughed, but I was never jealous. It never occurred to me that she'd be unfaithful; she was too possessive, too passionate for that. She didn't want to go back, she said, to the small fishing settlement on the other side of the island. She liked scientists, that's why she'd come. She liked engineers too, and me best of all.

She got pregnant, of course. I hadn't exactly thought to stock up on supplies that might prevent that. I wanted her to leave the island then, to come with me on the red-hulled supply ship when it next called. She refused.

Unnervingly, she refused any help at all. The pregnancy couldn't have been as long as it seemed; I must have lost count of the months. She was restless and discontented, and liked to be alone, and one day she didn't come back for all my searching and screaming, or Mal's. She simply reappeared the next day with her infant.

She smiled, her dappled hair plastered to her head, but the dampness wasn't sweat, because when I kissed it and kissed it, holding onto her fiercely, it smelt of seawater, and ice, and penguin-shit, and blood.

I loved our baby so ferociously, fear settled into me and wouldn't leave. Children change things. Not outwardly, though; not for a while. I was too embarrassed to confide my suspicions to Mal, and I didn't want to argue with Elin, so as usual we'd sit in the evenings, all three of us—four, with our quiet, ravenous daughter—and we drank rum and talked and laughed and spoke about the fur seals and the supply ship and the weather coming in across the razor-edged hills.

Elin got along great with Mal, but nobody stays on the base forever; nobody, it seemed, except her. And now me, and our child. Mal's replacement, when he chose to leave, was a spiky little man called Thewlis. I didn't especially want a replacement for Mal, but then the base didn't belong to me or the others who came through. The base wasn't Elin's. A replacement for Mal had to come to count the penguins and the fur seals, to record them and measure them and send the data back.

Thewlis respected the leopard seals as much as Mal did. He'd get out of the water if there was one there with him. They weren't aggressive, only curious, but you never knew. You never knew, and you could only remember Shackleton's wild stories, and take account of anecdote and an earlier, less scientific age.

Thewlis understood a lot less about children than about sub-Antarctic fauna, but that was hardly his fault. He simply couldn't understand us keeping Sylvie in the wilderness. We beggared his belief, he said, when he got to know us better. It was mad, bringing up a child here. And soon she'd be of an age for school, and the nearest school was two islands away, and then what were we planning to do?

I hadn't planned anything, but I didn't like to admit that because I'd sound downright gormless.

Thewlis didn't like or understand Sylvie, but that didn't stop him worrying about her. She needed proper pediatric care and a decent education. He wanted us to take her away.

That's not quite true. I was useful; I knew the base and its innards. He wanted Elin to take Sylvie away.

It's not right, he'd say, stroking his little beard, all concerned. It's no environment for a youngster.

Elin said that Sylvie ruined the environment for him; that was his trouble.

"I think it's only right," he told me quietly, one evening after he finally browbeat me into agreement, the evening before the red-hulled ship was due to dock again and take us north to civilisation and nursery school and pediatricians. "The older she gets, the more she'll need to be away from here."

I knew he wanted the bleak beauty of the place to be child-free, but I also knew he was right. So I drank too much, and Elin stormed out in a temper, pulling her fur wrap around her winter clothes and slamming the door. She must have expected to be very cold. Indeed, she was gone all night and between alcohol and anxiety I didn't sleep at all. I turned over and stared into the dark and worried till the palest streak of dawn let me get up.

Stiff and bleary, I opened the blind. There was ice in the bay.

I saw Thewlis close to the base; he'd only just set out on his rounds of the ragged shoreline. He glanced up at me, waved. I waved back, and thought about the glitch with the generator and how I could fix that one last thing before I left.

I sighed and blinked hard at my headache, and that's why I didn't quite see the lunging shadow. If I saw it at all it was a blur on the edge of my vision, like a fleeting, flaring cataract.

I heard his hoarse howl, and then I was running, grabbing my boots on, not bothering with my anorak. I hoped Thewlis could keep his hold on the frayed edge of the ice, because he wouldn't live if he went in the water, not when something had pulled him there like a striking snake.

I thought I ran fast, but by the time I reached the brink of the land, scattering offended penguins, there was nothing on the ice but a smear of blood.

We found Thewlis later that day: me, two fishers, and my own replacement plus the supply ship's crew after it docked. We hunted for hours, and I thought we might not see him again at all. One of the fishers from the little town brought a pistol; it was too late for that, but I didn't say so.

When we found his sodden corpse, Thewlis was barely touched; I thought he might even be alive, till we rolled him over and saw his skull, crushed by a single bite.

When we told Sylvie she ran sobbing in shock to her mother, who stood soberly at the base door and wrapped the girl in her arms and kissed her dappled hair.

~

Later, the two of us argued so badly that the others left us alone to it, going outside to try to smoke in air that was minus ten and falling.

"It was a leopard seal," I yelled at Elin. "I'm not changing our plans. We'll still take Sylvie when the ship leaves. It's dangerous here."

"It isn't dangerous for her," she spat. "Thewlis antagonised it. He must have."

"You're being selfish," I shouted. "Because you don't want to leave."

"And neither does she. And she never will."

And of course she flew out again, slamming the door so hard it bounced. I rolled my eyes. Her rage was too much of a habit for me to care. Instead of caring I drank more, and laughed with the crew and the new engineer and the men from the settlement, and drank even more. Sylvie played quietly in the corner of the room with her plastic Sea Life animals, and looked morosely, but only occasionally, towards the door.

I drank beyond the point of not caring, to a state of suddenly caring very desperately. I was drunk and maudlin and angry, so when I stood up fast, I knocked over the chair.

I blinked, and stared at the abandoned Sea Life set. "Where's Sylvie?"

~

Sylvie wasn't far away. I saw her in the light of stars and ice: ice in the bay, ice on the edge of land and life. The child was laughing, dangling her bare feet into freezing water, leaning down to the sleek raptor head raised above the greasy slick of ice.

"No," I screamed. "No."

It bared dinosaur teeth as ancient as death. Sylvie hesitated, looked back at me, then at the seal. I was drowning its growls with my furious frightened yells, and I was outpacing the men behind me. I'd scared her. Sylvie began to cry.

"Daddy," she wailed.

As I hurtled towards her I saw that blurred shadow lunge again, and the seal had her leg.

And I had her arm, but only just. I looked at the seal and I knew it would tear her in half sooner than let her go. It glared hatred, my daughter's blood on its teeth, and suddenly I wasn't drunk any more. I wasn't drunk when I yelled "Shoot it! Shoot it!" and the man running up behind me fired a shot into the sleek reptilian head.

But my vision was blurred all the same, and my eyes stung with awful grief, and the head was sliding under the surface, wolf-eyes turning dull, full of hatred, then full of nothing but death, and then lost in the deep cold water, trailing a single tendril of blood.

~

I took Sylvie home. I didn't love the island any more. My daughter had health checks and hospital treatment and an education, but she walked with a limp ever after, a limp and a faraway sadness. She limped down the aisle on her wedding day, and she limped to the boy Culley's baptism, and I daresay she limped the day she went to the sea at last and didn't come back.

On that day and many days after, Culley's father howled with grief, so I got him drunk and patted his shoulder, but I knew I shouldn't cry myself because, after all, I'd cheated the sea of her for long enough.

And I did have Sylvie's son, because Sylvie was better than her mother. She was just selfish enough to go to the sea, but not quite selfish enough to take the boy with her.

Still I worry. I go down to the bay that's a mirror reflection of one in the far south, and I shiver in the darkness and count seconds, and wait for Culley to not-come-back.

And sometimes him not-coming-back isn't the worst thing I imagine, when he smiles at me and his canines gleam in moonlight, and his hug is so strong and fierce it could drag me under.

I keep the rifle in the Land Rover.

It's not as if I'll need it.

A KNOT OF TOADS

~

by Jane Yolen

"March 1931: Late on Saturday night," the old man had written, *"a toad came into my study and looked at me with goggled eyes, reflecting my candlelight back at me. It seemed utterly unafraid. Although nothing so far seems linked with this appearance, I have had enough formidable visitants to know this for a harbinger."*

A harbinger of spring, I would have told him, but I arrived too late to tell him anything. I'd been summoned from my Cambridge rooms to his little white-washed stone house with its red pantile roof overlooking St Monans harbor. The summons had come from his housekeeper, Mrs. Marr, in a frantic early morning phone call. Hers was from the town's one hotel, to me in the porter's room, which boasted the only telephone at our college.

I was a miserable ten hours getting there. All during the long train ride, though I tried to pray for him, I could not, having given up that sort of thing long before leaving Scotland. Loss of faith, lack of faith—that had been my real reason for going away from home. Taking up a place at Gerton College had only been an excuse.

What I had wanted to do this return was to mend our fences before it was too late to mend anything at all. Father and I had broken so many fences—stones, dykes, stiles, and all—that the mending would have taken more than the fortnight's holiday I had planned for later in the summer. But I'd been summoned home early this March because, as Mrs. Marr said, father had had a bad turn.

155

"A verrry bad turn," was what she'd actually said, before the line had gone dead, her r's rattling like a kettle on the boil. In her understated way, she might have meant anything from a twisted ankle to a major heart attack.

The wire that had followed, delivered by a man with a limp and a harelip, had been from my father's doctor, Ewan Kinnear. "Do not delay," it read. Still, there was no diagnosis.

Even so, I did not delay. We'd had no connection in ten years beside a holiday letter exchange. Me to him, not the other way round. But the old man was my only father. I was his only child.

He was dead by the time I got there, and Mrs. Marr stood at the doorway of the house wringing her hands, her black hair caught up in a net. She had not aged a day since I last saw her.

"So ye've left it too late, Janet," she cried. "And wearing green I see."

I looked down at my best dress, a soft green linen now badly creased with travel.

She shook her head at me, and only then did I remember. In St Monans they always said, "After green comes grief."

"I didn't know he was that ill. I came as fast as I could."

But Mrs. Marr's face showed her disdain for my excuse. Her eyes narrowed and she didn't put out her hand. She'd always been on father's side, especially in the matter of my faith. "His old heart's burst in twa." She was of the old school in speech as well as faith.

"His heart was stone, Maggie, and well you know it." A widow, she'd waited twenty-seven years, since my mother died birthing me, for the old man to notice her. She must be old herself now.

"Stane can still feel pain," she cried.

"What pain?" I asked.

"Of your leaving."

What good would it have done to point out I'd left more than ten years earlier and he'd hardly noticed. He'd had a decade more of calcification, a decade more of pouring over his bloody old books—the Latin texts of apostates and heretics. A decade more of filling notebooks with his crabbed script.

A decade more of ignoring his only child.

My God, I thought, meaning no appeal to a deity but a simple swear, *I am still furious with him. It's no wonder I've never married.* Though I'd had chances. Plenty of them. Well, two that were real enough.

I went into the house, and the smell of candle wax and fish and salt sea were as familiar to me as though I'd never left. But there was another smell, too.

Death.

And something more.

It was fear. But I was not to know that till later.

~

The study where evidently he'd died, sitting up in his chair, was a dark place, even when the curtains were drawn back, which had not been frequent in my childhood. Father liked the close, wood-paneled room, made closer by the ever-burning fire. I'd been allowed in there only when being punished, standing just inside the doorway, with my hands clasped behind me, to listen to my sins being counted. My sins were homey ones, like shouting in the hallway, walking too loudly by his door, or refusing to learn my verses from the Bible. I was far too innocent a child for more than that.

Even at five and six and seven I'd been an unbeliever. Not having a mother had made me so. How could I worship a God whom both Mrs. Marr and my father assured me had so wanted mother, He'd called her away. A selfish God, that, who had listened to his own desires and not mine. Such a God was not for me. Not then. Not now.

I had a sudden urge—me, a postgraduate in a prestigious university who should have known better—to clasp my hands behind me and await my punishment.

But, I thought, *the old punisher is dead. And—if he's to be believed—gone to his own punishment.* Though I was certain that the only place he had gone was to the upstairs bedroom where he was laid out, awaiting my instructions as to his burial.

~

I went into every other room of the house but that bedroom, memory like an old fishing line dragging me on. The smells, the dark moody smells, remained the same, though Mrs. Marr had a good wood fire burning in the grate, not peat, a wee change in this changeless place. But everything else was so much smaller than I remembered, my little bedroom at the back of the house the smallest of them all.

To my surprise, nothing in my bedroom had been removed. My bed, my toys—the little wooden doll with jointed arms and legs I called Annie, my ragged copy of *Rhymes and Tunes for Little Folks*, the boxed chess set just the size for little hands, my cloth bag filled with buttons—the rag rug, the over-worked sampler on the wall. All were the same. I was surprised to even find one of my old pinafores and black stockings in the wardrobe. I charged Mrs. Marr with more sentiment than sense. It was a shrine to the child that I'd been, not the young woman who had run off. It had to have been Mrs. Marr's idea. Father would never have countenanced false gods.

Staring out of the low window, I looked out toward the sea. A fog sat on the horizon, white and patchy. Below it the sea was a deep, solitary blue. Spring comes early to the East Neuk but summer stays away. I guessed that pussy willows had already appeared around the edges of the lochans, snowdrops and aconite decorating the inland gardens.

Once I'd loved to stare out at that sea, escaping the dark brooding house whenever I could, even in a cutting wind, the kind that could raise bruises. Down I'd go to the beach to play amongst the yawls hauled up on the high wooden trestles, ready for tarring. Once I'd dreamed of going off to sea with the fishermen, coming home to the harbor in the late summer light, and seeing the silver scales glinting on the beach. Though of course fishing was not a woman's job. Not then, not now. A woman in a boat was unthinkable even this far into the twentieth century. St Monans is firmly eighteenth century and likely to remain so forever.

But I'd been sent off to school, away from the father who found me a loud and heretical discomfort. At first it was just a few towns away, to St Leonard's in St Andrews, but as I was a boarder—my father's one extravagance—it might as well have been across the country, or the ocean, as far as seeing my father was concerned. And there I'd fallen in love with words in books.

Words—not water, not wind.

In that way I showed myself to be my father's daughter. Only I never said so to him, nor he to me.

~

Making my way back down the stairs, I overheard several folk in the kitchen. They were speaking of those things St Monans folk always speak of, no matter their occupations: Fish and weather.

"There's been nae herring in the firth this winter," came a light man's voice. "Nane." Doctor Kinnear.

"It's a bitter wind to keep the men at hame, the fish awa." Mrs. Marr agreed.

Weather and the fishing. Always the same.

But a third voice, one I didn't immediately recognize, a rumbling growl of a voice, added, "Does she know?"

"Do I know what?" I asked, coming into the room where the big black-leaded grate threw out enough heat to warm the entire house. "How Father died?"

I stared at the last speaker, a stranger I thought, but somehow familiar. He was tall for a St Monans man, but dressed as one of the fisher folk, in dark trousers, a heavy white sweater, thick white sea stockings. And he was sunburnt like them, too, with eyes the exact blue of the April sea, gathered round with laugh lines. A ginger mustache, thick and full, hung down the sides of his mouth like a parenthesis.

"By God, Alec Hughes," I said, startled to have remembered, surprised that I could have forgotten. He grinned.

When we'd been young—very young—Alec and I were inseparable. Never mind that boys and girls never played together in St Monans. Boys from the Bass, girls from the May, the old folk wisdom went. The Bass Rock, the Isle of May, the original separation of the sexes. Apart at birth and ever after. Yet Alec and I had done everything together: messed about with the boats, played cards, built sand castles, fished with pelns—shore crabs about to cast their shells—and stolen jam pieces from his mother's kitchen to eat down by one of the gates in the drystone dykes. We'd even often hied off to the low cliff below the ruins of Andross Castle to look for croupies, fossils, though whether we ever found any I couldn't recall. When I'd been sent away to school, he'd stayed on in St Monans, going to Anstruther's Waid Academy in the next town but one, until he was old enough—I presumed—to join the fishing fleet, like his father before him. His father was a stern and dour soul, a Temperance man who used to preach in the open air.

Alec had been the first boy to kiss me, my back against the stone windmill down by the salt pans. And until I'd graduated from St Leonard's, the only boy to do so, though I'd made up for that since.

"I thought, Jan," he said slowly, "that God was not in your vocabulary."

"Except as a swear," I retorted. "Good to see you, too, Alec."

Mrs. Marr's eyebrows both rose considerably, like fulmars over the green-grey sea of her eyes.

Alec laughed and it was astonishing how that laugh reminded me of the boy who'd stayed behind. "Yes," he said. "Do you know how your father died?"

"Heart attack, so Mrs. Marr told me."

I stared at the three of them. Mrs. Marr was wringing her hands again, an oddly old-fashioned motion at which she seemed well practiced. Dr. Kinnear polished his eyeglasses with a large white piece of cloth, his flyaway eyebrows proclaiming his advancing age. And Alec—had I remembered how blue his eyes were? Alec nibbled on the right end of his mustache.

"Did I say that?" Mrs. Marr asked. "Bless me, I didna."

And indeed, she hadn't. She'd been more poetic.

"Burst in twa, you said." I smiled, trying to apologize for misspeaking. Not a good trait in a scholar.

"Indeed. Indeed." Mrs. Marr's wrangling hands began again. Any minute I supposed she would break out into a Psalm. I remembered how her one boast was that she'd learned them all by heart as a child and never forgot a one of them.

"A shock, I would have said," Alec said by way of elaborating.

"A fright," the doctor added.

"Really? Is that the medical term?" I asked. "What in St Monans could my father possibly be frightened of?"

Astonishingly, Mrs. Marr began to wail then, a high, thin keening that went on and on till Alec put his arm around her and marched her over to the stone sink where he splashed her face with cold water and she quieted at once. Then she turned to the blackened kettle squalling on the grate and started to make us all tea.

I turned to the doctor who had his glasses on now, which made him look like a somewhat surprised barn owl. "What do you really mean, Dr. Kinnear?"

"Have you nae seen him yet?" he asked, his head gesturing towards the back stairs.

"I... I couldn't," I admitted. But I said no more. How could I tell this man I hardly knew that my father and I were virtual strangers? No—it was more than that. I was afraid of my father dead as I'd never been alive. Because now he knew for certain whether he was right or I was, about God and Heaven and the rest.

"Come," said Doctor Kinnear in a voice that seemed permanently gentle. He held out a hand and led me back up the stairs and down the hall to my father's room. Then he went in with me and stood by my side as I looked down.

My father was laid out on his bed, the Scottish double my mother had died in, the one he'd slept in every night of his adult life except the day she'd given birth, the day she died.

Like the house, he was much smaller than I remembered. His wild, white hair lay untamed around his head in a kind of corolla. The skin of his face was parchment stretched over bone. That great prow of a nose was, in death, strong enough to guide a ship in. Thankfully his eyes were shut. His hands were crossed on his chest. He was dressed in an old dark suit. I remembered it well.

"He doesn't look afraid," I said. Though he didn't look peaceful either. Just dead.

"Once he'd lost the stiffness, I smoothed his face a bit," the doctor told me. "Smoothed it out. Otherwise Mrs. Marr would no have settled."

"Settled?"

He nodded. "She found him at his desk, stone dead. Ran down the road screaming all the way to the pub. And lucky I was there, having a drink with friends. I came up to see yer father sitting up in his chair, with a face so full of fear, I looked around mysel' to discover the cause of it."

"And did you?"

His blank expression said it all. He simply handed me a pile of five notebooks. "These were on the desk in front of him. Some of the writing is in Latin, which I have but little of. Perhaps ye can read it, being the scholar. Mrs. Marr has said that they should be thrown on the fire, or at least much of them scored out. But I told her that had to be yer decision and Alec agrees."

I took the notebooks, thinking that this was what had stolen my father from me and now was all I had of him. But I said none of that aloud. After glancing over at the old man again, I asked, "May I have a moment with him?" My voice cracked on the final word.

Dr. Kinnear nodded again and left the room.

I went over to the bed and looked down at the silent body. *The old dragon*, I thought, *has no teeth.* Then I heard a sound, something so tiny I scarcely registered it. Turning, I saw a toad by the bedfoot.

I bent down and picked it up. "Nothing for you here, puddock," I said, reverting to the old Scots word. Though I'd worked so hard to lose my accent and vocabulary, here in my father's house the old way of speech came flooding back. Shifting the books to one hand, I picked the toad up with the other. Then, I tiptoed out of the door as if my father would have minded the sound of my footsteps.

Once outside, I set the toad gently in the garden, or the remains of the garden, now so sadly neglected, its vines running rampant across what was once an arbor of white roses and red. I watched as it hopped under some large dock leaves and, quite effectively, disappeared.

~

Later that afternoon my father's body was taken away by three burly men for its chestening, being placed into its coffin and the lid screwed down. Then it would lie in the cold kirk till the funeral the next day.

Once he was gone from the house, I finally felt I could look in his journals. I might have sat comfortably in the study, but I'd never been welcomed there before, so didn't feel it my place now. The kitchen and sitting room were more Mrs. Marr's domain than mine. And if I never had to go back into the old man's bedroom, it would be years too soon for me.

So I lay in my childhood bed, the covers up to my chin, and read by the flickering lamplight. Mrs. Marr, bless her, had brought up a warming pan which she came twice to refill. And she brought up as well a pot of tea and jam pieces and several slabs of good honest cheddar.

"I didna think ye'd want a big supper."

She was right. Food was the last thing on my mind.

After she left the room, I took a silver hip flask from under my pillow where I'd hidden it, and then poured a hefty dram of whisky into the teapot. I would need more than Mrs. Marr's offerings to stay warm this night. Outside the sea moaned as it pushed past the skellies, on its way to the shore. I'd all but forgotten that sound. It made me smile.

I read the last part of the last journal first, where father talked about the toad, wondering briefly if it was the very same toad I had found at his bedfoot. But it was the bit right after, where he spoke of "formidable visitants" that riveted me. What had he meant? From the tone of it, I didn't think he meant any of our St Monans neighbors.

The scholar in me asserted itself, and I turned to the first of the journals, marked 1926, some five years earlier. There was one book for each year. I started with that first notebook and read long into the night.

The journals were not easy to decipher for my father's handwriting was crabbed with age and, I expect, arthritis. The early works were splotchy and, in places, faded. Also he had inserted sketchy pictures and diagrams.

Occasionally he'd written whole paragraphs in corrupted Latin, or at least in a dialect unknown to me.

What he seemed engaged upon was a study of a famous trial of local witches in 1590, supervised by King James VI himself. The VI of Scotland, for he was Mary Queen of Scots' own son, and Queen Elizabeth's heir.

The witches, some ninety in all according to my father's notes, had been accused of sailing over the Firth to North Berwick in riddles—sieves, I think he meant—to plot the death of the king by raising a storm when he sailed to Denmark. However, I stumbled so often over my Latin translations, I decided I needed a dictionary. And me a classics scholar.

So halfway through the night, I rose and, taking the lamp, made my way through the cold dark, tiptoeing so as not to wake Mrs. Marr. Nothing was unfamiliar beneath my bare feet. The kitchen stove would not have gone out completely, only filled with gathering coal and kept minimally warm. All those years of my childhood came rushing back. I could have gone into the study without the lamp, I suppose. But to find the book I needed, I'd have to have light.

And lucky indeed I took it, for in its light it I saw—gathered on the floor of my father's study—a group of toads throwing strange shadows up against the bookshelves. I shuddered to think what might have happened had I stepped barefooted amongst them.

But how had they gotten in? And was the toad I'd taken into the garden amongst them? Then I wondered aloud at what such a gathering should be called. I'd heard of a murder of crows, an exaltation of larks. Perhaps toads came in a congregation? For that is what they looked like, a squat congregation, huddled together, nodding their heads, and waiting on the minister in this most unlikely of kirks.

It was too dark even with the lamp, and far too late, for me to round them up. So I sidestepped them and, after much searching, found the Latin dictionary where it sat cracked open on my father's desk. I grabbed it up, avoided the congregation of toads, and went out the door. When I looked back, I could still see the odd shadows dancing along the walls.

I almost ran back to my bed, shutting the door carefully behind me. I didn't want that dark presbytery coming in, as if they could possibly hop up the stairs like the frog in the old tale, demanding to be taken to my little bed.

But the shock of my father's death and the long day of travel, another healthy swallow of my whisky, as well as that bizarre huddle of toads, all seemed to combine to put me into a deep sleep. If I dreamed, I didn't remember any of it. I woke to one of those dawn choruses of my childhood, comprised of blackbirds, song thrushes, gulls, rooks, and jackdaws, all arguing over who should wake me first.

~

For a moment I couldn't recall where I was. Eyes closed, I listened to the birds, so different from the softer, more lyrical sounds outside my Cambridge windows. But I woke fully in the knowledge that I was back in my childhood home, that my father was dead and to be buried that afternoon if possible, as I had requested of the doctor and Mrs. Marr, and I had only hours to make things tidy in my mind. Then I would be away from St Monans and its small-mindedness, back to Cambridge where I truly belonged.

I got out of bed, washed, dressed in the simple black dress I always travel with, a black bandeaux on my fair hair, and went into the kitchen to make myself some tea.

Mrs. Marr was there before me, sitting on a hardback chair and knitting a navy blue guernsey sweater with its complicated patterning. She set the steel needles down and handed me a full cup, the tea nearly black even with its splash of milk. There was a heaping bowl of porridge, sprinkled generously with salt, plus bread slathered with golden syrup.

"Thank you," I said. It would have done no good to argue that I drank coffee now, nor did I like either oatmeal or treacle, and never ate till noon. Besides, I was suddenly ravenous. "What do you need me to do?" I asked between mouthfuls, stuffing them in the way I'd done as a youngster.

"'Tis all arranged," she said, taking up the needles again. No proper St Monans woman was ever idle long. "Though sooner than is proper. But all to accommodate ye, he'll be in the kirkyard this afternoon. Lucky for ye it's a Sunday, or we couldna do it. The men are home from fishing." She was clearly not pleased with me. "Ye just need to be there at the service. Not that many will come. He was no generous with his company." By which she meant he had few friends. Nor relatives except me.

"Then I'm going to walk down by the water this morning," I told her. "Unless you have something that needs doing. I want to clear my head."

"Aye, ye would."

Was that condemnation or acceptance? Who could tell? Perhaps she meant I was still the thankless child she remembered. Or that I was like my father. Or that she wanted only to see the back of me, sweeping me from her domain so she could clean and bake without my worrying presence. I thanked her again for the meal, but she wanted me gone. As I had been for the past ten years. And I was as eager to be gone, as she was to have me. The funeral was not till mid afternoon.

"There are toads in the study," I said as I started out the door.

"Toads?" She looked startled. Or perhaps frightened.

"Puddocks. A congregation of them."

Her head cocked to one side. "Och, ye mean a knot. A knot of toads."

A knot. Of course. I should have remembered. "Shall I put them out?" At least I could do that for her.

She nodded. "Aye."

I found a paper sack and went into the study, but though I looked around for quite some time, I couldn't find the toads anywhere. If I hadn't still had the Latin dictionary in my bedroom, I would have thought my night visit amongst them and my scare from their shadows had been but a dream.

"All gone," I called to Mrs. Marr before slipping out through the front door and heading toward the strand.

~

Nowhere in St Monans is far from the sea. I didn't realize how much the sound of it was in my bones until I moved to Cambridge. Or how much I'd missed that sound till I slept the night in my old room.

I found my way to the foot of the church walls where boats lay upturned, looking like beached dolphins. A few of the older men, past their fishing days, sat with their backs against the salted stone, smoking silently, and staring out to the gray slatey waters of the Firth. Nodding to them, I took off along the beach. Overhead gulls squabbled and far out, near the Bass Rock, I could see, gannets diving head-first into the water.

A large boat, some kind of yacht, had just passed the Bass and was sailing west majestically toward a mooring, probably in South Queensferry. I wondered who would be sailing these waters in such a ship.

But then I was interrupted by the wind sighing my name. Or so I thought at first. Then I looked back at the old kirk on the cliff above me. Someone was waving at me in the ancient kirkyard. It was Alec.

He signaled that he was coming down to walk with me and as I waited, I thought about what a handsome man he'd turned into. *But a fisherman*, I reminded myself, a bit of the old snobbery biting me on the back of the neck. St Monans, like the other fishing villages of the East Neuk, were made up of three classes—fisher folk, farmers, and the shopkeepers and tradesmen. My father being a scholar was outside of them all, which meant that as his daughter, I belonged to none of them either.

Still, in this place, where I was once so much a girl of the town—from the May—I felt my heart give a small stutter. I remembered that first kiss, so soft and sweet and innocent, the windmill hard against my back. My last serious relationship had been almost a year ago, and I was more than ready to fall in love again. Even at the foot of my father's grave. But not with a fisherman. Not in St Monans.

Alec found his way down to the sand and came toward me. "Off to find croupies?" he called.

I laughed. "The only fossil I've found recently has been my father," I said, then bit my lower lip at his scowl.

"He was nae a bad man, Jan," he said, catching up to me. "Just undone by his reading."

I turned a glared at him. "Do you think reading an ailment then?"

He put up his hands palms towards me. "Whoa, lass. I'm a big reader myself. But what the old man had been reading lately had clearly unnerved him. He couldna put it into context. Mrs. Marr said as much before you came. These last few months he'd stayed away from the pub, from the kirk, from everyone who'd known him well. No one kenned what he'd been on about."

I wondered what sort of thing Alec would be reading. *The fishing report? The local paper?* Feeling out of sorts, I said sharply, "Well, I was going over his journals last night and what he's been on about are the old North Berwick witches."

Alec's lips pursed. "The ones who plotted to blow King James off the map." It was a statement, not a question.

"The very ones."

"Not a smart thing for the unprepared to tackle."

I wondered if Alec had become as hag-ridden and superstitious as any St Monans fisherman. Ready to turn home from his boat if he met a woman on the way. Or not daring to say "salmon" or "pig" and instead speaking of "red fish" and "curly tail," or shouting out "Cauld iron!" at any mention of them. All the East Neuk tip-leavings I was glad to be shed of.

He took the measure of my disapproving face, and laughed. "Ye take me for a gowk," he said. "But there are more things in heaven and earth, Janet, than are dreamt of in yer philosophy."

I laughed as Shakespeare tumbled from his lips. Alec could always make me laugh. "Pax," I said.

He reached over, took my hand, gave it a squeeze. "Pax." Then he dropped it again as we walked along the beach, a comfortable silence between us.

The tide had just turned and was heading out. Gulls, like satisfied housewives, sat happily in the receding waves. One lone boat was on the horizon, a small fishing boat, not the yacht I had seen earlier, which must already be coming into its port. The sky was that wonderful spring blue, without a threatening cloud, not even the fluffy Babylonians, as the fishermen called them.

"Shouldn't you be out there?" I said, pointing at the boat as we passed by the smoky fish-curing sheds.

"I rarely get out there anymore," he answered, not looking at me but at the sea. "Too busy until summer. And why old man Sinclair is fishing when the last of the winter herring have been hauled in, I canna fathom."

I turned toward him. "Too busy with what?"

He laughed. "Och, Janet, yer so caught up in yer own preconceptions, ye canna see what's here before yer eyes."

I didn't answer right away, and the moment stretched between us, as the silence had before. Only this was not comfortable. At last I said, "Are you too busy to help me solve the mystery of my father's death?"

"Solve the mystery of his life first," he told me, "and the mystery of his death will inevitably be revealed." Then he touched his cap, nodded at me, and strolled away.

I was left to ponder what he said. Or what he meant. I certainly wasn't going to chase after him. I was too proud to do that. Instead, I went back to the house, changed my shoes, made myself a plate of bread and cheese. There was no wine in the house. Mrs. Marr was as Temperance as Alec's old father had been. But I found some miserable sherry hidden in my father's study. It smelled like turpentine, so I made do with fresh milk, taking the plate and glass up to my bedroom, to read some more of my father's journals until it was time to bury him.

~

It is not too broad a statement to say that Father was clearly out of his mind. For one, he was obsessed with local witches. For another, he seemed to believe in them. While he spared a few paragraphs for Christian Dote, St Monans's homegrown witch of the 1640s, and a bit more about the various

Anstruther, St Andrews, and Crail trials—listing the hideous tortures, and executions of hundreds of poor old women in his journal entries—it was the earlier North Berwick crew who really seemed to capture his imagination. By the third year's journal, I could see that he obviously considered the North Berwick witchery evil real, whereas the others, a century later, he dismissed as deluded or senile old women, as deluded and senile as the men who hunted them.

Here is what he wrote about the Berwick corps: *"They were a scabrous bunch, these ninety greedy women and six men, wanting no more than what they considered their due: a king and his bride dead in the sea, a kingdom in ruins, themselves set up in high places."*

"Oh, Father," I whispered, "what a noble mind is here o'erthrown," For whatever problems I'd had with him—and they were many—I had always admired his intelligence.

He described the ceremonies they indulged in, and they were awful. In the small North Berwick church, fueled on wine and sex, the witches had begun a ritual to call up a wind that would turn over the royal ship and drown King James. First they'd christened a cat with the name of Hecate, while black candles flickered fitfully along the walls of the apse and nave. Then they tortured the poor creature by passing it back and forth across a flaming hearth. Its elf-knotted hair caught fire and burned slowly, and the little beastie screamed in agony. The smell must have been appalling, but he doesn't mention that. I once caught my hair on fire, bending over a stove on a cold night in Cambridge, and it was the smell that was the worst of it. It lingered in my room for days.

Then I thought of my own dear moggie at home, a sweet orange-colored puss who slept each night at my bedfoot. If anyone ever treated her the way the North Berwick witches had that poor cat, I'd be more than ready to kill. And not with any wind, either.

But there was worse yet, and I shuddered as I continued reading. One of the men, so Father reported, had dug up a corpse from the church cemetery, and with a companion had cut off the dead man's hands and feet. Then the witches attached the severed parts to the cat's paws. After this they attached the corpse's sex organs to the cat's. I could only hope the poor creature was dead by this point. After this desecration, they proceeded to a pier at the port of Leith where they flung the wee beastie into the sea.

Father wrote: *"A storm was summarily raised by this foul method, along with the more traditional knotted twine. The storm blackened the skies, with wild gales churning*

*the sea. The howl of the wind could be heard all the way across the Firth to Fife. But the
odious crew had made a deadly miscalculation. The squall caught a ship crossing from
Kinghorn to Leith and smashed it to pieces all right, but it was not the king's ship. The
magic lasted only long enough to kill a few innocent sailors on that first ship, and then
blew itself out to sea. As for the king, he proceeded over calmer waters with his bride,
arriving safely in Denmark and thence home again to write that great treatise on
witchcraft,* Demonology, *and preside over a number of witch trials thereafter."*

I did not read quickly because, as I have said, parts of the journal were
in a strange Latin and for those passages I needed the help of the
dictionary. I was like a girl at school with lines to translate by morning,
frustrated, achingly close to comprehension, but somehow missing the
point. In fact, I did not understand them completely until I read them
aloud. And then suddenly, as a roiled liquid settles at last, all became clear.
The passages were some sort of incantation, or invitation, to the witches
and to the evil they so devoutly and hideously served.

I closed the journal and shook my head. Poor Father. He wrote as if the
witchcraft were fact, not a coincidence of gales from the southeast that
threw up vast quantities of seaweed on the shore, and the haverings of
tortured old women. Put a scold's bridle on me, and I would probably
admit to intercourse with the devil. Any devil. And describe him and his
nether parts as well.

But Father's words, as wild and unbelievable as they were, held me in a
kind of thrall. And I would have remained on my bed reading further if
Mrs. Marr hadn't knocked on the door and summoned me to his funeral.

She looked me over carefully, but for once I seemed to pass muster, my
smart black Cambridge dress suitable for the occasion. She handed me a
black hat. "I didna think ye'd have thought to bring one." Her lips drew
down into a thin, straight line.

Standing before me, her plain black dress covered at the top by a solemn
dark shawl, and on her head an astonishing hat covered with artificial black
flowers, she was clearly waiting for me to say something.

"Thank you," I said at last. And it was true, bringing a hat along hadn't
occurred to me at all. I took off the bandeaux, and set the proffered hat on
my head. It was a perfect fit, though made me look fifteen years older, with
its masses of black feathers, or so the mirror told me.

Lips pursed, she nodded at me, then turned, saying over her shoulder,
"Young Mary McDougall did for him."

It took me a moment to figure out what she meant. Then I remembered. Though she must be nearer sixty than thirty, Mary McDougall had been both midwife and dresser of the dead when I was a child. So it had been she and not Mrs. Marr who must have washed my father and put him into the clothes he'd be buried in. *So Mrs. Marr missed out on her last great opportunity to touch him*, I thought.

"What do I give her?" I asked to Mrs. Marr's ramrod back.

Without turning around again, she said, "We'll give her all yer father's old clothes. She'll be happy enough with that."

"But surely a fee…"

She walked out of the door.

It was clear to me then that nothing had changed since I'd left. It was still the nineteenth century. Or maybe the eighteenth. I longed for the burial to be over and done with, my father's meager possessions sorted, the house sold, and me back on a train heading south.

~

We walked to the kirk in silence, crossing over the burn which rushed along beneath the little bridge. St Monans has always been justifiably proud of its ancient kirk and even in this dreary moment I could remark its beauty. Some of its stonework runs back in an unbroken line to the thirteenth century.

And some of its customs, I told myself without real bitterness.

When we entered the kirk proper, I was surprised to see that Mrs. Marr had been wrong. She'd said not many would come, but the church was overfull with visitants.

We walked down to the front. As the major mourners, we commanded the first pew, Mrs. Marr, the de facto wife, and me, the runaway daughter. There was a murmur when we sat down together, not quite of disapproval, but certainly of interest. Gossip in a town like St Monans is everybody's business.

Behind us, Alex and Dr. Kinnear were already settled in. And three men sat beside them, men whose faces I recognized, friends of my father's, but grown so old. I turned, nodded at them with, I hope, a smile that thanked them for coming. They didn't smile back.

In the other pews were fishermen and shopkeepers and the few teachers I could put a name to. But behind them was a congregation of strangers who leaned forward with an avidity that one sees only in the faces of vultures at their feed. I knew none of them and wondered if they were newcomers to the town. Or if it was just that I hadn't been home in so long, even those families who'd been here forever were strangers to me now.

Father's pine box was set before the altar and I kept my eyes averted, watching instead an ettercap, a spider, slowly spinning her way from one edge of the pulpit to the other. No one in the town would have removed her, for it was considered bad luck. It kept me from sighing, it kept me from weeping.

The minister went on for nearly half an hour, lauding my father's graces, his intelligence, his dedication. If any of us wondered about whom he was talking, we didn't answer back. But when it was over, and six large fishermen, uneasy in their Sunday clothes, stood to shoulder the coffin, I leaped up with them. Putting my hand on the pine top, I whispered, "I forgive you, Father. Do you forgive me?"

There was an audible gasp from the congregation behind me, though I'd spoken so low, I doubted any of them—not even Alec—could have heard me. I sat down again, shaken and cold.

And then the fishermen took him off to the kirkyard, to a grave so recently and quickly carved out of the cold ground, its edges were jagged. As we stood there, a huge black cloud covered the sun. The tide was dead low and the bones of the sea, those dark grey rock skellies, showed in profusion like the spines of some prehistoric dragons.

As I held on to Mrs. Marr's arm, she suddenly started shaking so hard, I thought she would shake me off.

How she must have loved my father, I thought, and found myself momentarily jealous.

Then the coffin was lowered, and that stopped her shaking. As the first clods were shoveled into the gaping hole, she turned to me and said, "Well, that's it then."

~

So we walked back to the house where a half dozen people stopped in for a dram or three of whiskey—brought in by Alec despite Mrs. Marr's strong disapproval. "There's a Deil in every mouthful of whiskey," she muttered, setting out the fresh baked shortbread and sultana cakes with a pitcher of lemonade. To mollify her, I drank the lemonade, but I was the only one.

Soon I was taken aside by an old man—Jock was his name—and told that my father had been a great gentleman though late had turned peculiar.

Another, bald and wrinkled, drank his whiskey down in a single gulp, before declaring loudly that my father had been "one for the books." He managed to make that sound like an affliction. One woman of a certain age who addressed me as "Mistress," added, apropos of nothing, "He needs a lang-shankit spoon that sups wi' the Deil." Even Alec, sounding like the drone on a bagpipes, said "Now you can get on with your own living, Jan," as if I hadn't been doing just that all along.

For a wake, it was most peculiar. No humorous anecdotes about the dearly departed, no toasts to his soul, only half-baked praise and a series of veiled warnings.

Thank goodness no one stayed long. After the last had gone, I insisted on doing the washing up, and this time Mrs. Marr let me. And then she, too, left. Where she went I wasn't to know. One minute she was there, and the next away.

I wondered at that. After all, this was her home, certainly more than mine. I was sure she'd loved my father who, God knows, was not particularly loveable, but she walked out the door clutching her big handbag, without a word more to me; not a goodbye or "I'll not be long," or anything. And suddenly, there I was, all alone in the house for the first time in years. It was an uncomfortable feeling. I am not afraid of ghosts, but that house fairly burst with ill will, dark and brooding. So as soon as I'd tidied away the dishes, I went out, too, though not before slipping the final journal into the pocket of my overcoat and winding a long woolen scarf twice around my neck to ward the chill.

~

The evening was drawing in slowly, but there was otherwise a soft feel in the air, unusual for the middle of March. The East Neuk is like that— one minute still and the next a flanny wind rising.

I headed east along the coastal path, my guide the stone head of the windmill with its narrow, ruined vanes lording it over the flat land. Perhaps sentiment was leading me there, the memory of that adolescent kiss that Alec had given me, so wonderfully innocent and full of desire at the same time. Perhaps I just wanted a short, pleasant walk to the old salt pans. I don't know why I went that way. It was almost as if I were being called there.

For a moment I turned back and looked at the town behind me which showed, from this side, how precariously the houses perch on the rocks, like gannets nesting on the Bass.

Then I turned again and took the walk slowly; it was still only ten or fifteen minutes to the windmill from the town. No boats sailed on the Firth today. I could not spot the large yacht so it must have been in its berth. And the air was so clear, I could see the Bass and the May with equal distinction. How often I'd come to this place as a child. I probably could still walk to it barefooted and without stumbling, even in the blackest night. The body has a memory of its own.

Halfway there, a solitary curlew flew up before me and as I watched it flap away, I thought how the townsfolk would have cringed at the sight, for the bird was thought to bring bad luck, carrying away the spirits of the wicked at nightfall.

"But I've not been wicked," I cried after it, and laughed. *Or at least not wicked for a year, more's the pity.*

At last I came to the windmill with its rough stones rising high above the land. Once it had been used for pumping seawater to extract the salt. Not a particularly easy operation, it took something like thirty-two tons of water to produce one ton of salt. We'd learned all about it in primary school, of course. But the days of the salt pans were a hundred years in the past, and the poor windmill had seen better times.

Even run down, though, it was still a lovely place, with its own memories. Settling back against the mill's stone wall, I nestled down and drew out the last journal from my coat pocket. Then I began to read it from the beginning as the light slowly faded around me.

Now, I am a focused reader, which is to say that once caught up in a book, I can barely swim back up to the surface of any other consciousness. The world dims around me. Time and space compress. Like a Wellsian hero, I am drawn into an elsewhere that becomes absolute and real. So as I read my Father's final journal, I was in his head and his madness so completely, I heard nothing around me, not the raucous cry of gulls nor the wash of water onto the stones far below.

So it was, with a start that I came to the final page, with its mention of the goggle-eyed toad. Looking up, I found myself in the gray gloaming surrounded by nearly a hundred such toads, all staring at me with their horrid wide eyes, a hideous echo of my father's written words.

I stood up quickly, trying desperately not to squash any of the poor puddocks. They leaned forward like children trying to catch the warmth of a fire. Then their shadows lengthened and grew.

Please understand, there was no longer any sun and very little light. There was no moon overhead for the clouds crowded one on to the other, and the sky was completely curtained. So there should not have been any shadows at all. Yet, I state again—their shadows lengthened and grew. Shadows like and unlike the ones I had seen against my father's study walls. They grew into dark-caped creatures, almost as tall as humans yet with those goggly eyes.

I still held my father's journal in my left hand, but my right covered my mouth to keep myself from screaming. My sane mind knew it to be only a trick of the light, of the dark. It was the result of bad dreams and just having put my only living relative into the ground. But the primitive brain urged me to cry out with all my ancestors, "Cauld iron!" and run away in terror.

And still the horrid creatures grew until now they towered over me, pushing me back against the windmill, their shadowy fingers grabbing at both ends of my scarf.

"Who are you? What are you?" I mouthed, as the breath was forced from me. Then they pulled and pulled the scarf until they'd choked me into unconsciousness.

~

When I awoke, I was tied to a windmill vane, my hands bound high above me, the ropes too tight and well-knotted for any escape.

"Who are you?" I whispered aloud this time, my voice sounding froglike, raspy, hoarse. "What are you?" Though I feared I knew. "What do you want of me? Why are you here?"

In concert, their voices wailed back. "A wind! A wind!"

And then in horror all that Father had written—about the hands and feet and sex organs of the corpse being cut off and attached to the dead cat—bore down upon me. Were they about to dig poor father's corpse up? Was I to be the offering? Were we to be combined in some sort of desecration too disgusting to be named? I began to shudder within my bonds, both hot and cold. For a moment I couldn't breathe again, as if they were tugging on the scarf once more.

Then suddenly, finding some latent courage, I stood tall and screamed at them, "I'm not dead yet!" Not like my father whom they'd frightened into his grave.

They crowded around me, shadow folk with wide white eyes, laughing. "A wind! A wind!"

I kicked out at the closest one, caught my foot in its black cape, but connected with nothing more solid than air. Still, that kick forced them back for a moment.

"Get away from me!" I screamed. But screaming only made my throat ache, for I'd been badly choked just moments earlier. I began to cough and it was as if a nail were being driven through my temples with each spasm.

The shadows crowded forward again, their fingers little breezes running over my face and hair, down my neck, touching my breasts.

I took a deep breath for another scream, another kick. But before I could deliver either, I heard a cry.

"Aroint, witches!"

Suddenly I distinguished the sound of running feet. Straining to see down the dark corridor that was the path to Pittenweem, I leaned against the cords that bound me. It was a voice I did and did not recognize.

The shadow folk turned as one and flowed along the path, hands before them as if they were blindly seeking the interrupter.

"Aroint, I say!"

Now I knew the voice. It was Mrs. Marr, in full cry. But her curse seemed little help and I feared that she, too, would soon be trussed up by my side.

But then, from the east, along the path nearer town, there came another call.

"Janet! Janet!" That voice I recognized at once.

"Alec..." I said between coughs.

The shadows turned from Mrs. Marr and flowed back, surrounding Alec, but he held something up in his hand. A bit of a gleam from a crossbar. His fisherman's knife.

The shadows fell away from him in confusion.

"Cauld iron!" he cried at them. "Cauld iron!"

So they turned to go back again towards Mrs. Marr, but she reached into her large handbag and pulled out her knitting needles. Holding them before her in the sign of a cross, she echoed Alec's cry. "Cauld iron." And then she added, her voice rising as she spoke, "Oh let the wickedness of the wicked come to an end; but establish the just: for the righteous God trieth the hearts and reigns."

I recognized it as part of a psalm, one of the many she'd presumably memorized as a child, but I could not have said which.

Then the two of them advanced on the witches, coming from east and west, forcing the awful crew to shrink down, as if melting, into dark puddocks once again.

Step by careful step, Alec and Mrs. Marr herded the knot of toads off the path and over the cliff's edge.

Suddenly the clouds parted and a brilliant half moon shone down on us, its glare as strong as the lighthouse on Anster's pier. I watched as the entire knot of toads slid down the embankment, some falling onto the rocks and some into the water below.

Only when the last puddock was gone, did Alec turn to me. Holding the knife in his teeth, he reached above my head to my bound hands and began to untie the first knot.

A wind started to shake the vanes and for a second I was lifted off my feet as the mill tried to grind, though it had not done so for a century.

"Stop!" Mrs. Marr's voice held a note of desperation.

Alec turned. "Would ye leave her tied, woman? What if those shades come back again. I told ye what the witches had done before. It was all in the his journals."

"No, Alec," I cried, hating myself for trusting the old ways, but changed beyond caring. "They're elfknots. Don't untie them. Don't!" I shrank away from his touch.

"Aye," Mrs. Marr said, coming over and laying light fingers on Alec's arm. "The lass is still of St Monans though she talks like a Sassanach." She laughed. "It's no the drink and the carousing that brings the wind. That's just for fun. Nor the corpse and the cat. That's just for show. My man told me. It's the knots, he says."

"The knot of toads?" Alec asked hoarsely.

The wind was still blowing and it took Alec's hard arms around me to anchor me fast or I would have gone right around, spinning with the vanes.

Mrs. Marr came close till they were eye to eye. "The knots in the rope, lad," she said. "One brings a wind, two bring a gale, and the third…" She shook her head. "Ye dinna want to know about the third."

"But—" Alec began.

"Och, but me know buts, my lad. Cut between," Mrs. Marr said. "Just dinna untie them or King George's yacht at South Queensferry will go down in a squall, with the king and queen aboard, and we'll all be to blame."

He nodded and slashed the ropes with his knife, between the knots, freeing my hands. Then he lifted me down. I tried to take it all in: his arms, his breath on my cheek, the smell of him so close. I tried to understand what had happened here in the gloaming. I tried until I started to sob and he began stroking my hair, whispering, "There, lass, it's over. It's over."

"Not until we've had some tea and burned those journals," Mrs. Marr said. "I told ye we should have done it before."

"And I told ye," he retorted, "that they are invaluable to historians."

"Burn them," I croaked, knowing at last that the invitation in Latin they contained was what had called the witches back. Knowing that my speaking the words aloud had brought them to our house again. Knowing that the witches were Father's "visitants" who had, in the end, frightened him to death. "Burn them. No historian worth his salt would touch them."

Alec laughed bitterly. "I would." He set me on my feet and walked away down the path toward town.

"Now ye've done it," Mrs. Marr told me. "Ye never were a lass to watch what ye say. Ye've injured his pride and broken his heart."

"But..." We were walking back along the path, her hand on my arm, leading me on. The wind had died and the sky was alert with stars. "But he's not an historian."

"Ye foolish lass, yon lad's nae fisherman, for all he dresses like one. He's a lecturer in history at the University, in St Andrews," she said. "And the two of ye the glory of this village. Yer father and his father always talking about the pair of ye. Hoping to see ye married one day, when pride didna keep the two of ye apart. Scheming they were."

I could hardly take this in. Drawing my arm from her, I looked to see if she was making a joke. Though in all the years I'd known her, I'd never heard her laugh.

She glared ahead at the darkened path. "Yer father kept yer room the way it was when ye were a child, though I tried to make him see the foolishness of it. He said that someday yer own child would be glad of it."

"My father—"

"But then he went all queer in the head after Alec's father died. I think he believed that by uncovering all he could about the old witches, he might help Alec in his research. To bring ye together. though what he really fetched was too terrible to contemplate."

"Which do you think came first?" I asked slowly. "Father's summoning the witches, or the shadows sensing an opportunity?"

177

She gave a bob of her head to show she was thinking, then said at last, "Dinna mess with witches and weather, my man says…"

"Your man?" She'd said it before, but I thought she'd meant her dead husband. "Weren't you… I mean, I thought you were in love with my father."

She stopped dead in her tracks and turned to me. The half moon lit her face. "Yer father?" She stopped, considered, then began again. "Yer father had a heart only for two women in his life, yer mother and ye, Janet, though he had a hard time showing it.

And…" she laughed, "he was no a bonnie man."

I thought of him lying in his bed, his great prow of a nose dominating his face. No, he was not a bonnie man.

"Och, lass, I had promised yer mother on her deathbed to take care of him, and how could I go back on such a promise? I didna feel free to marry as long as he remained alive. Now my Pittenweem man and I have set a date, and it will be soon. We've wasted enough time already."

I had been wrong, so wrong, and in so many ways I could hardly comprehend them all. And didn't I understand about wasted time. But at least I could make one thing right again.

"I'll go after Alec, I'll…"

Mrs. Marr clapped her hands. "Then run, lass, run like the wind."

And untying the knot around my own pride, I ran.

THE ADVENTURES OF LIGHTNING MERRIEMOUSE-JONES

~

by Nancy & Belle Holder

Editor's Note: Just as a sumptuous banquet is topped off with a light dessert, we finish this literary feast with a whimsical tale that is a cross between Bram Stoker's Dracula *and Richard Peck's* Secrets at Sea.

To begin at the beginning:

That would be instructive, but rather dull; and so we will tell you, Gentle Reader, that the intrepid Miss Merriemouse-Jones was born in 1880, a wee pup to parents who had no idea that she was destined for greatness. Protective and loving, they encouraged her to find her happiness in the environs of home—running the squeaky wheel in the nursery cage, gnawing upon whatever might sharpen her pearlescent teeth, and wrinkling her tiny pink nose most adorably when vexed.

During her girlhood, Lightning was seldom vexed. She lived agreeably in her parents' well-appointed and fashionable abode, a hole in the wall located in the chamber of the human daughter of the house, one Maria Louisa Summerfield, whose mother was a tempestuous Spanish painter of some repute, and whose father owned a bank.

However, our story has little to do with the Summerfields, save that they shared living accommodations with the mice, and that it was Maria Louisa who named our heroine. Maria Louisa insisted that the tiny creature should be called Lightning because she was born during a terrible thunderstorm, although Mr. Summerfield argued for Snow. But Maria Louisa declared that she had already named the new kitten Snow, which she

179

had most certainly not done, but such was the nature of the little girl. For since she had not thought to name the infant mouseling Snow, no one else should be able to do so, either.

However, such were the Summerfields that they were content to allow mice to live in their home untrapped and untroubled, and for the parents of Snow to blithely ignore them, as the cats were so coddled and cosseted they would never dream of chasing after anything, much less their fur-clad neighbors.

Lightning she was, then, and Lightning was indeed as white as snow and together with her comely nose and delicate whiskers, she grew to become such a lovely young mousie maiden that suitors scrabbled from thicket and village to the Merriemouse-Jones residence in hopes of winning her hand.

Upon learning that she was expected to accept one of these suitors in marriage, Lightning became quite vexed indeed. But no amount of adorable nose-wrinkling could deter her parents' insistence that she choose the best of the lot, marry him, and bear his pups.

"It is the way of things, darling," Lightning's mother explained. "Your father and I long to see you settled, so that we will know you're taken care of in our dotage."

Settled was not a word Lightning appreciated. *Taken care of* were three more. The suitors who came to call upon her, bearing bits of cheese, corn, and pastry, were none to her liking. One was a mousy gray, one allowed as how he lived among the tracings of a coal mine, and one was actually a bow-legged rat.

However, we have promised not to dwell upon the circumstances of Lightning's life prior to the adventure we wish to recount; let us move forward, then, with the comment that it is well-documented that when Maria Louisa eloped with her second cousin, Juan Eldorado Adelante-Paz, Lightning hopped into the pocket of Miss Summerfield's traveling coat, and so was present during the untimely sinking of their frigate, *El Queso*.

It is also known that the errant lovers, Juan and Maria Louisa, were rescued by some Basques, and decamped to Catalonia. But the fate of Lightning was unknown for nearly a year, and her parents sorely grieved the loss of their enchanting and much-beloved daughter.

That is, until she managed to smuggle out the following communiqué:

Eeeek! Eeek! Eeekeekeek!

Which, for those not schooled in Received Standard Mouselish, translates:

31 October
Castle Dracurat, Transylvania
Au secours!
I am in great danger. Through circuitous means too complex to describe, I am imprisoned within the walls of the gloomy and foreboding castle of that dread rodent, Count Vlad Dracurat. I fear his plans for me will prove my undoing! I have pressed silver into the hairless palm of a young Gypsy named Marco, who promises to carry this letter to the priest of the nearby village. Alas, Mama! Oh, my poor, darling Papa! I fear you shall not see your Lightning in this life or the next!

At first determined to travel to Castle Dracurat himself, Mr. Merriemouse-Jones was forced by poor health to remain in London. His wife desired to go also, but at length acceded to her husband's entreaties not to undertake the journey: he could not bear losing both feminine rodentia he loved. Thereupon he hired a private detective who came highly recommended by highly placed persons who banked with him.

The detective's name was Quincey Dormouse. He was an American from Texas, quite courageous and resourceful; and Mr. Merriemouse-Jones directed that he travel posthaste to Castle Dracurat in the Catpathian Mountains. If their young miss was indeed there, he was to rescue her by any means possible from the paws of the fiendish nobleman.

However, upon arriving in the region, Mr. Dormouse reported back that the castle had been quitted, and locked up. There was no one there, and no evidence left behind to affirm that Lightning had ever been there, either.

However, shortly thereafter, the following page of a waterlogged ship's long was published in *The London Whisker*:

3 November
They are coffins. Would that the demon had brought extras for my crew, my poor men who have been nightly drained of their vigor, and have all died! I and I alone remain; I write this with some haste as I hear him coming for me now, he and his unholy mate, she who is a ghastly white possessed of such teeth as would tear this ship apart, had she but the opportunity and leisure to do so. Thus far I have thwarted them both, but now I fear they shall prove my undoing.
Hark! They come, swift and silent as cats!
Onze Vader in de hemel, uw naam worde geheiligd...

As is well known, Capt. Van Rattraap was discovered alive and unhurt in the wreckage of the *Fontina,* on the beachhead in the village of Hedgehogs-upon-Trivets, home of the Experimental Asylum for the Criminally Insane. Upon examination, he was determined by the excellent physicians at the asylum to be hopelessly devoid of his wits—that is to say, quite squirrelly. He was admitted into the asylum, and there remains to this day. The bodies of his crew were never found, although their widows and orphans pressed unceasingly for another inquiry to be opened.

However, though not widely known, there was one other survivor, whose presence was not reported by the excellent journalists of the day, in order that her delicate sensibilities might be protected from the glare of public scrutiny. She was discovered in a state of strange delirium, and was transported as well to the Asylum, not as an inmate, but as the private guest of the head of the institution, Sir Frederick Sewerat. Her parents were sent for immediately, and the Merriemouse-Joneses were soon stationed at her bedside. Her mother particularly remarked upon her pallor, for although the fur of the young lady was a snowy white, now her tiny nose, delicate tail, and lacy paws were ivory-complected as well.

Imagine the pitiable condition of Madame Merriemouse-Jones, to have pined so long for the return of her child, only to be confronted with the converse! She demanded vengeance upon the head of the person whom she heaped full blame: Count Dracurat himself!

Though there was no proof that it was of the Count whom Captain van Rattraap spoke, Lightning's mother produced the letter they had received from her, which, taken together with the captain's log, had convinced her that her daughter was grievously misused by Count Dracurat—who she claimed had escaped the wreck of the *Fontina* and was now at large on the village of Hedgehogs-upon-Trivets.

"A monster walks among us!" she concluded.

There were several asides made amongst the constabulary about the hysterical nature of females—none within the earshot of Madame—but she was as intelligent as she was worried, and so quickly deduced that her anxiety was not shared by those who were in a position to do anything about it.

Thereupon Mrs. Merriemouse-Jones told her husband that if the authorities would not take the matter into their own paws, then Lightning's devoted parents should do so, by re-engaging the services of Quincey

Dormouse. Quite happily, the Texan had entertained hopes of being sent for, and so had traveled from Catpathia to London on another ship. From there, it was but a train ride to the village where Lightning lay in her swoon.

Mrs. Merriemouse-Jones found Mr. Dormouse very strapping and youthful, cutting quite a figure in a suit tailored in the "Western" style. Upon being introduced, he doffed an enormous hat such as Texan cattle ranchers wore and swept a courtly bow.

Hardly had he stepped from the train platform at Hedgehogs-upon-Trivets than he studied the letter and the captain's log. He did not stop even for tea, and, upon conclusion, declared in his affable American way: "Something here sure stinks, and it ain't the Longhorn Cheddar."

He applied next for permission to observe Miss Merriemouse-Jones in her sickroom. There was some further discussion between Lightning's parents about the propriety of allowing Mr. Dormouse to visit their daughter; but her mother insisted that they had no one else to turn to.

And so, with Lightning's mother and a nurse present, Mr. Dormouse entered the chamber of Miss Merriemouse-Jones for the first time.

How can one describe the effect her ethereal loveliness had upon the youthful gentleman? Hovering at her bedside, he was struck dumb, then was heard to utter softly, "'Ah! She doth teach the torches to burn bright!'"

Mindful of her modesty, he nevertheless resolutely proceeded to examine her neck, and there discovered two tiny puncture marks. His mouth set in a grim line, he entreated first the nurse and then Mrs. Merriemouse-Jones to look as well.

Madame Merriemouse-Jones gasped in horror, inquiring what on earth they might be, while the nurse examined them with obvious confusion.

"How long have these been here?" he inquired of them both.

"Truthfully, sir, I've never seen them before," the nurse replied.

Mrs. Merriemouse-Jones was equally at a loss. Thereupon Mr. Dormouse entreated Dr. Sewerat to examine them as well. The good doctor was astounded by their presence, and assured Mr. Dormouse that they had not been there previously. Challenged by Mr. Dormouse to account for the last time he had examined Miss Merriemouse-Jones, he allowed as how he had not thought to do so since the day she was brought to the asylum, now some nine days previous.

It was apparent that his reply overset Mr. Dormouse, who blurted, "Y'all haven't been checking in on her?"

Dr. Sewerat reminded Mr. Dormouse that the oath of his profession required that he do no harm, and since he had had no inkling of the nature of Lightning's affliction, he had nursed no wish to compromise her privacy until he had some reason to do so.

Mr. Dormouse seemed displeased by this explanation. He took Mrs. Merriemouse-Jones aside. He said to her, "Madame, I don't know how else to explain this to y'all, but it is my belief that your precious daughter has, been, ah, *visited upon* by a vampire. And from what I saw on my previous assignment for you and Mr. Merriemouse-Jones, and what I have seen here, I can reach no other conclusion that that you were quite correct. I believe that Count Dracurat is that vampire! And I also believe that he has taken up residence in Hedgehogs-upon-Trivets, here to commit his nefarious deeds!"

Rather than succumb to the strong emotions one may expect from a mother under these circumstances, Madame revealed that she was made of sterner stuff. Her eyes glittered like Spanish steel as she held out her paw to Quincey Dormouse and said, "Then clap hands and a bargain, sir! You are my deputy in this wild work. I beg of you to locate and dispatch this monster to that unholy realm where his soul belongs!"

She spoke further of payment, at which point Mr. Dormouse put hand to heart and said, "Mrs. Merriemouse-Jones, pray, I entreat y'all, do not speak of money at a time like this. To see your beautiful li'l gal up and around will be recompense enough. I would gladly die in the performance of this duty, should it come to that."

The violence of this speech privately decided Madame Merriemouse-Jones then and there, that if her darling daughter should be restored to her, she would encourage a match between Lightning and Mr. Quincey Dormouse. He was a mouse's mouse, and surely her young lady would consent to such a dashing stalwart as a mate.

Whatever the outcome of that, Mr. Dormouse directed that garlic be hung about her chamber. Dr. Sewerat was rather uncertain about the efficacy of such a precaution, but consented, as he felt most culpable that the young lady had been ah... punctured... while in his care. It seemed to have no effect on Lightning, although her mother claimed that she became whiter still, taking on the pallor of death itself.

Quincey Dormouse next secured the services of an individual with the somewhat notorious reputation of having not only studied, but successfully hunted, Creatures of the Night in his native Switzerland. This was none other than Professor Abraham Van Lemming. He was a remarkable old fellow, quite gray and, one might say with some accuracy (if indelicacy), that he was mangy.

Embarking on a series of research expeditions, Dr. Van Lemming announced that it was his belief that Count Dracurat had transported his many coffins from the *Fontina* and placed them throughout the village of Hedgehogs-upon-Trivets. He revealed that he found several odd coffins in warehouses and beneath the wharf, and had placed hosts of holy water in them in the hopes of preventing the Count, if they were indeed his coffins, from resting in his native earth.

He said to Quincey, scratching at the mangy patches of his coat, "However, it is mine believing that he has other coffins in the village gehidden, and they must be found and destroyed!"

Quincey Dormouse was quite in accord. While Dr. Van Lemming conducted his searches, he guarded the beauteous Miss Lightning. Then, one night, he received a note from the good doctor:

Tonight. Catfax Abbey.

With assurances to Mr. and Mrs. Merriemouse-Jones that he would soon return, he met Dr. Van Lemming by moonlight at the appointed place. Dr. Van Lemming then produced two crucifixes, wooden stakes, and holy water. He presented Quincey Dormouse with one of each, and revealed to him his belief that Count Dracurat had set up residence in the shadow of the abbey itself.

"For when one searches for the things of the shadows, one does not look into the light, eh?" he asked, with a twinkle in his eye. "In other words, this evil Count flaunts his diabolical nature by dwelling in close proximity to a house of worship!"

Mr. Dormouse was much amazed by the professor's deduction, but as they crept beyond the abbey walls, such a sense of foreboding came over him that he perceived the truth of the professor's words: they moved in the presence of a great evil.

This they did not know, but at that precise moment, Captain Van Rattraap awoke in his cell and began thrashing about, raving, "My master comes! See how he comes, with his beady red eyes and his great, enormous teeth!"

He was quite inconsolable, though Dr. Sewerat employed all the most modern methods of psychic medicine at his disposal to ease his hysteria: a bath of cold water and a good beating. So distraught was the captain that

Dr. Sewerat raced from asylum to private rooms, alerting Mr. and Mrs. Merriemouse-Jones that something was amiss.

Together, the trio burst into Lightning's boudoir. And there, revealed to their horrified gazes, they discovered the silhouette of a great rat thrown against the wall!

Mrs. Merriemouse-Jones screamed as Dr. Sewerat and her husband darted forward, brandishing the gas lamp Dr. Sewerat carried as one would a weapon. The soft light from the fixture cast a revealing glow: an enormous, hulking rat stood with his back to the balcony door (for such was there, for the duration of this tale, but never spoken of previously.) He had ebony fur, large red eyes, and long, beaverlike teeth. He wore a black opera cape lined in red silk and a medal of honor around his neck, though what honor can a fiend of Hell possess?

Few can dispute the ferocity of the bonds that exist between mother and child. Without thought of her own safety, Mrs. Merriemouse-Jones advanced upon the villain and attempted to fling her arms around him. But as she did so, he spread forth his paws. He stared into her eyes, and began to chant in a language she did not know.

In an instant, she, Mr. Merriemouse-Jones, and Dr. Sewerat were mesmerized, standing still as statues, in a state of catatonia.

As they looked helplessly on, the dread Count Dracurat spoke these words:

"You have thought to keep me from this lovely maiden. Ah, foolish mices of England! Now that you have sent your varriors to my abode, I am free to make Lightning Merriemouse-Jones my new bride! For surely your menfolk vill destroy my old Countess, and I shall begin a new life of romance with this exquisite creature! Now, you, doctor of the insane, remove the odious garlic bulbs from the vicinity of her person!"

Imagine the despair with which Lightning's parents attended his pronouncement! Unable to stop himself, Dr. Sewerat did as he commanded, gathering up the garlic that prevented Count Dracurat from harming their child. As further ordered, he carried everything into the hall, and there remained.

The Count's smile was wicked and toothsome as he then approached their beloved daughter, opened wide his mouth, and prepared to bite down upon her neck!

But in the precise moment of her undoing, Count Dracurat drew back and cried, "Who has bitten this young lady?"

And in *that* moment of reprieve, via the aforementioned balcony, a second black rat with red eyes and sharp, protruding teeth flew into the room!

Yes, flew, as would a bat, although this creature was most assuredly a rat. This one wore a scarlet gown with a ruff of ebony; the apparently feminine monster seized Count Dracurat around the neck and began to shriek in a tone most shrill and ignoble:

"You cheating creepinski! How dare you leave me, a Countess and a Fancy Rat, in our matrimonial coffin for vampire hunters to find, while you cavort vith a common mouse girl!"

Then she squeezed her paws tighter and tighter still. The Count's eyes bugged, and he began to gasp. As the Countess Dracurat strangled her errant spouse, his hold upon the Merriemouse-Joneses dissolved. Yes, even the young lady was released. Her eyes flew open; she sat up in her bed, and cried, *"Mama! Papa!"*

Her elders raced to her, her paternal relative lifting her up into his arms while both father and mother kissed her sweet, furry face. Sobbing with joy, they were about to quit the scene of so much violence and disaster, when Abraham van Lemming and Quincey Dormouse also burst through the balcony door, stakes, holy water, and garlic bulbs in hand.

"Ah ha! You thought to escape!" Abraham van Lemming cried with what can only be described as glee.

"Mister Merriemouse-Jones!" Quincey bellowed. "Please convey Miss Lightning to a more yonderous location! These two are about to meet their Maker and I doubt it will be pretty!"

So it was done, and therefore, Gentle Reader, you are assured that the actual destruction of the two evil vampire rats was accomplished out of the sight of the gentle Miss Lightning Merriemouse-Jones and her beloved parents, just as it is accomplished out of your own sight. Suffice to say that it was bloody and horrible in the extreme, and that Quincey Dormouse nearly gave his own life in the ordeal.

When it was done, Van Lemming and Quincey reunited with the trembling family. Dr Sewerat joined them also, most contrite for twice remaining passive and offstage when his presence could have thwarted the plot.

All was revealed: The two fearless vampire hunters explained that the evil Count Dracurat had designs upon Miss Merriemouse-Jones back at his castle, of a nature which could not be detailed in mixed company. However, his wife was suspicious. Happily, Madame was also tired of living in the country. Therefore the Count suggested they quit the cold climate of Catpathia and mix in England, forcing Lightning to act as their interpreter in all things English—to serve as Beatrice to their Dante, in their presumption to enter civilized human congress. But in truth, he had hoped to find a way to rid himself of the Countess during their voyage on the *Fontina*.

Alas, Countess Dracurat proved tenacious and continually suspicious, and as before, his "dread bride" stood between him and the delectable young maiden he coveted with all the lasciviousness with which a fiend of Hell was capable. For it was of the Countess that Captain Van Rattraap wrote in the log, a fact he himself made clear, now that he had regained his wits.

The crafty Count devised a secondary scheme: he would made it easy for Van Lemming to discover the coffins containing the native Catpathian earth in which Count and Countess must rest, in order to continue their unholy lives. His ultimate object what that Van Lemming should discover the Countess asleep in the matrimonial coffin the Count so unwillingly shared. Once the vampire hunters dispatched his current Countess, the Count could honorably install Lightning in that position. Therefore, though evil, he was courtly, and he himself had never touched their young lady, preferring to wait until such time as he could "rightly" claim her as his own.

The marks that Quincey Dormouse had found upon the delicate neck of Miss Lightning had been made by the Countess. She had hoped to rid herself of her rival, but the wreck of the *Fontina* had interrupted her plans. However, once Lightning was ensconced in her room at the asylum, she had managed to attack her! But just the once; and then she was further prevented by Quincey Dormouse's order that garlic be placed in the room… which in the end, may have proved the saving of Lightning's life, and her immortal soul as well!

In deep gratitude for the great favor done his family, Mr. Merriemouse-Jones offered Van Lemming and Quincey each all his worldly goods, and each turned him down. Van Lemming assured the fatherly rodent that his calling to rid the world of vampires was on the order of a religious quest, and therefore, he had no need of material things. As for Quincey, he was, as he himself phrased it in the colorful American vernacular, "rich as all get-out."

Upon hearing this, Madame's eyes lit up and she gazed meaningfully at her child. But Lightning lifted her lovely white chin in an insouciant manner, as if to remind her dame that she had quitted the family seat rather than be forced to marry, and may do so again, if pressed.

However, when Mr. Dormouse inquired as to whether he may call upon Miss Lightning at the Merriemouse-Jones residence before his scheduled return to Texas, permission was granted.

A protest filed by Miss Belle Holder: Lightning is not white. She hates white. Why did you make her white? Why did you make this a vampire story? We did not discuss that. Also, there is too much talking! Except that there should be as many eeeks in the letter as there are human words. Listen, you need to grab your reader on the first page and go right through it with a beginning, a middle, and an end. Make things happen. People like to read about violence. That's why Buffy the Vampire Slayer is popular, Mom. Because of the Kung Fu.

ABOUT THE CONTRIBUTORS

Saladin Ahmed

Saladin Ahmed's poetry has earned fellowships from several universities, and has appeared in over a dozen journals and anthologies. His short stories have been nominated for the Nebula and Campbell awards, have appeared in numerous magazines and podcasts, and have been translated into five foreign languages. He has also written nonfiction for The Escapist, Fantasy Magazine, and Tor.com. *Throne of the Crescent Moon* is his first novel. Visit Saladin at www.saladinahmed.com.

Peter S. Beagle

Peter S. Beagle is the Hugo, Nebula, Inkpot Award for Outstanding Achievement in Science Fiction and Fantasy, and World Fantasy Award for Life Achievement winning author of *The Last Unicorn* and *Two Hearts*. *The Last Unicorn* ranked #5 on Locus subscribers' All-Time Best Fantasy Novel list. *The Last Unicorn* was adapted to an animated movie. Peter also wrote the screenplay for the 1978 movie version of *The Lord of the Rings*.

Heather Brewer

Heather Brewer is the NY Times bestselling author of the Vladimir Tod series. She grew up on a diet of Twilight Zone and books by Stephen King. She chased them down with every drop of horror she could find—in books, movie theaters, on television. The most delicious parts of her banquet, however, she found lurking in the shadowed corners of her dark imagination. When she's not writing books, she's skittering down your wall and lurking underneath your bed.

Heather doesn't believe in happy endings... unless they involve blood. She lives in Missouri with her husband and two children. Visit Heather at www.heatherbrewer.com.

Jim Butcher

Jim Butcher is the NY Times bestselling author of the Dresden Files series, the *Codex Alera*, and a new steampunk series, the Cinder Spires. His resume includes a laundry list of skills which were useful a couple of centuries ago, and he plays guitar quite badly. An avid gamer, he plays tabletop games in varying systems, a variety of video games on PC and console, and LARPs whenever he can make time for it. Jim currently resides mostly inside his own head, but his head can generally be found in his home town of Independence, Missouri or at www.jim-butcher.com.

Kami Garcia

Kami Garcia is the NY Times bestselling coauthor of the *Beautiful Creatures* novels and the Bram Stoker Award nominated novel *Unbreakable*, and the sequel *Unmarked*, in the Legion series.

Kami is fascinated by the paranormal, and she's very superstitious. When she isn't writing, she can usually be found watching disaster movies, listening to Soundgarden, or drinking Diet Coke. She lives in Maryland with her family, and their dogs Spike and Oz (named after characters from Buffy the Vampire Slayer). Visit Kami at www.kamigarcia.com.

Nancy & Belle Holder

Nancy and Belle Holder have written two adventures starring Lightning Merriemouse-Jones; the other appeared in *Pandora's Closet*. Belle races autonomous vehicles and is a frequent presenter at MakerFaire and GeekGirlCon. Nancy is a Bram Stoker Award winning and NY Times bestselling author (the Wicked Saga) also known for her novels and episode guides based on *Buffy the Vampire Slayer*, *Teen Wolf*, *Beauty and the Beast*, and other TV shows. She also writes and edits comic books. They live in San Diego. Visit Nancy at www.nancyholder.com.

Gillian Philip

Gillian Philip's books include *Crossing the Line*, *Bad Faith*, *The Opposite of Amber* and the Rebel Angels series - *Firebrand*, *Bloodstone*, *Wolfsbane* and *Icefall*. She has been nominated and shortlisted for awards including the Carnegie Medal, the Scottish Children's Book Award and the David Gemmell Legend Award. Her home is in the north-east Highlands of Scotland with her husband, twins, three dogs, two cats, a fluctuating population of chickens and many nervous fish. Visit Gillian at www.gillianphilip.com.

Jane Yolen

Jane Yolen, often called "the Hans Christian Andersen of America," is the author of over 300 books, including *Owl Moon*, *The Devil's Arithmetic*, and *How do Dinosaurs Say Goodnight?* The books range from rhymed picture books and baby board books, through middle grade fiction, poetry collections, nonfiction, and up to novels, graphic novels, and story collections for young adults and adults.

Her books and stories have won an assortment of awards--two Nebulas, a World Fantasy Award, a Caldecott, the Golden Kite Award, three Mythopoeic awards, two Christopher Medals, a nomination for the National Book Award, and the Jewish Book Award, among others. She is also the winner (for body of work) of the Kerlan Award and the Catholic

Library's Regina Medal, and named a Grand Master for both the Science Fiction Poetry Association, and the World Fantasy Association. Six colleges and universities have given her honorary doctorates. Visit Jane at www.janeyolen.com

Henry Herz

Henry writes fantasy and science fiction books for young readers, including *Nimpentoad* and *Monster Goose Nursery Rhymes*. He enjoys moderating sci-fi/fantasy convention panels and eating Boston Crème Pie. He lives in San Diego with his wife and two co-author sons. Visit Henry at www.henryherz.com.

CPSIA information can be obtained at www.ICGtesting.com
Printed in the USA
LVOW12s1916260814

401013LV00003B/444/P